THE
MASTERPIECE
AFFAIR

Kenneth Royce

A Simon and Schuster Novel of Suspense

SIMON AND SCHUSTER · NEW YORK

SBN 671-21566-3
LIBRARY OF CONGRESS CATALOG CARD NUMBER: 73-6524
DESIGNED BY EVE METZ
MANUFACTURED IN THE UNITED STATES OF AMERICA

1 2 3 4 5 6 7 8 9 10

WITH ACKNOWLEDGMENTS AND THANKS TO
TERRY MEASHAM
OF THE TATE GALLERY
AND REG CLARKE
OF THE MAIN DRAINAGE SERVICES,
ALSO OFFERING MY PROFOUND APOLOGIES FOR
TURNING THEIR RESPECTIVE WORLDS UPSIDE DOWN.

1

THE DOUBLE GLASS DOORS swung behind us, and Maggie grasped my arm as we descended the few steps to the street. It was dark and reasonably quiet, the night air mild yet fresh for this part of London. A hopeful taxi crawled past with its flag up. We stood at the foot of the steps, Maggie's auburn hair reaching just above my shoulder.

"Which way?" I asked. There weren't that number of options for a walk in Holland Park at this time of night.

"Let's head for the park." Maggie gave my arm a tug and we moved off. I'm not keen on walks; they remind me too much of circling exercise yards in the various nicks I've been in. But I conceded there was no restriction and no screws eying us. So we set out without the ball and chain.

We didn't get far. A hunched shape turned the corner of the flats and hustled toward us, head down, hands in trouser pockets. He didn't see us, his sights firmly on the ground a few inches from his hurrying toecaps. I squeezed Maggie's arm to keep her quiet, and we stood still firmly in the path of the preoccupied oncomer. Had we not moved at the last moment he'd have bumped into us. His head shot up as if he had suddenly snapped out of deep hypnosis and he was momentarily bewildered. "I'm so sorry, I . . ."

"Wrap up, you big-footed copper. Just watch where you're going."

His eyes strayed to me as Maggie gurgled. "Oh, Dick," she gasped. "You should see yourself."

He was still late in recognizing us, and when he did it was apologetically instead of warmly; he'd aged in the short time since we'd last met.

"You all right?" I peered at him in the bad light.

"Yeah." He tried to smile but hashed it. "I was coming over to you; thought you'd be at Maggie's."

Maggie was quicker to catch on than I, sensing that Dick was far from himself. "You want to see Willie?"

"No, it's all right, Meg. I don't want to bust anything up."

"You're not interrupting anything. We were only going for a walk. You carry on with Willie and I'll go back to make some coffee for when you return."

I belatedly grasped Maggie's perception; Dick was in a state, his mind elsewhere.

"No, Meg . . ."

"Willie, get that young brother of yours mobile. I'll see you both later." To avoid argument she turned on her heel and headed back toward the main entrance.

When she'd disappeared Dick shook his head in anguish. "Oh, hell. I didn't mean to spoil your evening."

I placed a hand on his shoulder. "You're not. You know Meg. Now what's up?"

We walked slowly toward the park while Dick collected his thoughts. I didn't hurry him. He appeared noticeably shorter than me, but that was because he was hunched; in fact we are both tall, but I shaded him by about a half inch. His dark hair drooped untidily over one brooding eye, and it seemed to me that he'd lost weight, although he'd never carried excess. I wish I could always claim the same. He was muscle and bone, and his straight but slightly splayed nose above what might be termed an aggressive jawline ran in the family. The differences between us were largely of the mind; our attitudes were different. Hell, they had to be with my prison record and his

8

police career. Dick was as straight as I had once been bent. In my heart I knew that he was particularly straight *because* I'd been bent, as if to compensate for my lapses.

For all that, there was an unusual bond between us. No two brothers could be emotionally closer. A few years separated us, enough for me to remember the violent fracas between our parents and for him to have missed them. Because I am what I am, because I still have a periodic urge to return to crime, because I can look my shortcomings in the eye and recognize them, it has always been vitally important to me to insure that Dick remained straight, not that he needed my help, but I was fully aware of the disadvantages he carried in having a bent brother. I had once screwed the Chinese legation to protect his career; I'd even do more porridge for him if it would help, and that, to me, is the biggest nightmare of all. This terribly strong feeling of protectiveness for him might well be prompted by my own guilty conscience, but I believed it to be much deeper than that. After all, he felt the same for me without the compulsion of conscience.

As we strolled along I watched him covertly. Dick was strong stuff; he didn't upset easily. Usually he was a ball of good humor, always ready to pull my leg and sharpen his wits on me. But he could be dedicated too; he was to his job, so it was easy to guess that his present somber mood was connected with it.

We walked on in silence, turning up toward the park and one of the quieter streets below it. Suddenly Dick took a vicious right-footed swipe at an empty can some late litterbug had discarded; the can rolled and clanged in the empty street until it pinged to a halt. Even that emphasized a difference between us; I am left-footed, though right-handed; we played on opposite sides of the park in our footballing days.

"Feel better for that?"

"Sod it," he said. His face was screwed up angrily, as if he'd like to swipe someone; peas in a pod—externally.

9

"We're not getting far," I prodded.

"I've been suspended." It came out in a short explosion like a cork.

I stopped dead and grabbed his arm. "You've been *what?*"

"Suspended. Corruption charges."

"You've got to be kidding." We stood facing each other, almost oblivious of a young hurrying girl who stared curiously at us and decided to give us a wide berth; she must have thought we were measuring up for a scrap. I couldn't grasp what he was saying: corruption? Dick? I was going mad. "Start slowly," I groaned. "Take your time." We started walking again but were barely moving.

Dick seemed relieved to have blurted it out. "A newspaper has provided information against me alleging corruption. They haven't printed it, merely passed it on."

"That can't be enough to suspend you, for God's sake. They'd have to prove it."

Dick shook his head slowly. He would be feeling how I would feel, frustrated and livid and wanting to throttle whoever had worked it. It never once occurred to me that he might be guilty.

"It doesn't have to be proved at this stage," he explained. "The newspaper contacts the police, an investigating officer is appointed, he demands to know the source of information; if the paper refuses to give, then it's dropped there and then. But if they pass on the name of the informant, then the officer will see that person. If he's satisfied there is a case for investigation, the accused—that's me, matey—is suspended at once—on full pay," he added bitterly.

"Just like that."

Dick grimaced; he was looking for another can to thump. "The person who's tipped the paper need not be the real informant; someone can have put him up to it, providing chapter and verse, real or false. It's not new, Spider; it's an old, old story."

I was beginning to feel better. "Look, if you're clean, you've nothing to worry about. You know the fuzz are fair game with villains. Am I right in saying that most coppers are cleared of these sort of charges?"

"You're right," he agreed. "But this one's not so simple. It depends on how deep they dig."

I got his drift. "You mean they may unearth our relationship?" Dick nodded. "For chrissake," I said, "they can't blame you for me."

He put a hand on my shoulder and squeezed. "Not officially." Then realizing his low delivery, he patted my back. "Don't take it the wrong way, Spider. Nothing can destroy what's between us; I'm just being realistic, thinking out loud."

"Who's supposed to have paid you?"

"I'm not supposed to know at this stage, but it's Max Harris. That's why I came to you, to ask your opinion."

"Max? Old Max?" I felt slightly sick. "Max knows you're my brother. He wouldn't do it."

"Not unless he had an angle."

"I know Max pays coppers, but he wouldn't be doing himself much good, would he? Max wouldn't cross me." Max would cross anyone, but I had a lot of feeling for the old rogue and used to do jobs for him a few years ago.

"Look," I went on. "Maybe someone is gunning for *him*." I'd had an idea, but if I told him he'd probably worry about me.

"That occurred to me," Dick said. He brightened suddenly as if making up his mind about something. "I won't come back to the flat, Spider. Explain to Maggie for me. She'll understand." He grinned, not too convincingly. "I'll keep you in touch. Thanks for listening."

We shook hands and he moved off a great deal faster than when he'd arrived. I watched his disappearing back, and to show that he knew he held up a hand and waved it without turning round. Rather foolishly I gave a brief wave back. I was deeply worried about him. If we had our differences, then we had our similarities too; I just hoped that he wouldn't act impulsively.

When I got back to the flat Maggie was hiding behind a pair of square-framed, green-tinted spectacles as if to shield herself from what was coming. "Trouble?"

"Trouble." I put my arm round her shoulders, wanting her reassurance and knowing that she could give none. Dick needed someone like Maggie, I reflected, someone to love and who was always ready to try to understand, no matter what. Her sublime faith in justice sometimes frightened me, but she was straight right through and had not been contaminated by me—the reverse, in fact. But that was only one reason why she meant so much to me; there were so many others.

"His job's in jeopardy," I told her. "And you know what that means to him."

"And to you," she answered quietly.

I explained things to her and it didn't make our evening.

We were busy at the office and I had to show my face for most of the next day at the XYY Travel Agency, which was at last making a reasonable profit. When the crime figures increased, so did my company's, for most of London's villains booked through me. The staff remained loyal, with young Lulu still dipping her overmade-up yet oddly innocent face over a typewriter and between times trying to be maternal to me as an elderly teenager—a plumping bundle of energy with a ready cockney wit. Young Charlie Hewitt was growing his fair hair longer but was a good lad, and the tag of manager I'd given him was well deserved. Things ran smoothly without me, and the staff had increased to six. But there were times when I helped out to take some of the strain, and this was one of them.

So it wasn't until evening that I was able to set out for Max Harris's. I'd phoned Maggie to delay our meeting, and as it happened she was working late for the United Nations, so I was all set.

Max lived in a big corner house in Maida Vale. It was an area of Edwardian shabbiness in which he fancied he sank into anonymity. Externally there was little difference between the houses except woodwork painted like a variety of lipsticks on uncompromising lips. There was just room to open the iron gate without it scraping the front of the house, and I hammered on the old-fashioned knocker in preference to using the bell. A silver-gray Daimler Sovereign preened itself by the sidewalk. I guessed Max had no trouble keeping the parking space clear for himself unless he'd changed a lot.

His wife opened the door, her suspicious eyes hardening as she recognized me but pretended not to. She'd gone a harsh tight-curled blond which made her granite all round. She had good looks if you didn't mind them chipped from stone. A three-carat diamond beamed on me as her hand rose to grip the door.

"Yes?"

I grinned. "I'm Detective Superintendent Scott, ma'am. May I have a word with your husband?"

She bridled but gave in quickly. "Oh, it's you. Thought you were still doing time. I'm not sure that Max will want to see you."

"Why not ask him, Chrissie, my old love? If you keep me on the step much longer the neighbors will talk."

"You'd better come in."

I'd been in before. A long time ago. The decor had grown richer, the furniture a harsh mixture of old and expensive woods. Max could always identify value but had no damned taste. Ostentation to Max meant showing people you were good for credit. As he didn't need credit you'd have thought that he'd have honed down the visible bank balance crowding the walls. Chrissie reluctantly showed me into the drawing room; it wasn't that she really disliked me, but I wasn't big enough fry to mix socially with Max, and she strongly believed in differentials.

13

"You're a snob, Chrissie," I whispered as I moved toward the rising figure who'd been hunched in front of a color television set.

"Spider, me old pal." Max came forward, strong teeth showing in a wide smile beneath a trimmed heavy mustache. I was surprised to see that he'd been tinting the gray out of his thick mass of hair that somehow grew as it liked without appearing untidy. No comb could win with that jungle. His rough frame looked incongruous in a red velvet smoking jacket which Chrissie had probably told him was "with it." Max had never struck me as being vain before. Perhaps money and middle age had softened him. But his handshake was still strong, and his slightly shifty eyes seemed genuinely pleased to see me.

"Come to work for me again, 'ave you? Take a pew, boy, take a pew."

I disappeared into a mass of brocaded foam and tried to get comfortable.

He'd worn well, but then he didn't have to worry about the next crumb. He hadn't been inside for over fifteen years, and the knowledge gave him an easy confidence. His features had a craggy attraction although his skin looked as if it had been roughed over with a rasp. If Max had twinges of conscience, which is a fantastic thought, then they must have eased every time he shaved and saw his pitted face to remind him of a starving, tough childhood. Max was rough and tough and totally committed to being the biggest fence in the country.

To show that he didn't forget, he handed me a glass of apple juice, made only from Cox's and Bramleys, and poured himself a half-tumbler of Scotch.

"What about me?" whined Chrissie.

Max gave her a glance, then turned to me. "This business, Spider?"

I nodded.

Max grabbed a bottle of Pimms and shoved it at Chrissie. "Drink yourself silly on that. In the other room."

She shot me a look of undiluted hatred because she was afraid to direct it at Max, then flounced out, slamming the door.

"Cheers, Spider."

I wasn't deceived. Max needed Chrissie's razor-sharp wits when the chips were down, and she knew more about disposing hot goods than he did.

"Well," he said after the first swig. "I heard you were out of the game. Want to come back?"

I shook my head, wondering how to stand on the egg without cracking it.

"I could use you," he said warmly. "The craftsmen are disappearing. It's all mob stuff these days."

I looked round the room. There'd be nothing in it remotely bent. I looked back at the chunk of man that was Max Harris and remembered how he'd reached the top of his particular tree. Had he mellowed or did he still react like a bull? He seemed happy with me, but then he'd made a lot of money out of me. And I'd always kept his name clear. I liked him.

"There's a story going round that you won't like." I'd given him the opportunity to plead ignorance.

His eyes narrowed and his hand tightened on the glass. "That a fact?"

"It is said that you have leaked certain allegations to a national newspaper."

"Get away." He was smiling. "Doesn't sound my style." And it didn't the way I'd put it.

"A young jack has been suspended from duty as a result. The charge is that he's been taking bribes from you."

Max turned to stone. He lost some color and his eyes flicked from side to side as if monitoring his own thoughts. His pose was just short of murderous, but he got his senses back, and the glare he shot at me outdid the hardness of Chrissie's diamond.

"What's 'is name?"

So he *was* bribing the fuzz. "You must know."

"Don't play with me, Spider. What's his bloody name?"

"Dick Scott."

He looked stunned, then confused. Some of his rigor went and I'd almost swear that he sighed with relief. "Not your kid brother?"

I nodded.

"For chrissake, do you think I'm bloody stupid enough to try to fix your brother? And if I was, how raving mad would I have to be to leak it to the press? What're you trying to pull?"

Max rose to his feet, shed his velvet jacket as if suddenly realizing how ridiculous he looked in it, loosened his tie awkwardly and glowered above me.

"Steady on, Max. I'm merely giving you the form."

"Steady on be buggered. You're accusing me of slitting my own throat and your brother's too." He sat down heavily, glaring at me. "I've never paid him a cent. I don't even know him, let alone advertise it."

"Someone has leaked. If you're clean on the bribery bit you might try to fix a copper, knowing that you'd come out all right and the copper would be left with a stigma."

"There are other ways of fixing coppers without dragging my own name into it."

"Meanwhile, Dick's suspended and the inquiry will dig deep into your affairs."

"That's what's steamed me up. I'm not the suicidal type."

It began to look true. Max was a blunt instrument; he hadn't changed.

"So who?" I asked. "Who'd want to nobble Dick or yourself?"

Max started thinking. Aggression was part of his makeup, but he was still a very astute fence. His fingers explored his mat of hair. "There's only one bastard I can think of who'd go this far. Norman Shaw."

"I was going to ask what's happened to him."

Max poured himself another Scotch. He was quite calm now but angry. "We broke up the partnership some time ago. He's been trying to take over ever since."

"I should have thought there was plenty of room for two."

"I've too many advantages. Been at it too long. So 'e's been chipping away with his own smooth brand of cunning. A crafty devil, as you know."

When I had done jobs for Max, Norman Shaw was working with him. They made a good team. If Max could be described as a machete hacking a quick path through a jungle of problems, police and villains, then Shaw was the rapier with his polished and effective finishing. He was smooth and he was educated.

"But wouldn't he know Dick is my brother?"

"Not from me he wouldn't. I can't see why 'e should know."

"Then why would he try to fix him?"

Max peered across wearily. "Stop thinking of your brother; he's been just a name in a pot. It's me he's out to fix by bringing Old Bill about my ears."

"Yet you say you'll come out clean. On this issue at least."

Max frowned. It was too subtle for him. "It's queer, ain't it?" he agreed. "Bloody queer. It's time I dealt with Norman."

"Is it *so* bad between you?"

"Nothing I can't handle. But this is different. I didn't think he'd be so thick as to try this one on me."

"Just how many jacks are you paying, Max?"

Max scowled. "You know 'ow it is. One or two have to be squared to turn a blind eye, get the odd tip off. It's no different from your day except that it's now costing me a fortune. Boy, you wouldn't believe. But your brother isn't one of them."

"If Norman has pulled this he must be very sure of himself or he really hates your guts."

Max thought about it. "The rift wasn't all that serious at first. He was mad keen on paintings, top art stuff, and I was still concentrating on the easily movable stuff like tom and maybe furs. I just thought him a fool. But he soon found out that the best operators were monopolized by me. They knew me, knew that if I set them up for a job it was safe and the return was good. So he tried to buy them over with a bigger cut. Once that starts and they see rivalry they start turning the screws and the whole business goes arse-about-face. Now it's really getting out of hand." He reflected somberly, then quite seriously said, "I'll have to top him."

From Max this wasn't idle talk. If he decided that killing was the only solution, then he'd do it. There was nothing else to be learned. Yet I didn't believe we had arrived at the right answer.

Maggie knew that I'd been up to something. She always did. While she laid the table, her green eyes, bright with doubt, would all too often come sweeping my way, trying to intercept my guilt. Her hair had been cropped close to her neck in a style I wasn't sure about, and I was glad of the distraction from Dick's problem. She wore a short tartan skirt that swung with her movements.

I still kept my own flat, but it was increasingly becoming a superfluous expense. More and more I was staying with Maggie, yet I still carried the shadow of my past and the instability of my future that made me stop short of marriage. I still felt that keeping it like this provided an escape hatch for her if I really landed in it. Fighting the intermittent urge for the excitement of creeping was still a big problem, and while I had it I'd leave her free if she wanted.

Suddenly I smiled at her and she caught my glance and smiled back, but I could see that she was worried. "The sun's brought out the freckles across your nose," I said.

"Damn you, Willie, I thought I'd covered them."

"Then don't try. They look fine."

She said quickly, "What've you been up to? And don't lie because you always look silly." She finished laying the flatware.

With her I was a bad liar. There were times when I wished I wasn't. She wasn't going to like it because she didn't approve of me looking up old acquaintances. Whenever I hesitated at moments like this she knew I'd been seeing villains. I gave it to her straight. When she realized I'd been trying to help Dick she understood but still didn't like it. She had good reason to worry over my connections.

She disappeared into the kitchen and returned with some table napkins. "What does this Max Harris do?" She wasn't meeting my eyes.

"He's a villain."

She smiled wryly, realizing that I was trying to dodge the issue. "Even I know that, Willie. What does he do?"

"Love, I can't see that it matters. I thought you didn't like this sort of discussion."

"I don't. But Dick's involved. What this man does may have some relevance."

Puzzled, I said, "Sit down and I'll tell you."

Maggie sat opposite me, which meant that she was placing herself out of reach of any sidestepping distractions from me. But sitting there upright, her long legs crossed, was distracting enough.

"He's a fence," I explained. "And I don't mean a bent jeweler or antique dealer who fences stolen goods at random. Max Harris is big and he's a natural for the job. He has an intuitive flair for knowing where to dispose of his goods, and on that particular side his wife is even better. They very rarely take stuff out of the blue. Most times Max sets up the jobs himself. In spite of his coarseness he has enough money to move in rich circles whichever side of the track they come from."

I stared across at Maggie, disturbed by her neutral attitude and the fact that I'd never talked like this to her before. "Go on," she said, almost as if I was a stranger.

"Look, sweetie . . . I don't want to upset . . ."

"Go on," she repeated. "Perhaps it's time I stopped burying my head in the sand. Perhaps I should take a long look at the other you without pretending he doesn't exist."

This wasn't only a rundown on Max but a betrayal of myself. I mutely pleaded, but all she said was "Please, Willie," but more softly.

19

"Max has contacts all over. There is always a fringe of society and the arty set who cling to people like Max as if they enjoy a reflected glory of law-breaking and violence they're really incapable of themselves. It's easy for Max to set up jobs, not too frequently but always profitably, and laugh behind these morons' backs. Then there are the wealthy contacts from his legitimate business. People who don't know he's bent."

"But he never robbed people himself?"

"No," I agreed uncomfortably.

"He used people like you? Told you where to go and whether people would be in and things like that?"

I wriggled. It was like looking at myself in a prison mirror.

"Yes." I swallowed. Was she deliberately making me look at myself? I didn't like the image of the lackey that emerged.

"Then what?"

"How d'you mean?" Subtly my explanation had been replaced by her interrogation.

"When something was stolen it was then taken to Max?"

"Hardly ever. That's part of Max's brilliance. He knows where to place the stuff before it's nicked. Most times he doesn't even see it once it's hoisted."

"And then you got a percentage of what the buyer paid?"

"Max would pay, yes."

Maggie suddenly looked exasperated. "Willie, am I reading you right? Are you trying to tell me that you don't know what Max received for the goods and yet you believed you got a percentage? A percentage of what?"

My blood rose. "Don't make me look a fool," I snapped. It was the nearest to losing my temper with her I'd been. "I wasn't *employed* by Max Harris; I just did odd jobs for him that I wouldn't otherwise have known about. It was easy money." I pushed myself further in with every mouthful. Belatedly I escaped: "Anyway, I thought it was *him* you wanted to know about."

Maggie came over to stand beside me. Her hand caressed my cheek and pulled my face against her thigh.

I stood up roughly. "Stop treating me like a child!"

Quietly she said, "Then stop acting like one."

Even as I stood glaring I knew that she was right. I hurt easily over this subject. I was too open to ridicule. She hadn't made a fool of me but had let me show myself what a fool I'd been. It was no use explaining to her that I'd been a craftsman, that I'd got a kick out of it.

"Well, anyway," she said brightly as if nothing had happened, "Max has been bribing policemen from what you said earlier. And this Norman Shaw is trying to take over." She stood by the settee, glumly thinking it out, then suddenly smiled wanly. "Thank God you're out of all that, that's all. Thank God. Let's have dinner."

It must have been nearly midnight when Dick arrived. We weren't expecting him and were on the point of turning in. We took one look at him and Maggie dived for the brandy bottle. "Don't sip it, drink it," she instructed. His hands trembled round the goblet while his widened eyes signaled a mute thanks. He took a long pull at the spirit, coughed briefly and sprawled into a chair, his raincoat flopping back from a polo-necked sweater and tapered checked slacks. His neatness didn't conceal the wildness in him. There was desperation in the way he finished his drink and abstractedly wiped his lips with the back of his hand. Briefly he shuddered.

"Max Harris is dead," he said bluntly.

Maggie and I exchanged alarmed glances and I gestured her to leave it to me.

"How do you know?"

Dick looked across impatiently. "I still have mates in the force. Ron Healey told me. Max Harris's wife came home and found him. She's screaming blue murder right now. His head was bashed in."

"Oh God!" Maggie was horrified. Her long fingers were a vise at the sides of her temples. She quickly realized that to some degree we were all implicated.

Max dead. Tough, rugged, villainous old Max. It didn't matter what he'd been. I'd been talking to him only hours ago, when he was still full of fire; it was too recent not to feel a profound effect.

"So he was top-murdered." I changed for Maggie's benefit.

"Yep. And not neatly. Among other things his wife was complaining of the mess on the carpet."

I wished Dick would remember that Maggie was here but I could see that he was half dazed, tumbling out harsh thoughts as they entered his head.

"Are you worried about the inquiry? You think this won't do it any good?"

Dick appeared as drained as his goblet; Maggie gently took it from him and recharged it. "Worse," he replied. "They could blame me for Max."

"Max's murder? Don't be bloody silly."

Dick glanced apologetically at Maggie, then studied the mahogany tint of his liquor. "I was there not more than three hours ago."

"There? At Max's?" An iced rod passed right through my body.

"I went to see him. Wanted to straighten things out."

I couldn't believe it. "You're supposed to be a jack and you did something as stupid as *that?*"

"I know." He shrugged, spilling his drink. "It didn't seem so stupid at the time."

"Did anyone see you?" I was thinking like a copper, but thoughtwise there's not much difference between villains and fuzz.

"Look, don't get too worked up. I didn't see him. I went there and hung around outside for a while, torn between common sense and trying to resolve the matter the quick way. I wanted to talk to him; he must have had some ideas. I can't believe he'd fixed himself, so we had something in common. I rang the bell and waited but no one answered. I could have rung again but I didn't. I took it as an omen and left."

"You must be raving mad." I waited. "What sort of copper can you be? Someone might have seen you."

"Yes," he suddenly shouted, rising to his feet. Putting down his drink, he stabbed a finger at me, his face emotionally contorted. "It might be difficult for you to understand, but I went about it in a perfectly straightforward way. I had nothing to hide, do y'see."

"Nothing to hide," I groaned unbelievingly. "If the inquiry finds out you went, even if Max hadn't been knocked off, you'd have dropped right in it."

"It was because of the inquiry that I went." Dick stood heaving like a bull. He suddenly sat down again, rucking his coat behind him. Maggie was quiet, bewildered by what was going on and watching us both anxiously.

I stared at Dick as if he'd lost his senses. "You'd better explain." I sighed hopelessly.

"I found out today who's heading the inquiry: Detective Chief Superintendent Jack Harvey. He's got several similar inquiries at the moment and, of course, he's not from our division. Right now there are seventy C.I.D. officers under investigation in the Metropolitan district. Most of them will be proved not guilty, but to the public it's a lot. And it is. Fifteen of them are already committed for trial.

"It's a strange fact that Jack Harvey has always paid lip service to the belief that 'I'm not my brother's keeper.' You being an ex-villain and me being a copper is unusual but not unique. Jack Harvey's view of us would be that what you do is none of my responsibility. But he has a queer twist to this viewpoint. While he upholds the right of my joining the force, he doesn't think that the degree of extra responsibility I have to carry is fair to *me*."

"What extra responsibility?" I queried warily.

"Other coppers' talk. The pointing finger when something goes wrong, like now. It-must-run-in-the-family sort of thing. Blood's thicker than water and all the other trashy platitudes and proverbs that spring to a biased mind."

23

"Are you saying that he doesn't really agree with letting people like you join the force?"

"For their own good, you understand. Nothing to do with their integrity—but to protect *them*—save *them* getting a rough deal and gossip."

"So he's a bloody hypocrite."

"Perhaps an unconscious one. Perhaps he really believes it. What matters is that guilty or no he'll subconsciously reckon that I'll be better out of the force."

"If he knows about me."

"If he doesn't already—not many coppers do—the Guv'ner will almost certainly tell him or he'll find out by sheer digging. When I heard he was on, it didn't seem so unreasonable to try to sort it out with Max Harris in advance."

I thought it over. "I still think you were a fool."

"Maybe. But it's not your career at stake, is it? It's me who's on the block. It's me who's going to be asked the questions and some of them could be about you. You've worked for Max."

I still thought he'd been rash but began to see his viewpoint. From Jack Harvey's position it would begin to stink. Dick accused of taking bribes from a villain I used to operate for and then calls at the house shortly before the villain is found murdered? Already it looked a good circumstantial case against Dick.

"Right," I said. "So you're in bad trouble. Then who did do it?"

Dick looked blankly. "You don't expect me to answer that?"

"Certainly I do. Not to prove it but to give a qualified guess. Put it another way. Who had most reason for knocking Max off?"

"How would I know? There must be a score of villains who have been diddled by him."

That was near the bone. "I'll throw one in. I heard that Max and Norman Shaw have problems over their manors."

"I've heard that too. That doesn't make Shaw a murderer. I mean there's nothing to go on." And then reluctantly, "He'd certainly be a chief suspect."

I was keeping my fingers crossed that Maggie wouldn't innocently blurt out that I'd seen Max.

"I heard on the grapevine that Max had a copper or two on his payroll. Would you know them?"

Dick looked at me suspiciously. I was making him think and that meant he would begin to conjecture on the grapevine that had conveniently and so quickly coughed to me.

He looked vaguely embarrassed. "I have suspicions."

"This is no time to close ranks, Dick. If you can't tell me, who can you tell?"

"Two jacks; one a sergeant, the other an inspector; Newton and Durrant."

"If Norman was trying to take over from Max maybe he tried to take Newton and Durrant too. Coppers on Max's payroll might have a better idea than anyone who wanted Max knocked off."

"They might," Dick conceded. "But they won't cough of their own accord and there's not a hope of ever proving them bent now, is there?"

"Well, someone thinks they can do it to *you*."

"That was put into operation before Max was topped. It just makes it more difficult to clear me now. I don't want the case dropped through lack of evidence against me—that leaves all fingers pointing; I want off the hook."

The phone rang and startled us. Maggie answered it and passed it to Dick, who was surprised. "Yes? . . . Oh. Thanks, Ron. Yeah. I'll come in."

The room was very quiet as, grim-faced, Dick replaced the receiver. He gave a strange half laugh and stared at Maggie. "That was Ron Healey, a mate I can trust. I told him I'd be here." He turned his gaze to me, and I didn't like the look of him at all. Something had happened.

"I was seen all right," he said. "Two witnesses. There's a call out for me to be picked up. It would be better if I go under my own steam." He gave a little nod to each of us and went to the door.

25

"I'll go with you." But before I could reach him, he turned. "No. No, Spider," he said. "I'll do this on my own." When he'd gone it was as if the room was empty. Maggie and I both stood staring at the door as though willing it to open and for Dick to reappear. Something about his abrupt departure reminded me of how little we really saw of each other. We lived in opposite worlds; his was the more defined. The only person who could possibly hold Dick back was me. As kids he'd always looked to me as leader, and what a bitter disappointment I eventually turned out to be to him. Yet he'd clung closer, as if he'd wanted to understand and didn't really believe I was bad. The only difference in Dick was that he stopped boasting about me to the other kids and what shame he felt he hid. Reflecting like this upset me, made me realize not for the first time that he was of stronger stuff than I. He'd stuck it out, avoided the pitfalls I'd enjoyed falling into and by some compensatory strength of will and courage had gone the other way. And yet young Dick had never deserted me even when I'd been sent up.

He'd even traveled to Dartmoor on his day off when I was doing porridge there and must have risked ridicule from any of his colleagues who might have found out. And seeing this younger image of myself gradually emerge had frightened me to death in case he went my way. But he didn't. And he managed without discarding me, grew closer in fact. We didn't need to see a lot of each other, and it could have been embarrassing to him if we had although it wouldn't have stopped him. In times of crisis we'd fly back to each other. To see him now in this kind of trouble, the sort that he had deliberately avoided all his life, choked me beyond description. I couldn't trust myself to speak just then.

2

I RANG MAX'S WIFE from the office next morning. I felt rough and moody but knew that I'd have to handle her carefully. There'd been little if any love lost between them; they'd both had affairs on the side when I'd known them better and I didn't suppose things had changed. But *in crime* they had been a highly successful partnership, and without Max, Chrissie Harris was in for big problems. Some of the boys would try to take advantage and Norman Shaw was bound to move. She wouldn't be able to handle them as Max had; she was tough, but Max could always manhandle when necessary.

"Chrissie? It's Spider Scott. Hell, I'm sorry about Max. I had a weak spot for him, as you know. May I come and see you?"

She asked why, as I expected. There was only one line that she'd bite. "I'd like to talk to you about who did it."

She didn't bite readily, which suggested that she had her own ideas, but she told me to come over for a beer at lunchtime.

"What about the fuzz? Are they still there?"

She told me what she'd told the fuzz to do, so the coast was clear.

The Daimler Sovereign was still outside the house and nobody had tied a black ribbon to it. I cut out my preferences and this time rang the bell. Chrissie was dressed in black with a single strand of real pearls. She hadn't been crying, but her

27

hard-cut features somehow conveyed a sorrow, which in her was quite touching. Her eyes were dangerously brittle blue, her blond hair much too compact round her head. She'd never learned to let her hair down in a true sense. As we went into the lounge I wondered how she'd stand up to the pressures in Max's absence.

She poured me a small can of beer and a half tumbler of vodka and orange for herself. And she'd gone out of her way to make me welcome with a plate of thinly cut sandwiches. This was a generous handout, for Chrissie was notoriously mean, a fact which wouldn't help her a bit without Max's compromising hand.

To be fair to Chrissie she didn't want sympathy or platitudes. Right from the start she made it clear that all she wanted was the bastard who'd done Max.

I sipped my beer and looked slowly round the room.

"He's left you all right? No money problems or anything like that?"

Chrissie looked at me in disgust, one red lip curling. That was another thing she'd have to learn to curb from now on—showing her feelings too readily. It was going to be hard after Max's protection.

"I've got enough to live in comfort for the rest of my days. That's not the point, is it? I can't stop working. I've still got to run the bloody show for Max and get the cunning bastard who did him."

"Any ideas?"

"You phoned me to say that you have." It wasn't true, but the blue eyes pinned me into the foam of the chair. It was like being smothered.

"I have some," I said carefully, "but I asked first."

"I know who did it." She swigged her vodka and sat staring at me. Chrissie had a good figure and features, but I still couldn't find the woman in her. Failing to draw me, she added, "Norman Shaw." It ejected like a shot.

We stared each other out in a silence measured by a long

case clock. Chrissie was sitting straight-backed on the arm of her chair looking very sure of herself.

"You're very emphatic."

"Because I know he did it. What's your interest in it? Not Max, that's for sure."

There was no point in trying to deceive her; she was in a dangerously perceptive mood. Her sharp gaze would sweep up any hesitation on my part. I told her how Dick was involved because she already knew of him and because Max might have told her. Also she might know of his visit last night, although I didn't mention it.

"I see, so all you're trying to do is protect your kid brother. I don't think there's anything you can do for me, Spider."

"I can help you be sure who did it."

"I'm already sure."

"Would it hold up in court?"

Chrissie shot me more contempt. "It doesn't have to. You don't think I've told the fuzz, do you? I'll deal with this my way."

I started chewing on a sandwich with a suggestion of cheddar cheese between a scraping of butter. At least the bread was fresh.

"Revenge, Chrissie? It means putting your own head on the block."

She didn't rate it a reply. Chrissie was getting tired of me because I had nothing to offer. I had to try something before she kicked me out.

"Chrissie, if you have Norman Shaw topped, Dick goes to the wall for something he hasn't done."

There was no crack in the image; the pearls showed more warmth.

"That's your problem. I owe you nothing, Spider. Nor did Max."

"He wouldn't have agreed. I was sent up for one of his jobs. I kept him out of it."

"That's the sort of creature you are. You didn't do it for him but for your own satisfaction. Anyway," she added, "it wouldn't have paid you to grass."

Chrissie had shaken me. Was it true? I'd never grassed. Was it because I owed it to my own self-respect, egoism if you like, or out of loyalty to another? Could I ever answer that one?

Chrissie laughed like a smoker's cough.

"You should see your face. Bit near the mark, was it? Come on, Spider, out you go. I won't charge you for the sandwich."

"Wait a minute, Chrissie. Wait." I was getting desperate. "You may as well fill in a little of your time with me as remain in this empty house. Without Max there are going to be times when you'll even be glad to slum with people like me. What's an extra few minutes to you now?"

It was brutal, but she briefly saw the truth of it. Slowly she crossed to the drinks cabinet and half filled her glass again. She didn't offer me another beer. "You'd better have something to say or I might think you're in with Norman."

"Tell me first why you think it's Norman."

She gave me the hard stare, trying to decide whether I was big enough for harsh truths. "All sorts of small things. They've been at war for some time. None of it Max's doing."

I couldn't visualize Max with a halo but I didn't interrupt.

"The crunch came yesterday after you called. Max rang Norman and told him he'd fix him for good. Norman suggested that they meet to talk things over. It was the sort of approach that slimy bastard would make. Max invited him over, but Norman said that he would be out until at least eleven, that if he got back not too late he'd ring Max to see if he could still come over or fix another time."

"It sounds reasonable."

"It meant that he knew Max would be here."

It didn't seem a lot and my thoughts must have reached her.

She riveted me with a glance and stood up angrily. "My God, how trusting can you get. When Max invited him round he told Norman that it would be a good time to come because I would be out. *He knew that Max would be alone.*"

30

That made much more sense. Max could take care of Norman, but if Norman had called he may not have been alone.

"Have you asked Norman if he called or phoned?"

This time Chrissie really swept me under the carpet with a look so pitying that I had to admit to myself that it was a naïve question.

"I rang him after the fuzz had finished. He made all the oily noises I would expect from his smooth gullet. And then he told me that he had telephoned at half past eleven and that Max had told him he couldn't see him then and had slammed down the phone. I ask you. Max had been waiting for him."

For a moment I thought Chrissie was going to cry but quickly realized that her emotion was rage against Norman Shaw and my stupidity for not catching on more quickly. She had a very strong case. One the police should have, but they'd never get it from her. She was shrewd enough to know that legally it might leak, that Norman would have made damned certain that he wasn't seen. Just before midnight this wouldn't have been too difficult.

"For what it's worth, my guess is Norman too."

"Oh, thanks," she sneered. "Now I feel better."

"But don't do anything, Chrissie," I pleaded quietly. Somehow I had to cool her. "I'm going to pin it on Norman in a way that will keep your hands clean."

"I don't want my damned hands clean. For chrissake I want them round his scraggy neck."

"All right. All right." I held out my hands like a conductor signaling *pianissimo,* but it had no effect on her volume.

"Please, Chrissie. You can't lose by it. You can have your revenge but cut me in on it. My motive binds me to your side. Think about it. Give me a little time to do it my way and if I fail, then do what you like, for you'll be doing it for me too; I won't be around if I slip up."

She was staring hard. There was no crack as she mulled it over.

I followed up softly. "If you top him too soon the word will get out that you put up the money. You know fine that these things leak. You can't do it yourself. You'd be enlarging the war, for *his* wife wouldn't sit on it from what I hear of her. Now we can fix it without any of this. Nice and cool and permanent."

"You're too soft," she accused.

"Chrissie, my brother's up to his neck in it. I can't afford to be soft."

She gave me a cool look as if taking notice of me for the first time. "What are you going to do?"

"Go back to work," I said.

Chrissie hesitated with a flicker of interest. "You mean your old job?"

"That's how I see it."

I had her full attention now. "I'll say this for you, Spider, you were good at it. Max was always sorry he lost you."

"Yes, I know. He offered me work yesterday. But it'll not be your empire I'll be working for."

"I can't give you long. I'm not letting this slide."

"At least promise to let me know before you do anything."

She nodded. "All right. You accused me of putting my head on the block; what d'you think you're doing?"

I stood up. "That's how it's got to be."

"Well, you always had guts; don't get them spread over the gutter."

I grabbed another sandwich and left.

Maggie knew something was on the moment I told her I was moving back into my own flat. I couldn't operate from her drum; it would be too dangerous for her. She guessed that it was connected with Dick and that it wasn't straight. This was more difficult than dealing with Chrissie, for there was nothing I could tell her, and this worried her sick.

I stayed the night against my better judgment. Maggie was tender as she always was when she was afraid I was heading back to nick. The one possible advantage of our association was that my intermittent gambols into the wilderness provoked so much uncertainty that we could never take each other for granted. That was one aspect; the other was the terrible effect it had on Maggie. I had to weigh it up against deserting Dick and I told her this. The dreadful thing was that she said she understood.

I tried to contact Dick next morning, but there was no response from his digs. I rang his nick and asked for Ron Healey. He turned out to be a detective sergeant and he quickly arranged to meet me at a pub in Wardour Street, well away from his own manor. It had to wait till evening, which meant another day gone, but I had to be sure.

Detective Sergeant Healey picked me out in a crowded bar with a strata of tobacco smoke floating at ceiling level. When I asked him how he knew me he told me I resembled Dick's father. He said it with a smile. Recognition of him in future would be no problem. He was slight, with carroty hair and an open Celtic face from which two very clear gray eyes spanned a snub nose. Worry or laughter lines round his mouth robbed him of some of his youthfulness, but when he did grin it was spontaneous and boyish. For a copper his looks were far too innocent, which must have been a great asset. I liked him on sight and guessed that he was older than he looked—early thirties.

He ordered a couple of pints and said, "I'm glad we're meeting like this instead of me holding out a warrant card and giving you a caution." His eyes were quietly mickey-taking.

I took it as it was meant and smiled. "You'd have to catch me first. Where's Dick?"

"Still at the nick being questioned."

"Is he under arrest?"

Ron Healey wiped froth from his lips. He aged several years as his features set in reflection. "No. He sleeps at home but he's having a rough time."

"From Detective Chief Superintendent Harvey."

"He's only in charge of the bribery and corruption inquiry; at the moment the murder squad is grilling him about Max Harris."

"Do you think he did it?"

"Dick? Of course he didn't do it. But I'm his friend and I'm not on the case." He sipped his beer slowly, then said seriously, "You must understand something, Spider."

There was nothing boyish about him now. A weary lifetime of lies and deceit, crime and violence and twisted minds showed on his face. Much of what he saw in C.I.D. would sicken most people, and some of the ugliness of his experience shadowed the color from his eyes as they flickered to mine.

"It doesn't matter a damn whether they think he did it or not. And not all of them will think as I do. All they can do is follow the evidence, and if that's strong enough for an arrest, then that is what will happen. It's worse for him as a copper. They dare not lean in his direction because the press would love it if they did. On a murder inquiry he will be treated as a stranger, and with that over his head that's exactly what he'll become. You'd be surprised how many of his so-called friends now avoid his eye. Bribery charge, then a murder suspect. There's not that much smoke without a blaze, is there?"

This Ron Healey might know his onions but he wasn't making my day. "Isn't there anything on the credit side?"

"No there isn't. Only his record, and that's only useful in mitigation."

"Christ, you're talking as if he's already banged away."

"There's nothing that I can see that will prevent it short of knowing who did do the job." He held up a restraining hand as I was about to dive in. "Don't worry, Spider. It's being worked on. You'd get a shock if you saw the thoroughness of a murder inquiry, the indexing, cross-indexing of every single item from every single source or interrogation. It's more thorough than thorough. But at the end of the day we have

34

to have something to work on. Right now everything points to Dick, and he didn't help himself by calling on Max Harris, let alone doing it on the wrong day at the wrong time. Add to that a biased investigation and he's in a mess."

I knew most of this already but I thought that he might have something else. "So he's all you've got?"

Ron Healey finished his beer and I called for another. The blue strata had sunk to a swirling level just above his head. "The murder weapon is still missing. A blunt instrument."

"It'd be in the Thames. Tell me how I can help."

Healey smiled wryly. As the talk had gone on his innocence had disappeared into the smoke. He was tough beneath the carrot top.

"I can't teach you how to help, Spider. And I can't protect you if you do, not even in my own manor. So be careful of what you do or it might rebound on Dick. And that would upset me."

I nodded. Then he said, "If you come across anything, let me know."

I nodded again. We were being jostled at the bar, so we moved away from it at the price of a small loss of beer. I thought he was about to take a swig when he slipped out over the glass, "You didn't see Max Harris yourself by any chance?"

His gaze was wide-eyed, too steady. I thought quickly, for he was watching me closely. "If you thought that you'd have had me in by now."

He grimaced. "Two chance witnesses picked out Dick at an I.D. parade. We can't ignore that fact. It was dark when they saw him, but there is a street light almost directly opposite the front door. People's memories play tricks even after a short time. If they haven't visual memories they can get confused, and these two weren't particularly bright. One of them swears that he saw Dick go in. Now Dick says the door wasn't answered. It occurred to me that had you been on the I.D. instead of Dick they might have picked you out."

I felt sick. It was me who had been seen going in. There

35

couldn't have been much time separating our calls but seemingly enough for someone to do the job unless he was already inside when Dick rang the bell. "Are you suggesting that I put myself up and take Dick off the hook?"

"I hadn't thought about it," he lied. "Dick has admitted that he called on Max."

I caught his trend. "So I could insist that he's protecting me? I know Dick too well. He wouldn't wear it."

"But it would confuse the issue, bring in a strong element of doubt."

"And possibly land me in his place. Try doing three stretches of bird, including the Moor, and then tell me how I should answer. No, matey. We don't want confusion; we want the bastard who did it. And to achieve that I'm of more use to Dick out of nick than in it." If I hadn't meant that I'd have told him of my visit right then.

"Please yourself, but bear in mind that if you operate as I think you might, you'll finish up in nick anyway. Or worse."

As he put down his empty glass he said casually, "There's one thing. For God's sake keep it under your hat. The charlie who gave chapter and verse on corruption to the paper was Micky Evans. Know him?"

My blood rose. I knew him all right. My face must have been giving me away but I couldn't help it. Just then I felt like murder. Micky Evans had worked for Max and Norman when they'd operated together. As Max was dead, that left Norman. The bastard.

"I wouldn't try to find Micky," added Healey easily. "He's gone to earth."

I glared, still seething. "Under police protection?"

He shrugged. "If you find him you'll be weighed off for intimidation. Don't look for him and don't lean on him—for Dick's sake. Leave this to us."

I was too choked to answer. He was right. Knocking the truth from Micky Evans would be repudiated the moment he was free of me. And I'd be in it. But I had no faith in the police breaking him down.

I had a Chinese meal in Soho and felt lonely without Maggie. I took my time trying to find an alternative to what I had in mind but came up with nothing. From Piccadilly I caught the Bakerloo Line to Baker Street and changed for Westbourne Park. I left the West End to the inflow of teenagers and the theatergoing straights.

I walked to the block of flats that had digested mine, to the fifth-floor back facing the wall and the green stamp they called a garden. It was mid-evening, with people crouched over their television sets and later wondering why they bothered; like smoking, they couldn't give it up.

There were cars parked all round the block. Mine used to be one of them, but I'd found little use for it in town and had sold it, buying Maggie a three-diamond ring from the sale which looked better on her than a car draped round me. I loved fast driving and she had been very touched by what she called my sacrifice; any sacrifices between the two of us had strictly come from her. I have a quick eye for a good car, and as I approached the entrance to my wing of the flats I spotted a sand-colored Bentley making the street lamp above it hang its paltry lit neck in shame and the saloons round it tawdry—a queen among the peasants. The offside front door opened as I approached and a nylon-clad leg thrust out, a neat crocodile shoe touching the pavement. A mink jacket bunched above some form of short lamé dress that did its best under the poor light. This unexpected vision of Bond Street quality suddenly snapped as I saw the harsh, tightly groomed blond hair appear as her body straightened.

"Chrissie! For a moment I thought the Duchess of Kent was doing a spot check of the district."

"Very bloody funny." The final illusion was shattered.

"You've come for a loan then," I suggested.

She peered at me through too much makeup, and her hostility hadn't softened with the application of Estee Lauder. She had been out for the evening. It hadn't taken Chrissie long to forget Max, now dead almost twenty-four hours. But then Chrissie always had been a practical woman.

"What happened to the Daimler Sovereign?" I asked, curious.

"The ashtrays are full," she snapped. "I want to see you. I've been waiting some time."

"You could have rung."

"I'm not using the phone until I'm sure the fuzz aren't tapping it."

"O.K. Do you want to slum in my place? I can give you a can of beer and almost a sandwich."

"For someone who's asking me favors you've got a lot of lip. We'll walk round the block and don't be funny with me or I'll change my mind damn quick."

She didn't say that she wouldn't be seen dead in my place but she conveyed it through a cutting glance. We started to walk slowly.

Chrissie might well destroy her image with her brassy hair style and stiff good looks but she walked well. Maybe she'd spent her youth carrying buckets of water on her head, but she had a regal movement of limb that was quite beautiful. We stepped out slowly and she slipped an arm through mine but not from affection; Chrissie wanted a natural scene. I couldn't help but wonder about her. She had to chip the ice sometime, yet even when I worked for Max I could not recall her unbending. It had always been business; maybe she bought her lovers or had one special one tucked away.

"Something's missing," she said quietly. "I should have noticed it before but I had too much on my mind."

"Something that could have done the job?" I prompted.

"Something I'll lay odds on that did do the job. A bronze."

We turned the corner in silence, and off the main street it was quiet but for our own footfalls. There was no comfort in having Chrissie next to me even in the darker road. She was concentrating, so I left her to it until she said, "It wasn't Max's normal taste in things; he never understood Norman's taste, but over the bronzes they were in agreement."

"Bronzes?"

"They had one each; had to split a bloody pair to stop their rows over possession."

I'm old-fashioned enough not to swear in front of women; it didn't sound right from the opposite direction either. Chrissie somehow picked up some of my disapproval. She turned in surprise although I'd said nothing. "What's wrong with 'bloody'?" she demanded. "The number of times you've been inside you must live on the four-letter lingo. Would you prefer 'bleeding,' then?"

There was no doubt about it: I could needle Chrissie without twitching a muscle. "What are they like?" I asked.

"The bronzes? Eagles with outstretched wings perched on rocks. Kneeling on one is a young boy and on the other a girl, each holding a flame up high. Nice pieces about eighteen inches tall."

"And they had one each?"

"I don't know what they saw in them to fight over. I'm inclined to think that they used them as an excuse to explode a row that had been brewing up anyway. They weren't nicked; they were bought in Wigmore Street, but they argued like bloody children as to who saw them first."

"Which one did Max keep?"

"The boy."

"And you think that Norman used it on Max?"

"It's missing. And he called that night."

"Maybe he just wanted it to make up the pair and used another weapon for the murder."

"Either way, if he's got it he'll never explain it away."

"It's a hell of a long shot, Chrissie. If he used it he'd be raving mad to keep it."

She shrugged. "I'm just passing it on for what it's worth."

I wondered if it had been worth her waiting to tell me this. She'd gone out of her way, which wasn't like Chrissie at all. We continued round the block until her car was in sight again. We stopped a short distance from the Bentley.

"Have you told the fuzz about the bronze?" I asked.

She snapped on her hard-paste stare. "Don't be stupid." Then she ran quickly to the car, pulling away smartly.

I took the lift up to the fifth floor, saw the light strip under the door of my flat, remembered hastily that I wasn't on the run and opened the door normally. Maggie had a cup of Ovaltine by her side with some French bread and cheese and was watching television. She didn't look round but held up a hand to indicate silence. She was wearing black patterned stockings with a short-skirted, high-necked maroon dress and was hiding behind an unusually large pair of round-framed, pink-tinted glasses. Maggie was delicately made up, well groomed, exuded a suspicion of Mitsouka and looked superb. I was in for trouble.

It was ten minutes before I could speak while she watched the end of some period play. "That was super," she said at last. "Where've you been?" I turned off the set.

"Out," I said, wondering what to tell her.

"Hark at the man. Am I too young to know?"

"All right, I've been chatting up a friend of Dick's."

Maggie took a bite at the cheese-laden French bread and kept me waiting. I knew that it wouldn't be this easy. "It's a fine greeting," I grumbled, "in my own home. Not even a kiss."

"You don't deserve one. I've decided that I'm tired of being protected by you, Willie Scott. I'm tired of being treated like a little girl, fed only what's good for her. I'm sick of worrying over the unknown. Like a dying patient, I want to know what's going on. And don't lie."

I was about to answer when she caught me nicely in anticipation. "And don't soft-soap me, either. I'm as concerned as you

40

are for Dick. I know he's in deep trouble. You intend to do it your way, which means outside the law. I want to know what it is you're going to do."

"It'll worry you silly."

"I'm worried silly now."

I crossed to her, gently took her hands and pulled her to her feet. I took off her glasses and placed them on the occasional table by her chair. I held her firmly but tightly, relishing the warm contact, unheeding of her lack of response. "I just can't hurt you, Maggie," I whispered, my face against the soft texture of hers.

"You *are* hurting me. Every time you cut me out."

"I cut you out because you bring out the best in me. I don't want you to know the animal inside my skin. I'm more afraid of him than you are."

"I know that, Willie. But he was the man I first met, the villain. He was the man I fell in love with. I can't pretend he's not there, but I can help him."

"Not in this, my love, believe me."

"Is it so dangerous?"

I stiffened and she noticed it.

I felt her vertebrae under my fingertips as she stiffened with me. Then her arms came round my back and her hands pressed hard against my shoulder blades.

"Not really," I replied far too late. "But tricky."

"You never lie well to me." Her face was still against mine and some of its warmth had gone. "The truth, Willie; a half truth will worry me far more."

"It's a bit dodgy," I admitted. "But it's got to be done."

"Tell me about it. All about it."

I told her. That night she stayed at my place. The Ovaltine didn't make her sleep.

3

I SORTED OUT my problems at the office and checked with young Charlie Hewitt that the business could run without me for a bit; he managed not to smile. Lulu gave me an old-fashioned look; they all knew that strange things sometimes happened during my absence. They never discovered how strange, which was as well, for I couldn't have coped with the turnover of staff. I signed sufficient checks to last them for a few days and Charlie locked them away.

I went home at half five, showered and changed into a fawn lightweight suit and slipped into some casual brown shoes. I wore my favorite oyster-gray silk tie against a white nylon shirt. Maggie would have approved of my image but I wasn't dressing for her. I took the Underground to Chiswick and turned down Hanger Lane. I was on time; I took it slowly, noting the faded turquoise sky, relishing it, and hoping I'd be able to recall its beauty when pollution finally changed it to midnight blue. The traffic was thick, exhausts adding their bit to the inevitable.

The *trattoria* lay back from a layby, an image of latticed windows, trellis and big bunches of artificial grapes. On the forecourt it was still warm enough for clientele to enjoy a long drink under gaily striped umbrellas before hurrying home. It was nice and it was cozy and it could turn out to be a death trap.

One car in the line of the layby impressed me—a Mercedes 250. It could be his; it was this year's model and gleamed with care. I crossed the forecourt, weaving between the tables, and entered the grotto gloom of the interior. More bunches of grapes hung from phony vines under subdued lighting. A faint smell of cooking reassured me that the food, at least, was not plastic.

"Spider." A slow cultured voice conveyed mild pleasure. My sight not yet adjusted, I turned to see two dark shapes by the quarter moon of a bar to the right of the door. The larger of the shapes laughed softly. "Follow the sound of my voice; there is no usherette." I could now see that the woman with him was smiling, the lack of light giving her great beauty, the shadows catching her in the right places, under the cheekbones, narrowing her temples and tapering her long neck to the hollow of her throat.

"Hello, Norman." Our handshake was perfunctory. He sat crouched on the bar stool, a big yet elegant man, thick gray hair brushed straight back in strong, distinguished waves. As far as I could see in the bad light he hadn't aged much; his features were still lean. The lines running either side of his mouth might have deepened fractionally but his looks were still good; an easy manner suggested a relaxed personality. His eyes were clear but misleadingly casual. The cut of his suit was modern Continental.

"I don't think you've met my wife. Ulla, meet an old friend, Spider Scott."

It wasn't difficult meeting her. Her eyes were unusually violet, her accent in her brief "Hello" north European. Her fair hair hung loose. She had a soft, calculating gaze that in purpose was as hard as Chrissie's. But I reckoned her to have far more all-round intelligence coupled with a Continental charm that Chrissie might consider a simper, but there was little soft about it. Norman, in his early fifties, had done well for himself. Ulla I guessed to be a little younger than me, about thirty-three maybe, and well cared for. I felt Norman's gaze and switched mine quickly. I didn't need his jealousy just now.

"Spider used to do jobs for Max and me," explained Norman for my benefit. Ulla wouldn't be here at all if she didn't already know. "He's a great professional and there are few left."

"You are tall for a burglar," she observed when the barman was out of earshot. She said it as a compliment, as if to be on the creep was the most natural thing on earth.

"He's as agile as a cat, my dear." Between them they were setting me up for something. "I'm glad you phoned," he added. "I wanted to contact you, though I heard you'd retired." He signaled the barman, then to me: "Still on the wagon?"

"More or less," I said. "Tomato juice with an extra dash of Worcester."

Norman ordered, smiling like a television *compère*. "The food here's good." And then with a mild wink: "And it's away from the usual haunts."

For a few minutes we talked about everything bar crime and they made an excellent team. I sometimes wondered why Norman had ever gone bent. When I knew him before he also had a perfectly good import-export and packaging business. I asked him if he still had it. He had. It was clear as we talked that he had no secrets from Ulla and that he doted on her. It was difficult to reconcile her quiet, accented image with a man who must now be the top fence in Britain.

In his own line, now that Max was dead, Norman must rank with Reisen in importance. Rex Reisen was a mobster and carried a much bigger organization for higher returns, but his expenses were much higher too. So were his risks—which placed another surcharge on his expenses. Norman, on the other hand, operated much more subtly, making almost risk-free use of myriad contacts, bent, straight and don't-knows. I rated him higher than Max Harris. Max's roughshod methods had died with him. As the three of us chatted away I tried to see Norman as a murderer and couldn't.

The waiter signaled that our table was ready and we moved over to the darkest corner. Ulla moved ahead of me, a blue-sheathed figure with Norman attentive at her elbow.

As Norman knew the restaurant, I left things to him, and he and Ulla discussed the ordering like gourmets. There was no affectation here; they both knew what they were at. I don't much care for wine, but I rode along with them and could discern the quality if not relishing the taste. The dinner was tremendous, the small talk amusing and relaxed.

The business started with the liqueurs and coffee, and it was Norman who slipped it out as if he was still discussing a play they'd seen. "I can't pretend to be sorry about Max but I am sorry about how it happened." He looked mildly over his cigar smoke at me. "You *have* heard, of course?" He brushed his hair back carefully with one hand; he had always been vain.

I nodded, focusing on a huge platinum-mounted sapphire on Ulla's right hand. "That's why I rang you. The King is dead, long live the king."

"That's observant of you. And complimentary too. Yet I thought you'd retired."

Ulla had pushed her chair back slightly, and I was aware that she was watching me closely for my reaction to Norman's questions. If they were as good a husband-and-wife team in all departments of fencing they'd have knocked spots off Max and Chrissie at their best. "I had. But I recently saw Max and he offered me work. He said he'd missed me and I must admit that I'm getting bored. Now I shall never know what the job was."

"What about Chrissie?"

"Working for her?" I laughed. "You couldn't have forgotten that much about me. She's finished. The boys wouldn't stand for her."

Norman smiled thinly. "I'm inclined to agree. She's brash, but I can't see her giving up easily, can you?"

The peculiar thing was that the whole tone of talk seemed no different than before, yet I knew that it was. Behind Ulla's pleasant smile and soft-eyed gaze was an intense vigilance. These two would protect each other to the death. My impression was that she wasn't so emotionally entangled as he was, so her reasons might be hard cash, and if that was true she hid it well.

"I don't think you need worry about her."

"My dear fellow, I don't. Without Max she is nothing. Have you seen her lately?"

I had to take a calculated risk or their teamwork would pay off. "No. Not to speak to." Now could Ulla bore through my head without hardening her expression? The red alarm sounded, but Norman nodded as if he understood. I had a tremendous urge to enlarge but recognized in time that it would be a mistake.

"She's an extraordinary woman," Norman observed, "but lacking in many ways." He reflected behind drooped lids while a perfectly steady hand rested on the table with the lighted end of the cigar held high as if he wanted to avoid nicotine-stained fingers—and I noticed that he had. "Did you hear about Max and me?"

I wished Ulla would look at him for a while. "How d'you mean?"

He rolled off some ash. "The night he was murdered he rang me. Wanted a meeting. As you know, he was a rough-cast individual and I think he was beginning to see that his methods were antiquated. He strongly resented my own success and possibly imagined that I was trying to interfere with his. Anyway he wanted to talk about it."

"It was very lucky you didn't go, my darling." Faithful Ulla came in on cue, but it didn't sound contrived.

"What happened?" I asked obediently.

"Nothing actually. I had an appointment that evening, but I did tell him that if I returned reasonably early I would ring him to ask if he still wanted to see me that night. In the event

46

I did ring him to have a most extraordinary reception." Norman smiled wryly at the recollection and glanced at his wife. "He told me that he couldn't see me then and to get off the line."

"*Told* you?"

Norman smiled. "You knew him too well. He *shouted* at me. After his first call I was quite unprepared. I must admit that it shook me."

"So you didn't go?"

"Naturally not. When Chrissie telephoned later I told her what had happened. You know Chrissie. She didn't believe me, of course. I only hope that she does nothing silly."

"She'd better not try."

For the first time I saw a brittle flaw in Ulla. She'd ejected the words quickly, like four lethal darts. Her accent had noticeably sharpened with the threat. I'd remember to wear wing mirrors if I ever walked in front of her.

"Do you think Chrissie will stir it up? I believe she was very possessive of Max." If they were conning, then I was adding my own bit.

Norman's face straightened and I noticed that at last Ulla had switched her gaze to him; her features had hardened and I detected a suggestion of cruelty about her lips. For perhaps three seconds she concentrated on Norman, as if she too was unsure of his reply.

He shrugged uncertainly. "The only indication I have is that the police haven't called." Norman had always avoided criminal slang although he knew it well enough. How can you be snobby in his game? "I would normally have expected them in view of the phone calls. That must mean that Chrissie is playing her own game."

"Or that she has no game to play. Chrissie wouldn't help the fuzz under any circumstances," I suggested.

"I hope you're right, Spider. For her sake I really do."

So now they had both opened up. What had happened to the pleasantries of half an hour ago? But how much of any of it was true? Their life was embedded in subterfuge. As I looked at them both, their smiles now returned, it was difficult to believe. But I'd better believe it, by God. From now on I'd better keep that wholly in mind.

"So now you want to work for Norman?" Ulla had returned to sweetness.

"Not entirely. I'm basically a loner, always have been. But if something crops up where you feel I can be useful, sure, I'd be interested if the return justifies the risk."

"You've grown wiser, Spider. Good man. Max used to diddle you, y'know. He was always tight-fisted." His echoing of Maggie's assertion irritated me because it was true. "I could almost keep you wholly occupied," he continued. "And I am talking of jobs most suitable to your talents." He was studying me now, trying to detect possible changes. "Although you have had a long layoff," he added as a warning.

"Not as long as the last stretch of bird I did."

"No, but serving time is rather like a refresher course; you run into old friends, compare notes, bring methods up to date even if you can't practice them, and as you well know many things can be practiced even inside. So they tell me," he finished, just to let me know that he'd never done time himself.

He was ferreting. "Don't use me if you feel I'm a bad risk. I'm not desperate for work."

"But the urge is uncomfortable, is that it?" He chuckled quietly. "You're a bad businessman, Spider, but a damned fine craftsman. No, I have no fears about your layoff; you're too good a professional. In fact I have a job for you."

I hadn't expected it so soon. I glanced at Ulla, who seemed to have lost interest in me, but it didn't make me less wary. This was the crunch. Suddenly I found that I was acting, showing an outward interest while my nerve ends screamed no.

"Fill me in," I said not too eagerly.

Norman smiled stiffly. "Nervous already?"

"Just careful," I replied. "It's part of the game."

48

Ulla flickered to life again, her violet orbs soaking up the scene. All the pleasantries had led to this moment. I was on the rack. As that was the idea, I found it difficult to complain.

"You want to know about it?"

I managed surprise. "That's why I'm here."

Norman sat back, his lean looks half disappearing in shadow. His eyes were suddenly sharp, as if individually spotlighted from the gloom. Ulla was back to her concentration act, and tempted as I was to glance over, I kept my gaze riveted on Norman. It was as though the drinks and the dinner had never happened. Time started now. I could feel my heartbeat.

"What do you think, darling?" he drawled but still watching me.

"Wait a minute." I thumped the table with the flat of my hand. I stared arrogantly at Ulla, who seemed slightly amused. "Let's be clear about this. I'm not having a woman as boss, not in this game. Norman, if you can't make your own decisions, then I'm out. Right now."

Norman's eyes crinkled but the spotlights remained. Then he laughed, grasping Ulla's soft-fingered hand and squeezing it. "The same old Spider, thank God. That's exactly how I remember you."

The crafty bastard, I thought.

"Tomorrow night," he said. "My place. Half ten. I enjoyed meeting you again, Spider. Let's start to profit from it."

Ulla gave a dutiful smile that contained just a hint of enigma, and then I was brushed from her mind.

Maggie was out to prove that she could stand up to the strain of reality and she was determined to see it through. But she was suffering. I protected her to some degree by a mixture of truth and lies, but it wasn't easy.

She wore a lime-green trouser suit and a rakish cap to match. We caught a bus to Dick's pad.

His perky-faced landlady let us in and we found him with open-necked shirt under a grubby pullover, sprawled in his one-roomed den with a glass of beer by his side. He clambered to his feet white-faced with strain and red-eyed through sleeplessness. He smiled sheepishly. "Now I know what interrogation is all about from the receiving end." His hair was ruffled and he was bewildered by what had happened to him.

"Why haven't you contacted us?" I asked. "We've been worried."

Dick shrugged apologetically; he was near to being all in.

"I thought it better not. Anyway, I've been getting home too late to phone."

"Have you had a proper meal? Can I cook something?"

"No thanks, Maggie. Really. Mrs. Gee looks after me well."

"Anyway," I said, taking a pew, "they haven't nicked you yet."

He grimaced. "The only reason why not is political, I reckon. A copper arrested for murder is national news. They're holding back until they're cast iron, that's all."

"Well," I said, grinning, "you're safe then."

His answering grin was sickly. Then he ticked off the points against him, pulling back one finger at a time.

"There is the bribery charge now stinking to high heaven. My station chief called me in, suspended me from duty and produced forms of allegation from the complainant—the *News*. Then there's my visit to Max near the time of murder. Believe it or not, one of the witnesses saw me go in. Rubbish, but what can I do about that? There's a slight variation of the time I was seen between the two witnesses, but one admits that he wasn't clock watching so couldn't be exact. And there's the little matter of my dabs on the front door lintel. I must have put my hand up to lean against it."

I felt wretched about this, but my instinct still warned me not to tell him of my own visit. If I failed to get him off, then I reckoned that would be the time to do it. Maggie would back my judgment.

I took in the room, chintzy and homely with sports photographs around the walls; the Metropolitan Police boxing team with Dick standing with folded arms in the back row as a light heavy. Three silver cups for the same sport were on the mantelpiece. A little uncharacteristic untidiness had crept into the room—his jacket and tie slung over a chair, the evening paper crumpled on the table, small things showing his state of mind.

"Look," he snapped, "don't pity me, for God's sake. That won't help any of us. I'm doing something positive. I've been in touch with my snouts and the word is around. Ron Healey is also working on it in his spare time. The murder weapon's still missing and I don't think we're likely to find it now. The difficulty is that time's running out; they'll have to pull me in soon whether they like it or not. Don't forget that I'm involved in two separate cases, which will make it look far worse to the public."

He made no mention of Ron Healey contacting me, which meant the sergeant had wisely kept it between us. With Dick I had a similar problem to the one I'd had with Maggie but more clear cut. I had no intention of telling him how I was becoming involved with Norman Shaw. He'd do his nut. He felt as strongly for me as I did for him, so I left it there. Maggie understood.

When we left Maggie was despondent. Even she was beginning to realize that the straight and narrow path was as crooked as the rest. "He's too young to be looking so old" was her only observation.

The house was in wealthy St. John's Wood. In a quiet back street, not too far from a main road, it was the middle one in a pillared terrace. Cars were parked like status symbols on both sides of the street, with residents' stickers on the windscreens. Outside Norman's house was crouched the Mercedes, but he probably used it only to drive to the nearby row of lockups, where his Rolls Silver Cloud slummed it under bricks and mortar. I'd done some homework. It's a fact that in some areas I'd feel reasonably well breached, comfortable in my wallet; here my wallet felt empty. I was a servant looking for a job, and the analogy was almost true in both senses. I belonged here only if I was back on the creep.

I did my usual casing stint along the row of houses. There wasn't much point, but it was a habit I didn't want to break. They all had old-fashioned sash windows; anything else in the plastered façades would have looked wrong. I walked up the steps to the portico, standing between the white-painted pillars like a dark intruder. Respectability cloyed the air like sickly perfume. No one could miss it unless they lived here, and they would carry it with them as a protective shield against the disease of poverty. In the darkness I had to smile. The biggest fence in the country certainly knew where to fraternize in safety. Max would never have got away with it here. I thumbed the button. Subdued church bells summoned the angels.

One of them opened the door—an attractive teenager clad in something from a wagon train of the American West. Skirt reached the floor but she wasn't carrying a gun. Above the high, tight bodice a young face, too arrogant to be pretty, stared at me as if I'd forgotten to collect the dustbins that morning. Cold, piercing eyes rated me with no trouble at all, carrying the assessment into the tone of her voice. "Yes?"

I hadn't expected a maid and I hadn't got one. Norman wouldn't employ one unless she was deaf and dumb. So who had I got? I tried my famous smile and the image silently accused me of dumb insolence. "I have an appointment with Mr. Shaw," I explained.

"Oh? Which Mr. Shaw?"

"How many are there?"

"Does it matter? You must know which one."

I thought, To hell with it. "You're a polite little bitch," I said. "Now go and tell Norman Shaw that Mr. Scott is here."

"Oh—Daddy! Why didn't you say so at first? I suppose you'd better come in." The invitation was totally grudging. The mention of her father made little impression, and she made no effort to disguise what she thought of me. She showed me into a tall room with stucco cornices and a painted ceiling of Florentine design. My impression was of heavy drapes and walnut furniture and pale-green carpeting. With so much ormolu and glass I found the room too fussy.

As she was about to close the door I said, "Would it damage the furniture if I sat down?"

She eyed me coldly, as if actually debating my question.

"He shouldn't be too long." And she closed the door. Half amused, half annoyed, I sat down in a Bergere wondering how she could afford to be so haughty; she also struck me as being too old to be spawned by Ulla.

Ten minutes later Ulla came into the room wearing a low-cut dinner gown costing as much as Maggie's annual clothing allowance, tight on the breasts and hanging in well-trained folds below. She gave me a faintly coquettish smile, raising her brows in a vaguely challenging way and eying me with amused interest. Her face could really come alive when she wanted. "I'm sorry Norman's late. We've been out and were delayed, but he shouldn't be long now. Do please sit down."

She sat opposite me with her back to the door. Could it be that if Norman came in she wouldn't want him to see her expression? "How did you find Belinda?"

"Your daughter?"

"My stepdaughter."

I didn't miss the hardening of tone or gaze, but the smile stayed fixed.

"You can be frank," she added, seeing me hesitate.

"She wants her bottom spanked by a heavy hand. Mine, for instance."

Ulla laughed softly, throwing back her head and lengthening her neck line. This could turn out to be a dangerous game.

"I keep telling Norman that she's utterly spoiled. I'm glad you agree. His family mean everything to him and he overdoes it." She didn't say if she considered herself part of the family. The violet eyes were questing. I had an idea for what but couldn't believe it. Maybe I'm getting old.

"I can't see that being the daughter of a high-class villain is anything to be uppity about. How would she take it if he was banged away for a few years?"

Her eyes became iced lollipops. The stiffened smile accused me of spoiling a good thing. And so I was. I didn't want *my* head bashed by Norman.

"Are there any other children?" I asked conversationally.

"Not by me. There is Peter, also from Norman's previous marriage. He's still at university. A nice boy but too sensitive."

Sensitive to what? I wondered. Who was the nut who said crime doesn't pay? It was paying Norman and his family very nicely indeed.

"Have I raised a painful subject?" I probed.

"Painful? To me? Oh, Spider, how naïve!" Her smile projected half a dozen messages too confused to separate. "I raised it myself, did I not?"

She was still flirting with me but making no effort to go beyond it. Perhaps I wasn't being responsive enough. There was a cunning change of expression as the door opened and Norman came in. Ulla stood up, smiled brightly at him and slipped an arm through his. "I've been filling in for you, darling. Good night, Mr. Scott." She kissed Norman on the cheek and slipped out while he stood there thoughtfully for a couple of seconds wondering what he'd missed. In that pose he appeared a dangerous enemy. There was more than one Norman tucked behind that well-groomed, good-looking façade. There were moments when his eyes reminded me of Colonel Kransouski; that's another story but enough to chill me at the thought of it.

Norman sat where Ulla had been sitting, wriggling a little

as if the warmth she had left reassured him. He pressed the right button and was smiling again. "Sorry I'm late. Drink?" He didn't look as if he intended to get up and get one but perhaps he guessed I'd refuse. The grayness of his eyes was porcelain bright and as hard, the soft wall lights reflecting straight back from their glaze. I wondered how they would be if he knew that I had a brother in the police or if he could be sure that Ulla had been casually flirting with me.

He very carefully brushed back his hair with both hands, his fingers exploring for untidy strands. Then quite unexpectedly he drew in his breath, closed his lips and appeared to blow out his cheeks while trying to hold them steady. As he held his breath his color mounted with the strain. After a few seconds he exhaled with a rush of air, watching for my reaction. I didn't show one.

"Isometric exercises," he explained. "Force against force. Keeps the muscles trim. That one stops face sag."

I nodded with interest. Middle age had heightened his vanity.

Norman crossed his legs, gave me a measured look and said, "I have a job for you."

"*My* sort of job?"

"Made for you."

I didn't like the way he said that. "Where?"

"Here in London."

"Tom?"

"A beautiful collection of rings."

"They sound easily identifiable."

"Some will be. It's not too costly rearranging mounts and providing new shanks. In most cases it won't be necessary. The stones themselves I hardly think could be identified."

"Are they in a safe?"

Norman hesitated. He had the habit of squeezing his cheeks between fingers and thumb and gazing at the ceiling when uncertain. "I'm not sure. I'm of the opinion that they are not."

"You'll have to do better than that. I'm not screwing a drum on spec."

"Did I say it was a house? It is in fact. Oh, they're there all right. I have the feeling that they're hidden rather than locked up."

This wasn't the Norman I remembered; he'd been precise.

"It sounds dodgy. I can't go traipsing all over a place. They could be anywhere. It could take all night."

"Since when has that worried you?"

"If the drum's occupied it always worries me." Something was missing.

Norman remained unruffled and I think he was sounding my judgment. I couldn't believe he was this uncertain. Not calculating Norman.

"I like to place things quickly, preferably getting them out of the country that same night. Now I'm commercially interested in this particular collection because I can easily dispose of it. I don't believe they're in a safe because they could be embarrassing if found in a safe."

"You mean they're bent?"

"It wouldn't surprise me. The collector himself wouldn't have stolen them, but I strongly suspect he bought them knowing them to be stolen."

I smiled. "Not one of your own clients, Norman?"

He had his moments of humor. He laughed. "A delightful thought but not a good way to do business. No. I think they are hidden in the top part of the house. Probably the very top floor."

"How can you know?"

"How can I know they're there at all? Perhaps I'm being more obtuse than I should. Let's put it another way. If they're not on the top two floors, get out and I'll pay you compensation."

"How much?"

"Compensation? Fifty pounds. For successfully doing the job, two-fifty."

"That's as mean as Max." I chuckled. "Where's the percentage basis?"

"There can't be on this. It's easy money for an easy job. Let's face it, two hundred and fifty pounds for a couple of hours' work can't be bad. The research is all mine."

"You haven't done much so far as I can see."

"Enough. You'll find them."

"Who do I deliver them to?"

"To me."

This shook me. It wasn't like Norman to take unnecessary risks. He was baiting me in some way I couldn't see, but I had to make up my mind whether to ride along with it. If I turned this down he wouldn't ask me again.

"Is the place wired?"

"Not the part that affects you. And the people will be away for the next few days."

"Leaving tom floating around loose?"

Norman looked derisive. "Really! My dear Spider, I seem to remember that it was you who taught me that a really good hiding place was better than any safe. The trouble with people is that they are not sufficiently imaginative; I believe that this one is and that's the only reason I can't be more precise. The stuff is there and they'll be away. What more do you want?"

"I'll need to case it to make sure it's as simple as you say. Where exactly is it?"

"Next door," he said.

"*What?*"

"Next door," he repeated. "On this side."

4

I STARED at him for a while. I suppose there was no reason why it shouldn't be next door. But I was surprised that he was willing to take a chance on his own doorstep. Then I saw that it was typical Norman. Bold and safe.

He was smiling because he could see that he had startled me. "If it's of any help there is a house up for sale almost opposite. Need I say more?"

"When's the deadline?"

"Five days from tomorrow. The two upper floors are virtually a maisonette let out by the people below who may well be at home but there's no reason to disturb them, is there?"

"O.K.," I said. "It's on."

Norman pulled out his wallet. "Fifty in advance." He held out the notes.

I had to take them. It was a strange feeling accepting money for a job after all these years. I was committed, back in the game. Perhaps I'd never left it. I took the notes as if they were alight.

"They're good ones," he said in amusement.

I grinned sheepishly. "It's been a long time, Norman. It's a funny feeling." We rose together.

"I don't know," he said. "From what I hear you've kept your hand in, in a variety of ways."

"Don't believe what the papers say. Why did you break with Max?"

The question nipped under his guard. He frowned, eying me quickly.

"I should have thought you would have guessed. We didn't get on, had different tastes, ideas, *modus operandi*. Max lived in the past, couldn't move with the times."

"His murder will help you." I was careful how I said it, and he didn't seem too put out.

"Only in the short term. The rift between Max and me was inevitable, just as inevitable as my eventually taking over the whole scene."

"Max wouldn't have let you do it that easy."

Norman smiled confidently. "He would have fought, yes. But, you know, the trouble with Max was that you could see every blow coming. He was brutal but clumsy."

"I'd better get back," I said. I looked appreciatively round the room. "A nice place, Norman." There were no bronzes here. As he didn't offer to show me round the house in spite of my prod, I reasoned that I'd have to do it the hard way.

He led me to the front door with his hand affectionately on my shoulder. I hadn't realized until then that he was taller than me and I'm over six feet. He was every inch the business-man when he showed me out. His public-school education had done nothing for his morals but had at least helped him develop a natural presence. With his mature handsomeness it was a formidable combination. I wondered if Ulla really appreciated what she had landed.

The estate agent's keys jangled in my pocket. I was wearing my best suit with a white silk shirt and a green silk tie and turtleskin casual shoes. My friends wouldn't have recognized me. My hair was uncharacteristically tidy, held in place by some of Maggie's "hard to hold" lacquer. I felt as if I was going to my first interview for a job. But I'd needed the disguise, together with a fleeting, jacked-up accent which would have startled Norman, to convince the agent that I was sufficiently loaded to have an interest in the house near Norman's. Over one shoulder I carried a camera case.

I didn't give Norman's house as much as a glance as I approached from the opposite side of the road. There was a sale sign outside the empty house, and I turned into the gate, up the scrubbed steps between the pillars and turned the key in the lock. Inside the bare hall I stood still for a moment, knowing that my shape could be seen through the multicolored twin glass panels of the door. The place was musty and needed airing. By the browns and fawns of walls and woods I judged that whoever had lived here had a Victorian hangover.

Empty houses have always been unlucky for me. They've sprung some very nasty surprises. I went up the stairs without trying to reduce noise because the turning of the key and the closing of the door would have warned anyone. I trod loudly, getting some sort of pleasure from not having to creep for once. An army of echoes came with me, dying in the rising dust. I worked from top to bottom through all the rooms and finished up empty-handed except for an old bill for a dress hire. It wasn't a bad place; nice-sized rooms and high ceilings. But it was out of my bracket.

Now I got down to the serious work and went back upstairs again. The rear rooms overlooked a long narrow garden backing onto another. High wooden fences ran down both sides of an overgrown lawn. I examined the window catches. Sash windows almost inevitably overlap top pane over bottom from outside, which meant that a long-bladed knife went in between the two from underneath. In old, well-built houses catches are heavy and sometimes difficult to shift. Another nasty habit they can have is suddenly to spring back sharply, making a hell of a noise.

I then returned to a front room, standing well back from the curtainless windows. I was glad then of the brown and fawn backcloth. Norman's house faced me obliquely across the road, and the sun was reflecting off the windows like blazing medals on a general's chest. I opened my camera case and took out a pair of high-powered binoculars, focusing on the house next to Norman's. The sun was blinding in spite of my trying different positions. I thundered downstairs again.

It was better from downstairs but not the angle I really wanted. It had to do. Taking my time, I scanned every window from top to bottom. There were no visible alarms at any of them. Usually they can be seen down the woodwork. This meant that any wiring would be highly sophisticated. I began to think that Norman was right. The peculiar thing was that the downstairs windows were the same when he had intimated that they might be wired. It could be as easy as he suggested. It could be.

I went over it again; it was the Army that taught me that time spent in preparation is never lost in operation. Then I concentrated on Norman's place. The sun had moved very slightly and made it a shade easier for me. It could have been worse; it might have shone on my glasses. Norman knew what alarms were all about, of course. Yet I still didn't detect any. The curtains hanging down the frames might partially hide them—if they were there.

I thought about this. I've known other wealthy villains who never had an alarm in the place. They reckoned they had the best invisible alarm of the lot—reputation. Only an amateur wouldn't know whose drum it was, and amateurs as stupid as that never grew up to become professionals. Yet somehow I'd put Norman aside from the rest; he had struck me as the sort of character who wouldn't play down insurance but take out a double policy.

I locked up and went thoughtfully down the steps. I reckoned there was a good deal about Norman it would benefit me to know. I crossed the road, went past the house I was to screw and then Norman's. I took in a lot of detail without actually turning my head. From the empty house I'd naturally pinpointed the stout rain pipes at each house but was hoping that I wouldn't have to do a frontal job in full view of any sleepless character counting sheep at his window.

The street was quite long and there was no break between the houses. I turned the corner to find no break in the building line, no convenient little alleys between buildings. And the houses were solid and tall. When I had completed a tour of the block I knew that I had a problem. I'd also found another reason for a shortage of alarms. There was no back way in and only a mug would climb out front. Norman must know this.

When I got back to my flat I tried to telephone him. I knew he wouldn't thank me if I called in person. A youth's voice answered the phone, high-pitched and overcultured, yet it didn't sound like affectation. I asked if I could speak to Norman Shaw.

"I'm afraid he's out. Who's calling?" This voice was very high-bracket indeed and almost indifferent. The inquiry was pure reflex politeness.

"This is Spi—er, Scott is my name. I wonder if you would ask Mr. Shaw to ring me sometime this evening. It's important."

"Yes, of course. I'm afraid he'll be rather late. After eleven, I believe."

"That'll do. Who am I speaking to?"

"I'm his son, Peter. I'll pass your message, Mr. Scott."

What sort of children had Norman landed himself with? This one was more helpful than Belinda but an accent like that could only tumble down the scale like Belinda's haughtiness. But at least he hadn't talked down to me. I rang Maggie to tell her I was coming over.

"Why hide good legs under dirty dungarees?" I asked.

"Men," she complained. "They're not dirty and I've been dusting round the flat. It doesn't do itself."

She'd piled her hair high on her head. "You've got the wrong

62

nose for that style," I said. "You need a Grecian nose and yours is snub."

"Thank . . . you. When are you selling your travel agency for a beauty parlor?"

"I'm an expert on women," I said, grinning, ready to dodge if she threw something.

But Maggie looked at me archly. "What's all this banter covering up? We made an agreement, or have you forgotten?"

I told her about the house I had to screw, how I'd made my first inroads into Norman's confidence and how I didn't like it. I couldn't get used to telling her things like this, but she was entitled to know as long as she wanted to and as long as she was silly enough to stay with me. I could see that she was having difficulty in remaining calm about my involvement. I had returned to crime, whatever the reason. But apart from a little paleness and a sudden house-proud impulse to go round the room thumping cushions and repositioning articles already perfectly placed, Maggie took it well.

"Let's call it off," I said. "Let me just get on with the job and leave you right out of it. It would make us both happier."

She sat down, her hands fluttering because she didn't know what to do with them.

"Oh, Meg, be sensible. You're not cut out for it." I crossed over to kneel in front of her. I took her hands and felt their vibration. "Come on, love. I admire you for what you're trying to do, but you're too straight for this caper."

She took her hands from mine and placed them on either side of my face. They were like ice packs on my warm flesh, but I gave her no sign of this. Her face was so strained that I knew she was fighting tears. I could see the little laughter lines about her mouth and eyes but she was far from laughing now. Her eyes were tinged with a strange melancholy.

Suddenly she smiled and started taking the pins from her hair.

Then she said almost as an aside, "I'll help you."

63

I didn't get her drift. I got up from my knees to sit beside her.

"Which night are you doing the job?" she asked quite brightly as she fumbled with her hair.

"Tomorrow if the weather's right."

"If you're worried about climbing in full view, I can keep a lookout."

I stared at her disbelievingly. Maggie had never seen me do a job. The thought of it reviled me. If anything above all else threw up the past uselessness of my life, then the possibility of Maggie watching me screw a drum did just that. I was shaken badly.

"Oh no you don't," I said with a quivering voice.

"Why? Is there a difference between knowing you do it and actually seeing it done?"

"Never mind the differences." I was vehement. "It's not on and that's it."

She sat back from me as if looking at a stranger. "I've never seen you in a temper like this. I don't understand your anger. I'm trying to help you cut down the risk."

"And I'm saying no." I stood up.

My own temper turned on a sweet coolness in her. "So you can get me to make telephone calls to help you on a job; you can seek refuge with me after a job. What's the difference now?"

The blood had rushed to my head. "There *is* a bloody difference and that's that."

"You're swearing," she said sweetly. "And becoming inarticulate. You're not at all the man I almost married. Strange fellow."

I'd handled it wrong. At this rate she had me over a barrel and I'd just storm out. She was laughing quietly at me and in a perverse way I was glad to see her humored even at my expense.

"Oh, Willie, you *do* look furious. And you're so illogical. I thought that was a woman's prerogative. If you don't sit down you'll bust a valve."

I was saved by the bell. One long forlorn peal from the front door. We stared at each other. It was ten o'clock. I felt sheepish as I gazed at Maggie but was glad of the interruption. She went to the door reluctantly and I followed up behind just in case. A grim-faced Ron Healey stood there.

"It's all right, Meg. This is Detective Sergeant Healey, a very good friend of Dick's."

"I'm sorry to bust in," Healey said as he closed the door behind him. He nodded at me. "I tried to get you on the telephone. I hoped you'd be round here. They've arrested Dick."

Healey's carroty hair was windblown and he now looked his age. "Sometimes I wonder why I stay in this job with what they pay us for the hours we work." He was dejected and physically weary, his hands thrust into the pockets of an old jacket.

Maggie and I were stunned. We had both hoped without expressing it that it wouldn't come to this. "So they've got enough for a case?" I asked unnecessarily.

Healey kneaded his bloodshot eyes. "They always have had. They'd never admit it but they've hung back because Dick's a copper. They may not even realize that that is what they've done. But it's the truth just the same. The word has leaked out and don't ask me how. The newspaper boys were sniffing around and the pressure was becoming intense. They had to bring him in." He sank onto the arm of a chair.

"Which means they've now got to bring a case."

"That's right. He'll be up for remand in the morning." He suddenly looked up at me sharply. "Have you any ideas who did it?"

He took me by surprise, but I took my time. I looked him straight in the eye. "Yes, I have."

Healey jumped up. "Then you'd better tell me or I'll nick you for withholding information."

I waved an impatient hand at him. "Oh, sit down, Ron. Don't give me that bull. I'm withholding nothing. I know nothing. I have a hunch but no evidence at all. The only way we'll get evidence is my way. You haven't a hope in hell and you must know it. Your murder squad isn't stupid. They must at least have considered the same lines. But I'm not shackled by a ball and chain. They are."

"And if you do get evidence what are you going to do with it, Spider Scott, non-grasser of all time?"

I don't think he intended to sneer. He was on edge with the rest of us. Even so, I was stung. Like Ron Healey, Maggie was staring at me, waiting for an answer.

"For Christ's sake, we're talking about my brother," I burst out. "He's in nick. *In nick. My brother,* who's never been bent in his life. What do you think I feel about *that*—me, an old con? I could weep my eyes out. The one thing I've prayed for all my life was that Dick should be straight. Just what d'you think I'd do with evidence, you bloody fool?"

I was choked and frightened too. I hadn't answered the question, and from Ron Healey's strange look I knew the fact hadn't missed him. I couldn't have given Norman Shaw's name if my life depended on it, not now anyway.

"Will you keep me informed?" he mumbled.

"*Only* you. When I've got something." I meant it as a compliment. The stirring uncertainty growing in me was not Healey's suspicion or even Dick's arrest at this stage. It was the press. If they had got the scent, how long was it going to take them to discover that Willie "Spider" Scott is the brother of Detective Constable Scott. And when they did could they print it or would it be considered prejudicial to Dick? Trial by press. I had to hope so. I had to hope like hell so. If they printed it I didn't fancy my chances with Norman.

Ron Healey left not too convinced that I knew what I was at or that I was the best man to do it whatever it was. But at least he knew how I felt about Dick.

On our own again, Maggie said, "Now you've no choice. I'll help you, Willie. Please let me—for Dick's sake."

I couldn't answer. She was intent on full commitment. I just hoped it left her unscarred. I had to rush back to my flat in case Norman rang.

The phone was ringing as I unlocked the door. I grabbed it with the door still open behind me. "Scott. Hello, Norman. I've just come in. Hold on while I close the door." I was still breathless when I went back to the phone. "Thanks for ringing back," I said. "I wouldn't trouble you but it's important. I had a look at that house for sale today. Nice area but there are disadvantages. There's no access to the rear except through the house. I wondered if you knew an area where there is easier access." I didn't want to be too open over the phone, but he'd know what I was on about.

There was a silence while he mulled it over.

"I'd like to help you," he eventually said, "but I really don't see what I can do."

"Well, I know that you're very knowledgeable about houses, so I thought I'd ask. What happens if I lose the key? Would the next-door neighbor let me in?"

But he'd already detected my drift. "No hope of that, I'm afraid. He's a very cautious man; wouldn't help anyone in case they dirtied his carpet."

I could understand his reluctance not to let me through his house. He didn't want open involvement that could spring back on him. Yet I had to have some help. "That's a pity," I said. "I'm always losing keys and at least the back door could have been left open. There's another thing," I complained. "No parking space. I'd have to have parking space. I'm not traipsing half a mile to reach my car every time I go out."

Norman gave this one a bit longer before saying, "Parking can be arranged. Let me know if you intend to buy the house and I'll do what I can."

"I'm going to take another look at it tomorrow night, but it'll be very late. Thanks for the help. It's appreciated."

I hung up. Now that I'd have to go up the front of the house I'd never shake off Maggie.

67

I had one more call to make, one I'd promised and now dare not break. I could think of a dozen reasons for not making it, but all would rebound and I'd pay the price. I had promised. I must have been mad. I phoned Maggie. She was still up, waiting for the call. "Tomorrow night," I said listlessly. "Half twelve."

I hate having my shoulders and arms hampered, which is why I prefer the unrestricting lightness of a track suit. Yet I had to decide against it because Maggie would be with me. Alone I could always feign late-night training on quiet streets, but I couldn't get away with it with a woman. It was one of many niggling little things that had crept in due to her new and embarrassing determination. I could bite my tongue out for ever telling her the dangers of climbing the front of a house.

I went searching for a car at midnight in a bad mood, which is no way to start a job. I found an Imp near my flat. I had the louver open with a few harsh shakes aided by a long nail file on the catch. It was then easy to slip my arm through to open the door.

I nipped into the driver's seat, wound down the windows to pick up external sounds, then placed a shrouded torch on the floor with the beam shining up under the dashboard. It was awkward and I was out of practice but my fingers seemed to do their job without fuss. For a while Maggie was far from my mind as I sorted out the wires behind the dash. If I crossed the wrong wires I'd fuse the lot, but I wasn't *that* much out of practice.

The bitter mood Maggie had put me in at least kept me sharp. I heard the old familiar tread approaching like a slow, rhythmic drumbeat leading slowly in before the music grasped its mood. Torch out. Windows up. Door locks on. Down to the deck as far as possible. Matey had broken his tread and was doing a routine check of car doors. As he neared I squeezed myself as far under the bonnet as I could. There's a surprising amount of room in the front of an Imp, but I'm a big bloke and suffered.

Matey tried the door. He came round and tried the other. The car shook a bit, but who'd nick an Imp? Now I had to wait a hell of a time for him to get clear and he was in no hurry. It was some time before I could finish the wiring. Finally I connected up, the engine fired and I pulled out.

There was a little traffic on the roads, but the streets were largely deserted, reoxygenating themselves for the morning onslaught. At least it wasn't raining. I stopped dutifully at traffic lights in my lonely little prison and reflected that I'd never felt so bad about doing a job. I pitched up at Maggie's block with no enthusiasm. It was the first time that I can remember meeting her with complete abjection.

She stepped from the shadows like a tart waiting for a late pick-up. The analogy was instant and bitter on my palate. What was she trying to do? I opened the door for her and she climbed in without a word, not even of remonstrance for being late. She sank into the flimsy warmth of a dark raincoat and I noticed that she was wearing some sort of beret with a bobble, pulled rakishly over one ear. She knew that I found her insistence unsettling, which perhaps was why she kept silent. We acted like strangers.

"This is a stolen car," I rubbed in acidly.

The white blob of her face turned toward me but I watched the road.

"I didn't expect that you'd hired it. Don't be so bitter."

"For God's sake. What do you expect to gain from all this? You realize you've already broken the law."

"I told you. I've been running away for years, accepting just one part of you. It's time I found out just what it is I've tried to close my eyes to."

I took a corner too sharply and cursed at my nerves. "I can explain all that. You don't have to come on a caper."

"Don't I?"

I was tempted to meet her gaze but hadn't the courage to face her. If I had I'd have stopped the car there and then and we'd have finished up having the biggest row we'd ever had, and they were incredibly infrequent. I simply never wanted to quarrel with her.

"Willie, try to understand. Help me, please. I've *got* to do this. I can't really tell you why. There is Dick, of course, that might have prompted it, but it's not the real reason. I've got to find out about myself, about you—us. I can't go on as I did. I've got to know."

I didn't like the silence that followed that. I kept driving mechanically, somehow still keeping an eye open for the fuzz. They sometimes enjoy stopping lone cars at night; it passes the time for them. With great difficulty and in a very dry voice I said, "You mean this could finish us? That I might disgust you enough?"

Maggie put a cold hand on my knee. "You could never disgust me, Willie. Never think that. But I must discover my own reaction to real confrontation. Instead of sitting in a flat wondering what's happening, I will actually see. Perhaps having seen, I might never again be able to take the strain. *That* might finish us. I don't know." She turned in her seat so that she was fully facing me, but I still stared straight ahead through a soul-reflecting windscreen. "*You* know all about compulsion, Willie. I've tried to help you fight it. Help me see this compulsion of mine through, I beg you."

I swallowed. I licked my lips. My throat was dry. I was beginning to understand. I tried a different tack. "If we're caught we finish up in nick with Dick. There won't be much help for him then. And what do you think it would do to your parents?"

"What is more important is what it would do to you. Do you think I haven't thought it all through? Just as you do when you go alone and wonder how I might suffer if you're caught. At least we will have done it together."

Oh, God. It was like looking inside myself. I decided to try once more.

"Has it occurred to you that your presence might put me off, make me do something really stupid so that we *are* caught?"

"I've thought about it. I didn't notice my presence put you off when you climbed Thresher's wall."* She paused to let it sink in. "But if you are *really* afraid of that happening, Willie, then you must take me back now."

I glanced quickly at her for the first time. It was a mistake, for all I saw was innocence placing itself entirely at my mercy. I was on trial and this was part of it. Maggie was appealing to my honesty, what Fairfax, head of Defense Intelligence, had once described as integrity. I grappled and suffered strange, soul-twisting tortures. I couldn't look at her again. I tried to relax, using the steering wheel as an instrument of nerve therapy. The temptation to drive her back was enormous. "All right," I said, the sweat dribbling down my forehead. "Let's get it over with. But you must do what I say. No arguing."

"You're the professional," she said quietly.

I wondered if she realized how much that hurt. Only from a villain or a copper would I have considered it a compliment. From Maggie it somehow endorsed our relationship as being on trial.

* *The Miniatures Frame*

71

5

WE CRUISED in silence from then on. Nothing happened. I felt strange with Maggie sitting beside me, but I couldn't will her away. The feeling between us was strained because the whole situation was unreal. We drifted into the refined aura of Norman's street and I slowed down along the line of cars. The empty space looked like an extraction in a row of teeth. "Hold tight," I said.

I swung the car over past the gap that Norman had kept for me, then reversed in. I picked up an emanation of fear from Maggie and glanced quickly at her whitened face. She was scared, probably had been all along, but now she was showing it.

"You all right, Meg? I can run you back."

It broke the spell, but she was shaken. "Just a mini scare, that's all."

"It's like a bloke taking his wife to the office with him," I complained.

"Is it, Willie? It doesn't feel like it. Now what?"

"I get out to see if it's clear. I'll knock once on the car roof, then you go over to the empty house and hide behind one of the portico pillars. You'll be able to see me from there. If you see a copper or hear footsteps, one low whistle, then hide yourself as best you can. Once I'm inside there's nothing you can do but wait."

"At least I'll know where you are."

"It might be a long wait, Meg."

"I know."

I climbed out. The road was clear of people. Two ever-stretching rows of houses and cars with large regular tracts of darkness as if shrouds had been cast between the lampposts. It was a quarter to one. I tapped swiftly on the car and Maggie climbed out. She didn't look at me but walked straight-backed and soundlessly on rubbers toward the empty house I'd described to her. She didn't glance back. I gave her time to take up position, then entered the gate. Next door, Norman's house, like most of the others, was in complete darkness.

I started on up with my feet on either side of the pipe. It was an easy climb. The pipe was solidly fixed and the brickwork coarse under the soles of my feet, providing a good gripping surface. I went all the way to the top floor without incident. When I reached the guttering I let it take part of my weight as I gripped it with one hand and swung from the pipe to the nearest sill. Luckily the top floor was not so high-ceilinged as the lower ones or I might have had problems. My toe just reached the sill, so I let go the gutter and the pipe and took my weight on one leg. These old sills are thoughtfully wide. I let my body fall in gently toward the window so that my balance was forward. This was the most vulnerable moment—no man's land.

I held lightly onto the woodwork while I produced my clasp knife, using one hand and teeth to open it. I crouched still and listened once more and this time fleetingly thought of Maggie, who must be able to see me clearly. Beyond the roofs, from the main road, came the hum of a car, too fast to concern me. It was green all the way. I inserted the blade between the two frames, and the catch clicked back quite loudly. I waited but no lights came on, so I prepared to lift the bottom frame. A man's footsteps turned the corner farther down the road and started clacking my way. Maggie gave a broken whistle I only just heard.

I knew by the tread that it wasn't a copper, so I carefully lifted the frame while the footsteps neared. Maggie whistled again and there was desperation in the almost inaudible sound, as if she was having trouble transmitting. I climbed over the sill, pushed back some drapes and landed on a thick carpet. Leaving the window open, I ducked down until chummy had passed, then closed it.

Using a torch in a front room with the curtains drawn back is tricky; there are so many reflecting surfaces. So I left it off. I followed the lighter patches to the door like following a chain of holes in clouds. The landing was dark and empty and not a glimmer of light anywhere. I went back into the room, closed the door, crossed to the windows and drew the curtains across. By touch I could tell that they were lined and interlined and were of heavy fabric. No light would escape through them. This time using my torch, I located the light switch and depressed it. Red-shaded wall lamps provided a pleasantly subdued glow. I was in a study of some kind. There was a big leather-topped partners' desk and in one corner a studio couch, as if someone both worked and slept here. As it was an outside room, I decided to leave it till last.

I went out onto the landing again, treading a top-quality patterned Axminster. There were three rooms on this top floor, the other two being a very feminine bedroom with an ivory-colored, gold-stippled suite and pastel drapes and a sitting room of ultramodern furniture, button-backed leather-pedestaled armchairs that would keep you awake with movement. A luxury bathroom lined with opaque glass made the top deck self-contained but for a kitchen. Cozy. And definitely empty.

I took the bedroom first—obvious places like the dressing table and bedside tables. Apart from costume jewelry, cosmetics and an electric razor, I came up with nothing. Along the whole of one wall was a white built-in wardrobe with sliding doors and cupboards on top sparsely decorated with sprays of gilt. For such a big area there was little in the way of clothes. Two men's suits and, pushed to one end, as if forgotten or discarded, a woman's dress. I took a good look; the dress had a tear down one seam which might account for its apparent neglect. All were good quality; all had makers' or tailors' labels but without the wearer's name typed in as most tailors do with a hand-made job. The shoe rail was equally sparsely stocked. The men's shoes were size nine. Mr. average. I searched thoroughly and came up with nothing but the idea that the place was little used. It was like a doll's house. Furniture had been carefully placed, but there were no other indentations in the carpets, as if it was never moved about. It was a house of props, to view only. No one could really live here. And yet someone must. It was all too perfectly arranged with no soul in the place.

I was able to search quickly because there was so little in the drawers and not much in the way of reasonable hiding places. Even the toilet revealed only a blue flushing dye in the cistern, and when I unscrewed that I finished up with blue tops over my varnished fingers but no rings.

I went downstairs. There was a dining room, a big up-to-date kitchen and a library out of context with the rest of the maisonette, oak-lined and heavy shelves—a man's room, the only one in the place. There was a second bathroom. I worked quickly. Searching is largely a matter of deftness and experience of where to look. Safe places to the layman are usually obvious to the villain. I went through them all. Pot handles, jugs, vases, beds, lampshades, clocks, shoes, pockets, bookshelves, refrigerator, underneath furniture and so on. Nothing. Then I tried a few places villains use, like breadbins, powder boxes, bath salts, a three-quarter-full opaque liquor decanter, butter, soft cheese and more. Short of taking apart the television set and ripping every cushion and chair fabric there wasn't much else I could do. So far as I could see, the stitching of uphol-stery was untouched and I could feel inside the cushions. There was nothing of real value in the place.

Three original portraits hung in the dining room, but nothing adhered to their backs and they were worth little in their own right. Norman had landed me with an empty bowl that I could see through but couldn't escape from. Not yet. I roamed thoughtfully round trying to think up new hidey holes and examining them when I did. The only piece of real interest was the front door to the maisonette. At the end of a short lobby, it seemed innocuous enough until I went over it with fingertip care. It was steel-lined and had two locks on it. Interesting for a pad that had nothing to show.

Where do you hide rings? I looked down the sink and bathroom plugholes in case they had been strung down. I examined the wall-to-wall carpeting, especially along the edges. I cut open two rotting green peppers in the fridge in case the stalks had been cut out and resealed. It looked as if Norman was wrong, but that was as difficult to take as finding nothing.

I went back upstairs to the front-room study and searched it, especially the desk. These big old desks have cavities and sometimes secret drawers. This one had both and all were empty. I hadn't really expected to find anything in this room because of its accessibility but was just as thorough. I sat at the desk and tried to think as the owner had thought. In his seat I attempted to pick up his personality and to reason as he had done. What had I forgotten about creeping that was important? After a time I switched off the light and returned to the desk. I'd covered every angle. I knew it. The darkness helped me think. Something obvious had been missed. I could feel it. But I couldn't place it. Something was in the back of my mind. If it was my pad and I had to hide rings, where would I put them? Had I forgotten too much?

Norman could have back his fifty; when I failed I didn't want compensation. Reluctantly I rose and wandered over to the window. Time to go. Something was stirring in the back of my mind, irritating me. It wasn't until I was actually lifting the window that it clicked. I lowered the frame again and smiled bleakly in the darkness. It had to be. If they were here at all, that's where they'd be.

I used my torch to find a sturdy chair and pulled it over to the window. I stood on it and reached under the pelmet behind the top edge of the curtain. I found a curtain hook, and my exploring fingers found something else. Painstakingly I began to unhook each curtain. It was dangerous in full view of the street, and I raised the window a little to let sound in. I was disgusted with myself. I'd been away from the game so long that I'd forgotten some of the basics. A ring was placed on each curtain hook. The hooks had then been hooped through the curtain rail ring so that the jewelry was virtually impossible to detect behind the curtain.

It took no time at all to slip off the hooks but longer to put the curtains back, as it had to be done by touch. I reckoned it was time well spent. Anything that delays the discovery of a burglary is worth it; clues go cold, people forget faces and times and places. I felt the old thrill of success; I was back in the game, was robbing somebody and yet the only concern I could rake up was worry at *not* being concerned. I shouldn't be enjoying it like this.

With the curtains back up shrouding the room I shone my torch on the heap of rings I'd piled onto the carpet and was greeted by fire. All colors of the spectrum flashed back at me in blazing movement. I pocketed them about me, lifted the window, climbed outside and closed it. I fell toward the rain pipe, got good grip and climbed down. I waited at the gate.

Maggie came quietly across the road, hugging herself for warmth. I wrapped my arms round her and held her while she shivered. "We'd better not hang about," I told her gently. "I'll get the car heater going."

We got in and I connected up and the small engine sounded like a troupe of tanks. I drew out, concerned for Maggie, who was still shaking and hadn't uttered a word.

"I'm sorry it took so long, but I can't hurry a job."

She nodded and tried to steady herself.

"You sure you're all right?" I didn't like the look of her.

She nodded again. "It's not only the cold," she explained. "It was seeing you on that window ledge so far up with spiked railings below. Oh God!"

"Steady, Meg. It doesn't mean a thing."

"Not to you perhaps. When you fell toward the pipe I nearly screamed."

This shook me. It hadn't occurred to me that the climb itself might frighten her. As gently as I could I said, "I was against your coming."

"I know." Her voice emerged faintly from her upturned collar. "I won't do it again."

I didn't like the way she said it. For a minute or two I drove carefully, sweating blood when we turned into the main road and saw a white traffic car coming the other way. It shook Maggie too, for her hand suddenly shot out to clutch my arm. We swerved very slightly just as we were level and I felt naked. The last thing I wanted was a breathalyzer and questions on where we'd been.

"If we're questioned follow my line," I snapped. She gripped my arm tighter and she was really scared, not so much of being stopped but because she was no liar and was afraid of letting me down. Well, it was all part of it. So far she'd had it lightly. I watched my mirror and breathed relief when the fuzz's brake lights didn't go on.

"We were lucky," I said. When Maggie didn't answer I added, "My pockets are full of valuable rings."

I thought she was going to be sick. She retched and shuddered and then lay back with her head lolling on the seat. I was choked because I found difficulty in understanding her reaction to something I was used to taking for granted. I put out a hand to touch her to find it as cold as frozen fish. I thought she'd fainted, but she said tonelessly, "I'll be all right, Willie. I'm sorry I'm such a baby."

"You'd better come back to my place. I'll make some strong coffee." I gave her a brief glance and saw her whitened face against the seat back. I'd never seen such pained inquiry in her before. She was confused but was trying to find an answer in truth, and tonight truth had been ugly. My heart dropped as the knots tightened in my guts. The sickness I felt was different from hers. It suddenly hit me that I might lose her, and that was the most terrible sensation of all.

We coasted up to the flats and I stopped well beyond the entrance. "You go on up while I dump the car."

"I want to see it through."

"*Cut it out, Meg.* You've had what you wanted. You'll only double the danger from now on. Now go on up. Make some coffee." Everything was going wrong. We had lost touch in so short a time. She climbed out without a word and went slowly up the steps. I didn't wait to see her in but slid round the corner and parked the car from where I'd nicked it. I restored the wiring, closed the windows and climbed out.

I hugged the shadows back to the flats. We'd had a fairly straight run with no real complications, but the way it had knocked Maggie took some getting used to. Straights and villains are on different wave lengths, that's all. She couldn't operate like a villain if she took a long course on it.

In the flat Maggie's coat was flung over a chair, and that in itself was indicative of distress. I heard her moving in the kitchen, and she emerged with two steaming mugs. She glanced at me strangely, as if making a reassessment.

Taking the coffee from her, I sat down and said, "Meg, don't lose sight of why I did it. I must gain Norman's confidence. We're looking for a murderer and the only way I can get near him is this way. Don't forget Dick."

Maggie went over to the radiator and leaned against it, warming her hands on the mug. She looked thoughtfully at me. "I'm unlikely to forget Dick," she said evenly. "Take no notice of me. I thought I knew what I was letting myself in for. I didn't expect to be so shaken. I knew you took risks, but I didn't really understand how bad they'd be."

But it wasn't only that and I knew it. It wasn't like Maggie to hold back. "You're thinking that this was how it was before. Without the excuse of Dick. That I robbed people and lived by it. But you've known all along, stood by me while I was inside. What's so different now, Meg?"

She gave a little apologetic shrug. "I'm sorry. It's not you. It's me. I'm wondering how much I've unwittingly pretended not to see. I love you, Willie. I've been willing to close my eyes a good deal because of that."

"And now you can't?"

"Now I don't want to."

I took a swig at my coffee, watching Maggie still holding on to hers. "Reality stinks, Meg. I've a lot of sympathy for kids and dreamers."

She stared me straight in the eye, still pale but more composed and very lovely as she faltered behind a conflicting pattern of thoughts.

"I'm not a child and I don't really think I'm a dreamer. Reality shouldn't stink and if it does, then we can only blame ourselves. You're a cynic, Willie; I'm too soft to be one."

I put down my mug. "It's too late for this, Meg. Let's go to bed."

Maggie was eying me with a sort of questioning affection. She said sadly, "You go to bed. I'll sleep in here."

It was like ice down my back. I was going to argue but had one of my rare moments of insight. This was a new situation to us both. "All right. But you take the bed. I'll doss here." She was about to protest when I stopped her. "Leave me some pride, Meg."

She searched my face in a way that alarmed me, then took a sip of her coffee and put down the mug. "I don't want any more."

"You turn in. I'll see to the mugs." I took them out, washed and dried them and returned to the lounge. Maggie wasn't there. The door was closed and I guessed she'd gone to the bedroom. Nor would she be coming back. I could have done with a pillow and a blanket but I couldn't face going in there. She'd gone without so much as a peck on the cheek. It was a slow stab between the ribs to realize that she hadn't kissed me because she couldn't face it.

I sat down heavy-limbed and stared at the electric fire. It was like being back inside, all the old fears and heartbreaks and bleakness of future and that dull sensation of slowly dying. It was worse. In those situations I'd always been sustained by thought of Maggie, of her loyalty and patience, all the qualities that she had that I could admire and that I lacked. Now her image wouldn't come, not in the way that I wanted.

There was little night left and too much remorse for sleep. Being emotional, I've been on the deck a few times but never like this. Occupy myself. I took out the rings and laid them on the table under the central lamp. Normally I would have examined each one with a ten-magnification lens but had no inclination to get it from a nearby drawer. There were twenty-six of them—gold and platinum, diamonds, emeralds, sapphires and rubies. No rubbish but nothing world-shaking either. There were one or two really good ones—a three-carat brilliant-cut diamond, color, clarity, cut, all good. It would retail between fifteen hundred and two thousand pounds. It wouldn't fence at a quarter that price. One of the sapphires had a slight window on one side which depleted its value, but the emeralds and rubies were clear. A good tickle of tom. Not outstanding. I should have thought a bit primitive for Norman, who had high taste.

But it was no use trying to occupy my mind like this. It didn't work. Trying to shut out Maggie was like trying to stop the approach of dawn.

I went to the kitchen, opened the fridge and took out an unopened bottle of milk. It took me a little while to lift the foil without splitting or crumbling it. When it was off I dropped the rings in one by one. At the base of the bottle one or two dark patches were discernible, but when the bottle was back on its rack it looked perfectly normal.

I went back to the settee, took my shoes off and at last fell into an uneasy sleep. I don't know how long it lasted. A dog had got into the flat, for it was pushing my hand with its nose. I put out my hand to stroke it and felt long hair and then soft flesh. I struggled awake, bitter-mouthed and woolly-minded, to find a weight on my chest. The room was now in half-light. Maggie was on her knees by my side, her head on my chest, her face turned toward me, and her eyes, imploring understanding, were full of tears. Never had wakening from a thick head been so sweet. I held her head in both my hands and kept it where it was. One pajamaed arm was wrapped round my middle.

"I'm sorry," she whispered. "I'm so sorry."

I stroked her hair slowly, relieved beyond measure. She was quivering and crying quietly. There was nothing to say until she quietened. When she finally lifted her head I kissed her gently, feeling the salt on her lips.

"Well," I said. "That's settled one thing. You're not coming with me again."

"Why not?" There was still a trace of rear-guard defiance.

"Because you can't bloody well whistle," I said.

She started to laugh, harsh choking sounds mixed with sobbing. I couldn't stop her, so I let it come out and flush clear. "It's all right, Meg," I said, holding her. "It's all right."

I rang Norman after Maggie had left. He wanted to see me right away. I emptied the milk bottle, dried off the tom and went round to him. When the door was opened by a sensitive-faced young man in his early twenties I guessed that I had now met all the Shaw family. His hair, like his narrow, oval-chinned face, was fair, his eyes light blue. He was nowhere near as tough as his sister or stepmother and there was something in him that provoked instant sympathy. He seemed to place me in one quick-eyed appraisal and promptly looked embarrassed.

"My name's Scott," I said.

"Oh, yes. We spoke on the phone. Do come in, Mr. Scott. I'll tell Father you're here." He stood aside, a slightly stooped, thin figure. He was interested in me and tried to show that he was not, as if he was trying to figure what dregs his father associated with and not caring for them. I felt sorry for him.

If he was uncomfortable with me he was at least attentive. His sister emerged from a back room in a long suede coat trimmed with fur at collar, sleeves and bottom and sailed past into a hot day as if the sun wouldn't dare make it unbearable for her. She gave him a brief, almost professional smile and passed me as if I was a hat stand. The front door slammed, and Peter Shaw was holding the study door open for me.

"That was my sister," he explained apologetically. "She's always in a tearing hurry."

"A very positive young lady," I replied. I was beginning to like him. He smiled uncertainly, indicated a chair and pointed to the drinks cabinet. "Do help yourself. I think you'll find most standard brands there, Mr. Scott." He gave a little shy nod and left me.

Norman came in within seconds. Without Ulla beside him, his charm had a brittle quality. Steel traces escaped from hiding at odd times. Norman couldn't be where he was without ruthlessness. He turned a catch on the door, didn't waste time on offering me a drink, but offered a smile instead, not unlike that of his daughter's only moments ago. He crossed the room rubbing his hands together. "Well?"

"I got them. They were tucked nicely away. Almost fooled me."

"Not you, Spider, dear chap. Let's see them." He brushed his gray hair back with his hands in that vain action of his just short of feminine. Momentarily his eyes were too eager. Then as I started to pull the rings from my pockets he belatedly produced a velvet cloth, which he placed on a round walnut table. I laid them out and watched him.

He set the rings in straight lines and suddenly I realized that he was counting them. He wasn't noticeably examining them, not in any detail anyway, and this surprised me for a careful man. When he looked up he was obviously immensely pleased. "Well done," he said warmly. He didn't suggest that I might have kept some back. He wrapped the rings in the cloth and left them on the table. He produced a packet of notes and handed them to me.

"Two hundred," he said. "They're rather tatty but safe."

I stuffed the money into my inside breast pocket.

"Count them," Norman instructed.

I smiled. "I trust you."

"Then you're a fool. Count them."

I did as he wanted and pocketed them again. "All there," I said.

Norman went to the cabinet, looked questioningly at me, noted my brief shake of the head and poured himself a Scotch. We sat down and he said, "That's what I remember about you. No fuss. A good job done and no arguments afterward."

"There's nothing to argue about. Now I've seen the tickle I reckon I've been paid fairly enough."

"You don't think much of them?"

"They're all right. Good average stones."

"Max wouldn't have paid you as much."

"I agree. When *did* you break up?" I slipped in casually.

He eyed me sharply. "If you've been doing jobs for Max I should have thought you would have known."

"You know Max. He was tight-lipped. We could never talk like this."

"About two years ago." Norman mused over the thought. "Just before Ulla and I were married." He smiled reflectively. "Max and I got on well enough, I suppose. We had our problems, but there was no one to touch us. We made a lot of money. No, it wasn't Max's fault that we split."

Norman started to realize that he was being carried away by nostalgia, for he said at a tangent, "You met Peter on the way in. What do you think of him?"

"I met him only briefly. Strikes me as an upright citizen."

"That's a fact. He's studying law. He has a perception that augurs well for a career in law that could be most useful to me."

No wonder the kid had been embarrassed by someone he must have guessed was a villain. I saw a minefield ahead and back-pedaled.

"That's what matters to me," added Norman magnanimously. "My family. There's nothing I wouldn't do for them."

I still kept clear; a villain who boasted of his son's prowess at law had to have some form of mental blockage or intended to corrupt his son's career.

"Do you want another job?" Suddenly the social chitchat was over.

"I'll listen."

"A big one. Sensational. It will make the great train robbery look like a dummy run."

I prickled. Yet I was excited. I put out the warning scanners and tried to read his mind. I've done some big jobs. Very big. What was Norman's definition? He was waiting for me, so I humored him. "Go on."

"The Tate Gallery," he said seriously. "In the vernacular, how does that grab you?" He was doing his isometrics now.

6

IT GRABBED ME all right. It frightened the life out of me. And excited me at the same time. Some of the finest paintings in the world were in the Tate; they would be well protected.

"Paintings? But they're all known works. If you can get in."

"Come now, Spider. That's not like you. Since when have known works stopped illegal buyers. You think of the art thefts over the last decade and wonder who bought them. Anyway that would be my problem. Interested?"

"I have to be."

Norman was almost beaming an obsessional enthusiasm. He came alive and at the moment looked slightly mad.

"It's what I really wanted you for." He made a deprecating gesture toward the rings. "That was merely to see if you were still on your toes. You know your art. It's one of the qualities I've always admired in you."

"Not paintings I don't."

"You'd know a good one from rubbish, but in any event they will be pre-selected."

"They?"

"A few. The beauty of art theft is that the price does not necessarily have to be below market value. The crank buyer has virtually disappeared. The right people now buy for long-term investment, knowing that certain pieces will never reach auction."

Two hundred pounds were searing my shirt to remind me that I was back in the game. I didn't object to the money. I'd earned it, although Maggie would never agree. But what Norman was suggesting was in another league. I was getting in deeper, yet getting nowhere with helping Dick. And yet I had to continue or back out right now. If I did, then what? I could ask the same if I stayed, but I stood a better chance of truth if I won Norman's confidence and met other people round him.

"If I agree I would probably need help, and I only like working alone."

"I know you do. But it would depend on the prize, wouldn't it? To you it could represent anything from twenty to thirty thousand pounds. Perhaps more."

"What percentage would that be?"

Norman became evasive behind an easy smile. "I'd rather leave the detail until later. We can discuss it." He was trying to hook me a bit at a time. I considered the prices outstanding paintings fetch these days. "If you're offering me one percent, that leaves you a millionaire if you're not one already."

He flinched slightly. "We won't disagree about the figure, Spider, I promise you that! Take a look round the Tate and see what you think."

"But you've already thought," I accused. "You've thought an awful bloody lot."

"I have," he admitted. "But I'd like a second opinion. You're a top pro. Your judgment on this will be much finer than mine."

"So I case it?"

"It can do no harm."

I just hoped that Dick would one day appreciate what I was trying to do for him. "O.K." I stood up and slowly looked round the room. "I like your place. One day I'd like to look round it."

Norman opened the door for me. He was more pleased than I was about the way things had gone. "One day you will," he promised. As he showed me out I realized that that day would have to be before he invited me; Norman was in no hurry for me to see round. I had to do it before that Tate job grabbed me. I left trying to get used to the idea of Norman being a family man.

I couldn't visit Dick because I didn't want to be on a one-man identity parade. I wanted to keep our relationship as quiet as possible. Max had enjoyed some police protection; so might Norman, and a wrong word in his ear could put my head in the oven. So Maggie went. When she returned she told me Dick was bearing up well, but I guessed that she was protecting me. I knew just how Dick would be feeling.

Chrissie rang to invite me over for a snack at lunchtime. It wouldn't be social, so I had a decent meal before padding over to her place. The Daimler Sovereign was still outside, as if waiting for Max to return, but it looked lonely and a shade dirty. She had tarted herself up, which meant that she had elevated me to near her level or wanted something from me. Chrissie had looked after her figure, and the silk sheath she wore did it no harm. She was carefully made up and smiled to throw a little warmth. Her high-heeled mules made her wobble a little on the pile carpet either by accident or design. Chrissie was out for attention, which warned me to be careful.

We sat in the lounge, and there was the plate of wafer sandwiches. To show no ill feeling I took one and reckoned it was hard enough to be left over from the last lot. Chrissie didn't believe in waste. Her new image didn't bend sufficiently to put me out of the beer class; I found myself with another small glass of canned beer without having been asked. She held her vodka up and said "Cheers" without disturbing a single curl on her tight-packed blond head.

"I thought it was time you reported," she said flatly.

"Reported? About Norman?"

"Who else is there to report about?" Her eyes hardened, which wasn't difficult.

"You want to retain me?" I suggested. "We haven't discussed terms."

She was about to bite, checked herself, then said mildly for her, "Cut out the crap. Last time you pleaded with me to let you get on with it. I'm not holding off forever. Did you find the bronze?"

"Haven't had a chance. These things take time. I'm hoping he'll show me round."

"Since when have you waited for an invitation?"

"I've thought of that too," I admitted. "It's difficult to get a good look at the place without him knowing."

Chrissie drooped her lids and for a moment I was confronted by deep blue patches like bruises. "It's not wired," she flung over to me. Then she held her head back challengingly, daring me to ask her how she knew. I didn't.

Satisfied, she added, "Don't forget we used to go over there a lot in the old days."

"He may have made changes."

"Not our Norman. It won't be any different. So what are you going to do?"

"You know damn fine what I'm going to do. But it may be a washout, and if it is I've got to do it the long hard way, which is what I'm doing now. My brother's been nicked. The damage is done and I've got a lot of time before the trial. When I hang it on Norman it'll stay there."

"He's not soft, y'know. If he finds out he'll kill you like he did Max."

"I wouldn't expect him to kiss me. What do you know of his family?"

Chrissie stiffened so quickly that she spilled her drink. "Sod it." She moved and wiped her dress. It was a pity that someone so fundamentally attractive destroyed her image every time she opened her mouth. "What was that? His family? He dotes over them. He's bloody mad. He has an uppity bitch of a daughter who acts like a high-class tart, as if her old man's Prime Minister instead of a second-rate fence. A son who should have been his daughter and talks with a gobful of plums. I ask you! And he's crazy about them."

"They must know what he does."

"Of course they know but they don't want to know, do they? The old man brings in the bread and they don't care from which bakery."

"What about Ulla?"

Chrissie was guarded. And Chrissie wasn't as stupid as she could pretend. "I don't know much about her and I didn't know Norman's first wife. She died years ago."

"You must know something."

"What does it matter?"

"Chrissie, I'm looking for weak links. If Norman has an alibi and you can bet that he does, then I've got to break it."

She shrugged like a man. "You won't find a weak link among that bunch. They cling together. They've all too much to lose."

"Just an impression will do."

She swallowed her drink to pad out time, and it was unlike her to show reluctance over opinion on other people. "She hooked him about a couple of years ago. I don't know where she comes from but she's foreign. I think she's a calculating bitch after his money who'd jump in bed with any man—if she thought she could get away with it without losing her benefits. Norman is nuts about her."

"So you don't like her."

"I didn't say that. It's not my problem, is it? In a way I hope he catches her at it. It would serve him bloody right for what he did to Max."

"Shall I get you another drink?"

She gazed blankly at her glass, then held it out stiff-armed toward me, which meant there was still something else. Chrissie didn't need my company. I poured a liberal vodka and splashed in some bitter lemon. I still had some beer left.

"I ought to be going," I prompted.

"Where? You don't kid me. Sit down."

"I have a business to run."

"So've I. I thought it might interest you."

"What? Your business?"

"Without Max it's difficult. I need someone to help."

I stared in surprise. "I'm not a fence, Chrissie. You know that. I wouldn't know where to start."

"I wouldn't want you for fencing. I'll do that. I have all the contacts. You're just the bloke for operations."

"You're putting the clock back too far, Chrissie. I've given up creeping."

"Cobblers," she said. "Then what are you doing for Norman?"

"You know fine why I'm operating for Norman. It's the only way I can get close to him."

"But it shows you're still good at it. Max missed you a lot. He always said so. We both thought you were good."

Chrissie was busting her hair lacquer trying to be agreeable.

"Think," she said. "Once Norman is doing a lifer there's no one left with a grain of my experience at fencing. But I need a man to be on hand and to operate. You'd make a fortune."

That was the second one I'd been offered in twenty-four hours.

"Max would want it that way," added Chrissie, as if it mattered to her.

"I didn't think you cared that much for me," I probed laughingly.

Chrissie saw the danger in time. Shrewdness was as inbred as her language. "I don't. Not as a man. But isn't that the strength? A strictly commercial relationship. Nothing on the side. We'd slay them, Spider, the bloody lot."

I hesitated and she misread it. "A lot of credit Max got was due to me. I let him have it because it's better for business. People want a man up front in this game."

I nodded agreement. It was true on both counts. Chrissie knew her outlets and had a very sharp brain when it mattered. I wondered just how sharp she was being now.

"Let's do one thing at a time. Let's get my brother off the hook first."

"You see it that way. I see it as getting that bastard Norman onto it."

We went to the door. "I like your dress," I said, to change the subject.

"It's a Jean Varon. Exclusive. Your suits could be as expensive if we teamed up."

"It's a thought," I agreed.

The low wall of the Thames Embankment pointed a long untiring finger down Millbank toward Vauxhall Bridge. I crossed the wide road, thin of traffic at the moment, and walked with the swelling Thames creating its own world on my left—a gray, slopping waste of erratic motion and of people who were happier with their temporary severance of the lousy deal dry land could muster. A mild wind ruffled hair and water.

When I arrived opposite the Tate Gallery I stopped to face it with my back against the river wall. Too squat to be impressive in spite of its wide, white steps and Corinthian columns. Somehow it seemed oddly out of place, lying back from the wide ribbon road as though someone had got their periods mixed up and had dropped it there in error. A treasure house. And Norman wanted a morsel—from a palette.

It had stopped drizzling and clouds tumbled into each other to create blue gaps of sky. The few pedestrians were largely students shunting up and down the steps of the gallery, some risking damp behinds as they squatted like simulated Guy Fawkes' in their long coats on the damp grass of the small gardens either side of the entrance. It all looked very innocent and not a copper in sight. Typically British, you might say, until somebody's long arm shot out to grab you as you put a foot wrong. Mine started to go wrong as I slowly crossed over toward the gallery.

I went through the gates and turned left onto the recessed garden at the side of the protruding main entrance. I wandered round the grass, noticing sub-basement windows as if the whole building had suddenly sunk through being top-heavy. I looked down into a busy restaurant. I couldn't see any wiring; it was so damned innocent as to be ridiculous. If I believed its face value, then I'd believe anything. There were metal covers set in the grass as access to electric cables, phones and so on.

I crossed to the right wing and noted offices in the sub-basement occupied by human termites. To convince myself that this unattractive building housed fine works of art I climbed slowly up the steps and into the entrance hall. There were plenty of people about, and a circular counter like an enormous pay table with assistants in its center was filled with brochures and art literature. Stairs led down on either side of the hall. I took the left-hand set, which curled to the restaurant below. Was there a cellar beneath this?

I went along the corridor running alongside the restaurant toward the Gents, which opened out on the left. In front of me swing doors formed a cul-de-sac with the warning "Authorized Persons Only." I stood outside the Gents as if waiting for someone to come out, and in that time three people went through the swing doors and two came out. The only glimpse I had was of a further corridor. No stairs in sight. Normally I would have gone through and bluffed it out. No one had taken notice of me up till now. But I didn't want to do it at this stage; I had to know more from Norman before taking risks, however small. I went back upstairs to take a gander at some eighteenth-century portraits just to show willing, went further into the gallery to find one section blocked off in preparation for a special exhibition, past the flashing lights of a modern electronic art display not unlike an amusement arcade without the erks and went out the main entrance again.

Well, there it was—a virtually unguarded world collection. Nuts. It was all too subtle. But at least floor pads were out on the tiled floors. Outside, I turned left into Bulinga Street. Railings ran right along the perimeter of the gallery; left again into John Islip Street, where I noticed wooden huts in the gallery grounds but well detached from the main building, and turned left again into Atterbury Street. It was so quiet, so respectable, that it was difficult to believe it to be so near the heart of London. I completed the square back to Millbank and wasn't too happy about any of it.

Getting into the gallery grounds was easy, but the museum itself hid its security well. What I didn't like was the general area. It was too easy to seal off. The end of Bulinga Street and Atterbury Street could be cut with no trouble, and a single patrol car at each point would also cover an escape into John Islip Street. That left the front. And old father Thames left only two directions for flight along opposite ends of Millbank. Hidden alarms set off by a break-in would seal the place off like a tomb. I needed as many escape hatches as I could get. I couldn't see many here. I could always dive straight into the river, but if I'm going to nick I'd rather be dry.

I went back to the flats, stepped from the lift and saw the old familiar shape that proclaimed copper wandering the corridor outside my door. I don't know what it is about them; I think the plainclothes boys try to look too neutral. They're so busy trying not to look like coppers that they create their own breed apart. And they can't keep their sad experiences from their faces. This one wore an average raincoat over an average off-the-peg suit not too well pressed, stout shoes, of course, and a humorless, prematurely lined face. Black hair strayed across his head and hung in low clumps at the back. Somehow an untidy figure with active dark eyes.

I didn't like him on sight. I knew at once that he'd recognized me, which upset me because I'd never seen him before.

"Mr. Scott?" It's funny how they all ask the same stupid question. He *knew*.

"No," I said just to be awkward.

He tried to smile but his lips must have been frozen. I pulled out my front-door key.

"Is this where you live—sir?" He'd got the message.

"Push off," I said, "or I'll call the police."

"Oh, that's it? We're playing clever b———s. I'm Detective Sergeant Newton. I'd like a few words with you."

"You've had 'em," I said, turning the key. Then I almost froze but somehow continued to open the door. *Newton.* He was bent if Dick was right, had been on Max's payroll. My scalp prickled.

I went in. He tried to follow, but I stopped him in the doorway with a big hand on his chest. "How would you like me to ring the nearest nick and report you for breaking and entering?"

It stopped him dead. "All I want is to ask you a few questions."

"About what?"

"About Max Harris."

"Who did you say you are?"

"Detective Sergeant Newton."

"Let's see your card."

He pulled it out, hating me for it but trying to mask it. I took a good long look at the small photograph which made him look younger and fitter. I wasn't riding him for the sake of it but because I had to think damned quick. Suddenly I was part of the murder inquiry.

I let him in and relented enough to offer him a seat. They never take their coats off. He sat down and seemed relieved. He even tried to be friendly, trying his smile again with no greater success. I wondered if he'd been to the dentist.

"I'm sorry to call on you like this. It's routine really, but these things have to be done."

I stuffed my hands in my pockets and continued to stand so that I dwarfed him. He looked tired out and I felt a brief twinge of compassion. They work them too hard. Then I felt contempt, remembering he was probably bent.

"I don't think I can help, but carry on," I said.

"You knew Max Harris?"

"Many years ago. Your records probably show it."

95

"Have you seen him recently?"

"Ask him."

He tightened his already stiff lips. "If you don't intend to make this easy it's something I can bear in mind later on."

"What have I said?" I exclaimed with pained innocence.

"So you're saying you don't know he's dead?"

"What—Max? Dead? What did he die of?"

"When did you last see him?"

"Years ago. I can't remember exactly. Nobody could."

He eyed me bleakly. "What would you say if I told you you were seen at his funeral?"

This boy wasn't very good. I didn't go to the funeral. Anyway Max had been cremated. "I'd say we were talking of someone else. You'll have to do better."

"So you're saying that you haven't seen him for years, not even in a coffin."

"That's right." Mimicking him, I asked, "Are you saying that Max was topped, or am I reading too much into your visit?"

"You know damned fine he was, so cut it out."

I gazed at Newton almost feeling sorry for him. They should have sent someone better to an old lag like me. I felt insulted.

"Do you know Norman Shaw?"

Watch it, Spider. "I used to. About the time I knew Max." I didn't like the drift. What had he really called for?

"Have you seen *him* lately?"

"Why?"

"Because I'm damn well asking."

"You said you were inquiring about Max. Now you're asking about Norman Shaw. I want to know what you're on about."

"Mr. Scott, I'm on a murder inquiry. If you don't want to assist, then I'll take you back to the station with me and maybe someone of higher authority can persuade you to cooperate."

There was no reason why I shouldn't have seen Norman, but I couldn't judge what was on Newton's mind and I didn't trust him. He was up to something.

"No, I haven't seen him," I said, knowing that Norman would bear me out.

Newton looked wearily resigned. He rose very slowly, unwinding as if in pain. He ran a hand over his face and dislodged some strands of hair that fell across his eyes. He didn't seem to notice. "Do you know the sort of people who mix with Shaw?"

"How can I if I haven't seen him?"

"O.K. So you know nothing of Max Harris and nothing of Norman Shaw."

"You're quick," I said. "You've got it."

"And you're too quick," he said. "Why have you been seeing Shaw?"

"You certain you've been on a C.I.D. course? Your method of interrogation is terrible."

"When did you see him last?" he persisted.

"You need a team for this line. You can't do it on your own." This wasn't about Max. My flippancy covered a growing unease.

Strangely he nodded acquiescence. "For a man to be as evasive as you, you must have a hell of a lot to hide."

"Or nothing at all," I suggested.

"Are you Dick Scott's brother?"

Now he had me on my knees. It was a sneaky punch. If he looked a bit longer he'd know damn fine I was.

I teetered up and backed off. "Who's Dick Scott?"

"Detective Constable Richard Scott. I think he's your brother. The stupid thing about you is that I'm trying to help your brother and you're making it worse."

Suddenly Newton was being very crafty, but I couldn't change course. "Whoever heard of an ex-creeper having a brother with Old Bill. I ask you."

"I can find out," he said, almost managing a smile. "It'll just take a little longer." He opened the door and looked back at me in an oddly disturbing way. "See you in court," he said and closed the door behind him.

I stood staring at the door for some time. What kind of justice was it that allowed a bent copper to investigate one who wasn't? He should be in Dick's place so far as the corruption charges were concerned. It didn't *feel* right. And why had Newton been on his own? I didn't like it at all.

"I'd better keep my calls to you until after dark, as now."

Norman stopped pushing his hands together across his chest and looked surprised. His color gradually receded after holding his breath and pressing full power for six seconds. I reckoned he would wear himself out trying to keep fit.

"Why?" Norman asked. "There's no reason why you shouldn't be seeing me."

"The fuzz called on me this afternoon. I was asked about Max. How well I knew him and so on."

Norman got in a quick cheek puff while I was talking. "You should be used to that, Spider. Routine."

"Maybe. Have they called on you?"

Norman decided to give the isometrics a rest. "Eventually they did. I expected them to."

"Well, I was almost accused of knocking Max off. Did they try that with you?"

Norman laughed quietly. "They wouldn't have got anywhere if they had. No, the usual stuff. Where was I—you know."

Norman was thoughtful for a while and when he was like this his face was granite-hard. Without his applied charm he was simply a more refined version of Max. His basic emotions were the same; he merely controlled them better.

"Your seeing me has no possible bearing on Max, so what was he after?"

An iceberg formed in my guts. God help me if he realized his mistake.

"He was just groping. Perhaps he reckons one of us did it and is trying to stir it up among us."

"What's his name?"

"Newton. A detective sergeant." I realized my mistake. Newton seemed sure that Dick was my brother. If Norman found that out I might as well top myself. And Norman's reaction did nothing for my confidence. His face had stiffened and his eyes were suddenly active. The name had meant something to him and I cursed myself. Then he smiled a little stiffly, but I could see that he was worried.

"You're right, Spider," he agreed. "Keep to the dark in future. It won't make any real difference but it might be wiser." He stared at me so steadily and for so long that I felt panic, thinking that he'd rumbled me. His eyes were armor-plated with piercing black pupils while he was like this. He made me shiver in a way Max had never managed. I played it straight but was near to crumbling before he broke the lock. I was just about to make an uneasy remark when he spoke.

"I've been thinking an awful lot about you lately."

What was I supposed to say? I grinned. I must have appeared an idiot. "I'm not worth a thought."

"That's the trouble with you." Norman wagged a finger. "You always were self-effacing. That's why you never struck it rich. You were always too independent and where has it got you?"

"I prefer working alone."

"I know you do. But it's time you stepped into line. These days everyone needs somebody. Amalgamations pay off."

"I see them as takeovers."

"That's because you've never really studied the issue. There could be a great future for you, Spider."

My nape prickled. Everybody was suddenly forecasting my success.

"Where?" I asked dutifully, but I could see trouble.

"You could work with me. Permanently. I'm a rich man, Spider. I could retire and be wealthy for the rest of my life, but I'm too restless. I'd stagnate. I can make you just as wealthy."

"You've managed without me so far. Why change it?"

"There are jobs we could do that only *we could* do. At the moment I'm having to bypass them."

"Like the Tate?"

"Like the Tate. Until you came along it was only a dream. Fifty-fifty."

That was one hell of a jump from one percent. Two partnership offers in one day. It was enough to scare me to death. If I took neither I would be considered a risk, and if I took one of them I'd make a deadly enemy of the other. And this was quite apart from my real reasons for being here anyway. I could try to stall.

"Norman," I said heavily, "this is a great compliment. You talk of integrity. People change. I may have changed. You should give yourself longer to think it over."

He chuckled quietly. "My dear chap, you merely prove my point. Only a man with integrity could say such a thing." Then he was serious again. "There are other commercial reasons besides your prowess. You own a travel agency. What better outlet for the stuff we have to get abroad."

Oh, God. I couldn't be deeper in than this. Which was the way out?

7

I ROAMED the room well aware that his gaze was speculatively following me. I didn't want him to see my face just then.

"I haven't a freight license," I explained, "only passenger. I can't plant stuff on clients."

He sounded amused behind my back.

"You carry a lot of Reisen's boys from what I hear, but I'm pulling your leg. Reisen's mob would be the first under suspicion. No, I was thinking of your staff and yourself and perhaps carefully selected clients."

I turned. "The staff don't do many trips a year, perhaps two, each including their holidays. I'm a born Londoner. I don't like budging from it."

"We wouldn't need it often. We need to think about it, devise methods." Suddenly he laughed. "I am reminded of a ruse Max pulled. You must remember the woman and the baby he used to smuggle jewelry into the United States, how she pinched the baby's bottom to make it cry at customs and promised to change its nappies as soon as she could."

I chuckled with him. I remembered. It would have been a brave customs man to search the baby. If he'd been brave enough he'd have found a tidy tickle. But that sort of stunt could be pulled only once in one place. Norman was looking for a regularly safe outlet. I didn't like it.

101

"Think about it," Norman said. I was.

I was staring at the wall, wondering when I could really start on what I'd originally come for. I was beginning to think that I'd made a mistake in the first place, that I'd never really get anywhere. And yet what other line was there? Dick was inside, and unless something came up he would get life, as ludicrous as it seemed, or I would have to present myself to confuse the issue. At least Norman was getting friendly; something would break. It would have to. The fact that he never speculated on Max's murder was indicative. It was unnatural. I could feel his eyes on my back, so I swung round and looked straight at him.

"Who d'you think topped Max?"

It shook him and he appeared bewildered. "What a strange question. We were discussing a partnership and suddenly you ask that."

"I'm sorry. It came straight into my mind. You know me. You must have thought about it."

"Yes, I have," he said solemnly. He rose and flicked aimlessly with his foot at a chair. He ran his hands carefully over his hair and I knew that he was thinking fast. "It's a subject I've tried to keep off. And it worries me at times."

"In what way?"

He looked uncertain. "It depends on motive. I've sometimes wondered if I'm next."

A classic Norman answer. Bloody marvelous—evading the question and bringing concern for himself. I kept my thoughts from my voice.

"You mean someone is trying to move in on you both?"

"I don't know. It's crossed my mind. Max made enemies because he was rough and he was mean. There are so many reasons why he might have been killed."

"But you must have suspicions. You were near to him at one time."

"Indeed. I was on the point of suggesting a peace formula."

He gave me a long, puzzled sideways glance. "I didn't realize you were so interested."

"I'm bound to be. I worked for him. You might even think it was me." Crafty Spider forcing a reluctant smile from Norman.

"Not you, dear fellow. You couldn't hurt anyone. There's a lot I remember about you that you give me no credit for. There's nothing wrong with my memory." He straightened his jacket and plucked off an offending hair. "If you must have a name, why not Chrissie?"

"His wife? But she's been cleared by the fuzz. They'd have dug deep on that one."

"I know. But she is possessive and in truth put more brainwork into the business than Max. She is very, very shrewd. Very sharp. Their marriage had long been one of convenience."

I had to hand it to him that he was convincing. Chrissie had crossed my mind at one time, but she was going to miss Max commercially and she was never one to cut off her nose to spite her face. Not Chrissie.

I'd stuck my neck so far out that I might as well go the extra inch. "This is one time when I hope the fuzz find the bastard who knocked Max off. He didn't deserve topping."

"Until we know why he was murdered we shall never know whether he did or not."

Norman led the way to the door, quickly straightened his tie as he passed a mirror and smiled at me. At the flick of an eyelid Max had left his mind. "There's something I want to show you."

He led the way up the rich, maroon carpeting to a first landing discreetly decorated with banks of small pastoral water colors and then up a further flight of stairs. There were white doors, crystal handles and small, round gilt mirrors at intervals. He opened a door and ushered me in. I heard the key turn as he closed the door.

It was a study, its pale walls lined on two sides with crammed bookshelves. A window faced the rear of the house, and the remaining wall was partially filled by erratically placed box shelves, on each of which was a solitary, rare Staffordshire figure. There's Staffordshire and Staffordshire; this was the stuff you didn't see in the front of every antique-shop window. In two corners crouched large stereo speakers between which knelt a Jacobean chest flanked by two cupboards about four feet high built into the shelves.

Norman crossed to an oak bureau in the middle of this green-carpeted room and pushed a button. "It activates a red light on the landing," he explained. "When that's on not even Ulla will interrupt me. This is forbidden territory to everyone."

With increasing dread I realized the extent of my privilege. This was his sanctum, his operations room. Which showed how little I really knew about Norman. Unwittingly I had underrated him.

"Sit down." He indicated a green button-backed leather armchair facing the desk. He seated himself behind the desk and opened a lower drawer. His handsome features relaxed with a faint smile. Two glasses appeared and he poured some dark spirit from a Waterford decanter. "I know you don't normally drink, but I also know that you're not entirely teetotal. A special occasion demands a special drink." He returned the decanter to the drawer and closed it. "I find it evaporates too much if I leave it out. Cheers." He raised his glass and waited for me to reach for mine. Strong, mature cognac wafted under my nose. But I was cautious.

"What's the special occasion?"

"I've told you. To our partnership." He sipped his drink, letting it rest on his palate before slowly swallowing. Norman was in rare good humor.

I didn't rush it. I didn't even try the drink. "I haven't agreed yet, Norman. Cheers."

His smile became slightly rigid. "My dear Spider, if I thought there was the slightest risk of your refusing you wouldn't be in this room now."

There wasn't even a clock to break the silence. Then he added, "Mine's a logical conclusion. I'm not trying to force you. You've already agreed to work *for* me on the Tate. Now I'm offering an infinitely better proposition for the same job and others that may follow. The only difference is that you'll have more say and earn considerably more. Only a complete madman could refuse and you're certainly not that."

I grinned before he got suspicious. "I must admit it's certainly something to drink about." I took a swig at the cognac and its fire seemed to stab me in the heart. I had hoped to win his confidence but had never dreamed I'd get this close to him. Now that I had I was scared. I felt a Judas apart from the fear of real danger.

"So we're agreed?"

I nodded. "As you say, how can I refuse?"

Norman came over to me and held out his hand while I scrambled up. His grip was firm, and he placed his other hand on top to seal the contract. I was in the big time.

He went back to his seat, straightened his jacket behind him and observed, "You still seem surprised, but then you always did undersell yourself. You have a big contribution, Spider. Your expertise extends beyond burglary. You know and understand the same things that I do, and this is tremendously important."

He stood up and went to one of the cupboards at the side of the Jacobean chest. "Do you like music?" he asked unexpectedly.

"Jazz," I said. "Small-group American mainstream."

He looked vaguely disappointed that our tastes didn't touch at all levels.

Norman opened the cupboard door. "Look at this," he said.

I wandered over, glass in hand. There were banks of records and tapes filling the cabinet. "All classical music." He lifted the lid of the Jacobean chest. It was filled with hi-fi equipment from transistorized amp and pre-amp to stereo tuner and a magnificent tape deck.

"I like classics too," I said honestly.

He stood beside the tape library, put his hand in and seemed to push. There was a slightly wild look about him that unnerved me. "Now look," he instructed.

I peered in and the tape bank had gone. There was vague light some little distance beyond, but I could now see that the back was open.

"Follow me," he said and stooped to enter the cupboard. We bumped into each other beyond the wall line and material of some sort was hanging down on us like strips in a tunnel of horror. We were able to stand up and were smothered in clothes. Norman fiddled with the barrier in front of us, a door slid back and we stepped out into a room and suddenly there was light.

I stepped out of a wardrobe into a bedroom that was at once familiar. Norman pressed something in the wardrobe to close the aperture at the rear, then closed the wardrobe door. Before he spoke, he hand-dusted himself down, straightened before the dressing-table mirror and brushed his hair with a silver-topped brush from the set on the table.

"Do you recognize it?" he asked amusedly.

I did, with increasing concern. What was he trying to pull on me? I nodded behind masked feelings. I felt trapped.

"This is the bedroom of the drum I screwed."

"That's right. Don't look so disturbed."

I stepped uneasily into the center of the room. "What are you pulling, Norman?"

"Nothing to your detriment. You were rightly puzzled why I was certain of your integrity. You are quite right: some people do change. But not you, Spider. I have proof."

I began to see light. "This is your pad, of course. The tom was yours."

"My very secret one. Not even my family know of it. I have only the top part of the house. The lower part belongs to someone else. It's a useful bolthole if ever I need one and it has other advantages."

"What about the dress hanging in the wardrobe?"

His eyes glazed. "What about it?" He didn't like it.

I hope I smiled easily. "If your wife doesn't know this pad I wondered if it was merely a prop. It looks quite expensive."

"Let's say an old prop. It's not important to me."

I was feeling resentful over the deceit and was trying to see his angle.

"So you paid me half a monkey to screw your own drum and nick *your* tom. It doesn't make sense."

"It does to me, Spider, and it was well worth it. I want you on the Tate job. There are other experts, but I wouldn't trust most of them. When you called it was a godsend. But I had to make sure of two things—one that you are as good as I remembered and two that your character had not basically changed. Both were extremely important."

"You could have sent me on a proper job. I wouldn't have known the difference."

Norman wagged a finger to show how clever he had been. "It wouldn't have answered my second question: Integrity? How had time affected you? I believe you to be the only operator I know who would have handed over every ring. If they had been someone else's I couldn't possibly have remembered them all. But I knew what and how many there were. You not only didn't keep one but I'm willing to bet that it never crossed your mind."

I was sick of the word "integrity" because my very reason for being here was screaming the lie in his face. It was true that I hadn't considered hanging on to any of the rings because my kick is in doing the job and it's the only way I can operate. I gave him a sheepish smile and a shrug and wondered what it would do to his vanity if he ever discovered the truth. And what he would do to me.

Now that he'd shown me how clever he was we went to the front-room study where he'd hidden the rings. He pulled the heavy drapes and put on the lights. We sat down at the desk as if I was being interviewed, and in a way I was. There was something about a desk that gave Norman a sense of authority, although he didn't need it. Twice I'd underestimated him and it niggled. I told him what I thought of the Tate and of the many hidden problems there might be. He listened tolerantly, but I could see from his slightly supercilious air that he knew what I was telling him and had something else up his sleeve.

"Don't worry about external alarms," he said when I'd finished. "What I have in mind will obviate them."

I scrutinized him. He wasn't mad and he'd shown how thorough he could be. Nor was he weak. Isometrics might have tightened his muscles but he was strong anyway. I listened carefully.

"You will penetrate from under the ground," he explained. "I will arrange a thermal lance team of three to cut through reinforced concrete straight into the gallery."

Just like that. "Using a sewer?"

He nodded. I tried to dig up my scant knowledge of sewers.

"I suppose," I said heavily, "that there's a nice convenient sewer right outside."

"There are two. One directly outside which falls straight into a chamber and another across the road on the river side of Millbank."

He held up both hands to stop me raising more questions. "You're an operator, Spider. I am not. I've had a man planted with the main drainage service for a year. He gets paid for the job and I pay him a handsome taxfree retainer as well. There are possibilities other than the Tate from below ground. I think it best that you speak to him. Raise all the objections you like and satisfy yourself."

I couldn't argue with that. Norman smiled and flexed his fingers to keep them pliant to count his money. At least he was able to finance his own jobs.

When he'd closed the front door behind me I stood and reflected. Some of his inner excitement had transmitted to me, and this both annoyed and alarmed me. At the moment it was difficult to keep to my objective. There were a lot of risks but the prize was huge and that's the way it went. The poor street lighting shone on the car roofs like puddles of water along the roadside. Norman had already invested two-fifty in me; he'd want much more than that back.

I went down the steps, quite slowly and very thoughtfully. At the gate I stopped and crossed my arms along the top of it. In front of me was a dark dry patch among the light puddles; one of Norman's cars was missing. I looked up at the sky, at the slow, dark cavorting of clouds piling up to rain before a rising wind. It was very dark but my sort of night for pulling my kind of job. I belonged up there, not below the surface. I knew that I'd have to break into Norman's before the Tate job but instinctively felt that the timing wasn't right. I'd seen more of his house tonight—not much more and no sign of bronzes, but it was beginning to work. And Norman himself was opening up much more. In the short time I'd been at it I should've been satisfied. I wasn't.

A car pulled into the gap just as I was closing the gate behind me. Keeping my head averted, I started to walk away when a woman's voice called. "Mr. Scott. Spider."

I turned round. Ulla's face was just discernible in the dubious light from the street lamp as she leaned out of the car. Half lost in shadow, she was very attractive as the light and shade toyed with her features. The whites of her eyes had an appealing luminosity in the bad light.

"Are you going home?"

I nodded, not sure whether she saw it.

"Jump in. I'll take you."

Brakes on. "I enjoy the walk, Mrs. Shaw. Good for my waistline."

"Oh, don't be so stuffy. It's Ulla. Jump in."

I went round to the near side. She opened the door for me. I climbed in beside her, conscious of the pale expanse of leg reaching out from the dark line of skirt. She smiled to put me at ease and did anything but. I was thinking of what Chrissie had said. "It's all right. I'm early. Norman won't be expecting me for some time." And that didn't put me at ease either.

As she swung slowly from the parking line I saw a man approaching from the opposite side. It was Detective Sergeant Newton, who looked as if he was calling on Norman. I was glad then that I'd got to Norman first. Ulla didn't notice him because she was badly placed and she misunderstood my brief alarm.

"Why are you so nervous?" It was half a challenge.

"Norman might be a very jealous husband."

"He is. But I'm only taking you home, for God's sake." Her accent sharpened with irritation. I think she was vaguely disgusted that I showed apprehension over Norman. She was a good driver and kept her gaze on the road apart from the very quick glances she sometimes shot at me while we talked.

"It's good of you to do this," I said because I'd dried up.

"Oh, I like you. I think, too, that you'll be good for Norman."

Ulla was alarmingly frank. I somehow felt that she would not know of Norman's offer to me. I reckoned he kept business out of his domestic scene as much as he could.

"You think I might fill a useful gap, then?"

"Gap?" Her quick glance stabbed over.

"Now that Max has gone."

"Oh. He finished with Max a long time ago."

"But wasn't he renegotiating before Max was killed?"

She shrugged with one sensuous movement and conveyed a dozen answers.

"I don't know. Nor do I care much."

"But you must know Norman's work."

"Of course." That shrug again. "But I don't want to know the detail."

"And yet you seem interested in my influence on him."

Ulla laughed; it was short and expressive. "You are a man. Max was a wild bull. Dangerous."

"So you're glad he's gone."

She took a corner smoothly and the question didn't rattle her. "I'm indifferent. Chrissie won't miss him as a lover, that's for sure."

These two women loved each other.

"Any idea who knocked Max off?"

Her glance wasn't quite so quick; it lingered fractionally on my face.

"Does it matter? He was a brute of a man and upset many people."

"Including Norman?"

"Norman and he got on quite well until . . ." Suddenly she braked and the car stopped in the middle of an empty street. It was indicative of her coolness that she first looked in the central mirror before turning to me. "You mean do I think Norman did it?"

"Norman! No, no, no. It's not his style. I just wondered why they broke up if they got on all right together." I was banking on none of this dangerous conversation getting back to Norman on the grounds that Ulla wouldn't want him to know of this cozy meeting.

"It was Chrissie. She was too possessive of Max. She felt she was being left out, so she stirred it up."

"She's a hard woman," I agreed. "Anyway I can't see Norman knocking anyone off."

Ulla started the car rolling again. "I wouldn't say that. There are things he would kill for."

"You surprise me. What sort of things?"

"Us. His family. He's very much a family man, y'know. He wouldn't allow us to be harmed."

"You'd better let me out of this car then." I kept it light but I meant it too.

She smiled in the gloom and I thought that Chrissie, with her cold looks, should take a few lessons from Ulla. I'd rarely met anyone with as much suggestion in minimal movements. Ulla possessed the art of expression if only of sensuality. "You've lived dangerously and I can see from your face that you've knocked around."

"Looks are deceiving. You'd be foolish to upset Norman."

Ulla laughed. For once the sound was unattractive. "I agree. I have much to lose." She drove on in silence for a few seconds, then added suggestively, "That's why I'm so careful. Anyway, Norman would never blame me."

Which was probably true and made my seat hotter than it was. I gave her final directions to the flat, and soon she was gliding into the roadside outside the main entrance. We sat in our steel and glass cell looking out at nothing.

Ulla smiled mischievously. "Well?"

"I'm obliged to you for the lift." I started to open the door.

"Aren't you going to ask me up for a nightcap?"

"Norman might smell it on your breath."

"A coffee then."

This was crazy. If I followed her trend I'd be the meat in the sandwich of Norman and her. I remembered what Chrissie had said about her. Chrissie might be a bitch but she could be a shrewd judge of character. Glancing sideways at Ulla, I could see that she was taunting me. She was dangerous and unpredictable. Yet there was something half hidden that filled her with intense nervous energy. I could feel its charge. I suddenly had the feeling that she'd judged me too well. She expected me to get out. Yet if I did she'd use it against me in some way.

I put my hand high on her thigh, gently squeezing her warm, soft leg. Immediately I felt the tremor run through her. "If you don't mind risking a fortune, then why should I worry?" I moved my hand. She stiffened but didn't stop me. In the dim light I could see the desire in the dark searching depth of her eyes; if it once sprung out it would be uncontrollable. Chrissie was right about her. Two lusts were battling for control— passion and avarice. She left me in no doubt of which was the strongest urge just then, but she was petrified that submission to one would drastically affect the other. I was too close to Norman and she had miscalculated. She was trembling as I shifted position and her mouth was open. With a gasp she suddenly slapped my face hard and broke her own spell. Greed had won.

"If Norman knew what you'd tried to do he'd kill you."

I laughed. "I know. But you won't tell him. I've seen through you, Ulla."

"Get out," she snapped.

I was still chuckling. "Is that what happened to Max? Did he go too far and you clobbered him?"

She regained some poise and her eyes flashed. "You fool. Do you imagine I'd let that ox anywhere near me?"

I smiled at her. "What about that coffee now?"

"Get out," she hissed. "Get out."

"That wasn't how it started," I grumbled. I climbed out and watched her burn her tires as she pulled away. She'd given me food for thought.

8

WHEN MAGGIE CAME to the flat next evening I couldn't help compare her with Ulla, but she won hands down. She was like a fresh breeze blowing away the fog.

I brought her up to date, listened to her negative news of Dick and tried not to worry her too much. It wasn't easy as I had to meet a character that evening instead of spending it with her. I had a strange reluctance to kiss her goodbye, as if I was contaminating her after Ulla. She sensed a difference but said nothing.

His name was Ginger Douglas, but he was called the Arab. It wasn't difficult to see why. He wore an ankle-length multi-colored coat that added to variety by sundry grease streaks. He might have been called Jacob but for the fact that his long, curling hair was topped by a balaclava with a bobble. In his early thirties, he was a bit late for the gear but had compromised by not growing a beard and sported only a thick black mustache like a Western gunman. The one thing that really struck me was the easy job Old Bill would have if they ever issued a description for him to be picked up.

His hands were surprisingly clean, but his prematurely grooved face was nicotine-colored, as if years of leaving ciga-rettes dangling in his loose-lipped mouth had erratically stained him. Watery blue eyes had a dispassionate quality I didn't trust, and they jabbed about the airless cellar as if seeking light and, finding it, hiding away from it. We'd met in one of these sub-basement clubs that were nothing more than a legal loophole for drinking round the clock. In here, his strange garb was unnoticeable. I was the odd man out, the only straight, and I attracted some queer stares. And I mean queer.

We sat in a corner of this dark, smoke-infested hole that smelled of rank tobacco and third-rate pot bound by body odor. "What a place to pick," I complained. "It's the sort of dump the fuzz raid three times a week."

The Arab gave me a superior smile, and why not—he was playing at home. "Relax, man. They hit us last night. Tonight's O.K."

"God Almighty!" I exclaimed, and it *sounded* like blasphemy in this corner of hell. "How did they collar you?"

The blue eyes chipped away at my face like icepicks.

"Don't be like that, Dad. I know my job."

"Which is what?"

"I'm a flusher, Dad. You need me."

"And don't bloody well keep calling me Dad. I'd have been three to have spawned you, and I'd have topped myself if I had after one look at you."

"You don't have to be personal, Spider man. I haven't bugged you."

That was true, although there was time yet.

"Let's get down to it," I said.

He crossed his legs just to make sure I didn't miss his high-heeled knee-length boots beneath his coat. I tried to keep my feelings from my face. I've led too sheltered a life.

"Normally," he explained, "there'd be a team of four. One on top to signal bad weather and the other three, including the inspector, down the hole." In spite of his idle pose he was completely articulate and not half as dozy as he looked. I grudgingly notched him up a peg. "Someone must be on top to answer awkward questions if Old Bill arrives. The thermal lance men will be below. Easy."

"You go around thinking jobs are easy and you'll get a stretch. With this kind of caper they won't care too much about a first offense; you'll be in until you're forty."

It weakened his smile momentarily. "We've got to nick the gear," he went on, "and it can't be me. I've got to lay on an alibi so that no inside information is visible. You savvy, man?"

I savvied and I could see who would have to do the nicking. "Go on."

"The depot is down near Vauxhall. The old river Tyburn runs through it, coming into the open just there. I can make sure that the gear is available, but you'll have to take it out with one of our vans. I don't think you'll find it difficult."

He saw the queries in my face and added, "The vans are Wedgwood blue and I'll try to leave some gear in one of them —boots, long socks, dungarees, belts, lamps, gloves and some safety harness and safety lamps."

"It sounds too easy."

"Like I said, man, it is. A kid could open the gates."

Something was rankling in the back of my mind, something I'd read or heard. "I always thought that you had to have two covers open each end of the stretch being inspected."

"That's right, man. But it's not always done. It's an extra safety measure but they haven't always the time or the men. Those boys know how to get out quick enough."

"But we won't."

"You won't be moving. You'll be in a gallery with a sewer leading off. It's right outside the Tate."

I didn't press him for more detail then; I wanted the general layout, the broad feasibility. Although the Arab was Norman's man I knew that he didn't even know him, that Norman always used a front when dealing with operatives. Which emphasized the great compliment Norman had paid me and the complete trust he'd put in me. Just then I'd rather have been in the Arab's shoes.

We went over odds and ends and he was quite sharp when he wanted to be. I idly wondered what he was getting out of it. With the back hand Norman was dishing out to him and the half monkey to me there was no doubt that Norman had already dug deep. And he wouldn't do that without being certain of a good return. I didn't fancy my chances if I suddenly decided to opt out.

"What about gases?"

"What about 'em?"

"Well, isn't it dangerous down a sewer, gases build up?"

"They'll escape when the cover is opened. Anyway, there's the safety lamp to lower down with lead acetate paper to detect hydrogen sulfide."

I leaned nearer to him, keeping my voice down. "For chrissake, you're talking of using thermal lances down there. You could blow the whole bloody place sky high."

For a fraction his insolence left him. His quick eyes ferreted around, then fluttered back to mine. "Man, there's nothing to worry about. Use the lamp first. That sewer has no reputation for buildup." *He* wouldn't be with us, so why should he worry?

By the time I hit the relatively fresh air of Brewer Street I had the feeling that no sewer could be worse than the one I'd just left.

Maggie was with me when Ron Healey called at my flat. He stood in the doorway humped in a cheap sheepskin coat although it was still warm. His hands bulged in the pockets and he appeared as tattily defeated as his coat. He came in.

"Any news?" A weary question from a weary man.

"No. Have you?"

He shrugged and his coat seams suffered. "No. Wondered what you'd been up to."

"No real progress. I've asked a lot of questions and received a lot of convincing answers that only confuse the issue. I might have something for you fairly soon."

He didn't ask me what and his resignedness reminded me of Newton's tiredness. "There's one thing," I said. Ginger brows arched toward ginger hairline. "Your murder squad have roped me into their orbit."

He flickered to life, but warily. "Oh?"

"A Detective Sergeant Newton called on me. He was pushing at my old connection with Max and Norman Shaw." I was almost on the point of telling him that I'd spotted him at Norman's place but couldn't without him knowing I was there.

The news startled him for some reason, but when I pressed he was suddenly evasive. I had the impression that he was nervous, wanted to leave, which was strange, as he'd only just arrived. I kept him a little longer, unsuccessfully trying to draw him out, but he quickly covered his reaction.

"Dick all right?" I felt Maggie's quick stare of resentment.

"He feels how you'd expect a copper to feel the wrong side of bars. He's bearing up."

"So they still think he did it?"

"He's all they've got. Men have done porridge with far less evidence against them."

I nodded. Didn't I know it.

There were three of them—hard faces and calloused hands. They had form written all over their uncompromising quarried features. No smiles from this lot. They might not have worried my old friend Knocker Roberts, but they worried me. From the outset they displayed an unspoken contempt of me, as though creeping was for kids. Why creep when you can crack someone's head open with a tire lever and then take your time? They didn't like it either when they had to accept that they'd take instructions from me. It was no use my complaining that Norman should choose his men better; villains are villains, some worse than others. They'd know their jobs inside out.

We sat as a foursome in a workman's café off the Portobello Road with four mugs of steaming tea on the plastic-topped table. We were hunched like a rugger scrum. They were called

Big Fred, Slasher and Charlie. What their names were I never discovered.

"There's about four feet of reinforced concrete to cut through," stressed Big Fred, tapping the table with a finger like a hammer head. This didn't mean a thing to me, and because he sensed it he laid on the technical stuff.

"We'll need a gas-cutting blowpipe to ignite the lance—a lance holder and 'alf a dozen ten-foot, nineteen-millimeter lances. And that means an adaptor. Right?" He dared me to question him with an aggressive stare. I nodded. "To be safe," he continued, "we'll need four three-hundred-foot oxygen cylinders. You'll 'ave to be bloody sure that you've got the space in the van to take this stuff plus ourselves and the normal gear for the sewers. Goggles and gloves and leather aprons won't take up much room, but the lances are an awkward size. Right?"

I nodded again. To give an impression of intelligence I asked, "How long will it take you to bore a hole big enough for me to crawl through?"

The others turned to Big Fred, who looked me over. "Actual boring time, about fifty minutes or so. The lances will burn out about every eight minutes, and in that time we'll use about two hundred feet of oxygen. Right?" Fred leaned back, having expounded and feeling the satisfaction of knowing his subject.

I could see snags but they were a matter for the Arab to sort out. I saw myself bouncing between Ginger and this mob like a shuttlecock kept on the move by experts. Wisely, Norman didn't want the Arab to meet these three. As there was no hope of Norman himself seeing them it was left to me, and I was becoming an easy front man for Norman if things went wrong; he knew I wouldn't grass.

We'd need another man. I'd insist on it. We'd need the riverside manhole up as well as the one outside the Tate. With the heat of thermic boring I had to insure that natural gases had every chance of escaping.

119

"When the lance is burning is there any way of stopping it? Eight minutes is a long time if the fuzz are around."

Big Fred gave me a pitying look, then turned to each of his companions in hopeless surprise. He was trying to reduce my authority in front of them. "It's bleeding obvious, ain't it? You turn off the oxygen. I mean the oxygen reacts with the iron rods in the lance. No oxygen, no reaction. Right?"

"Right," I agreed. "Now listen to me, Fred or whatever your name is. You're not here to make me look a fool nor to show off in front of your mates. If you think you've enough brain to tie up the whole thing yourself, go ahead. And that will include nicking the right stuff. If you haven't, and I'm telling you that you haven't, then just answer questions simply or otherwise wrap up. Right?"

He didn't like it. He smoldered while Slasher and Charlie smiled sheepishly. Big Fred had been put in his place and he wasn't the forgiving kind. But being weak with a man like that can bring a more disastrous kind of trouble once a job has started.

I had no intention of doing the job, but participation like this brought me very close to Norman, and as that was the object of the exercise, then I was satisfied. I had to find out what I wanted to know before this job was scheduled; if I didn't I couldn't see how I could back out and stay breathing. It wasn't only Norman now but these three bonnies and, to a lesser degree, the Arab. Meanwhile I had to go through the motions. That apart, the job was beginning to intrigue me in a disturbing, all too familiar way. It could be done. I was sure of it once a few things had been sorted out.

I broke into the grounds of the Tate Gallery that night. It was no problem. All I did was to climb the railings in deserted John Islip Street, flit past the workmen's huts where the new wing was being built and ferret my way to the front of the building. I hid in the overhang of the steps, crouched on my haunches and settled for a long wait. Unless someone actually came into the grounds, I was well hidden and safe from the probing beams of coppers' torches. I wedged myself into a position of Spartan comfort and semi-dozed.

I sat there listening to the whine of tires and the much more occasional tread of footsteps. At the dead of night this was a very deserted, very lonely part of London. From beyond the river wall the water slapped and suctioned at the granite and sludge, and the odd tug churned along, identifying itself by the muted chug of engines and the backlash of wash, setting up a rhythm against the wall.

Only once during my stay did I hear a copper go past. During my more lively moments I spotted the odd patrol car. Behind me, in the Tate, would be night custodians. The building was never unmanned. But with all respect for honest bravery, there was no one in the building who could stop men like Big Fred, Slasher and Charlie if they cut loose.

I rummied on like this for three hours, passing the time with scattered thoughts but keeping basically alert. Even on a warm night the cold begins to creep in, and I moved before my limbs stiffened up. It had been enough. I went out the same way as I'd climbed in. Near Piccadilly, some life emerged like maggots from cheese, but I was able to pick up a questing cab.

I slept latish, phoned Charlie Hewitt at the office—we were still the right side of red—then went back to the Tate Gallery. Something about the apparent lack of security was niggling me. There were plenty of custodians but I wasn't thinking of that kind of security. I began to feel that there was an inner ring, that although the building was penetrable it didn't mean that the galleries themselves were. I'd brought with me a rolled bundle of dungarees tucked under one arm.

I went in through the main entrance. It was midday and loosely crowded in the foyer, which was what I wanted, down the left-hand spiral of steps, along the corridor and into the Gents, where I slipped on the dungarees. When I emerged the two swing doors marked "Authorized Persons Only" were on my left. I went through them and took the most obvious corridor, which virtually carried straight on. I wandered along stone corridors unimpeded. I saw odd bods, sometimes passed them, but no one stopped me. I received a mixture of blank stares, friendly little nods and smiles and was sometimes ignored. I went down some steps and came across some heavy double wooden doors and almost blundered. I spotted the wiring in time, retired to an adjacent corridor where I could watch, and I waited. Ten minutes later a white-coated girl pitched up in front of the doors and pressed a button. The lock whirred; she pushed the left-hand door and disappeared. This was what I'd suspected. I didn't think her button pushing had opened the door directly but had been a request to someone else who operated remote control over the door.

I went up to the doors and pressed the button. The lock whirred and I was in. I took good note that it was a Yale lock and that there was no draft-excluder strip covering the crack between the doors. I could have slipped not only mica through but a jimmy. I didn't have to go farther to know that I was in some kind of inner sanctum. Two massive pedestaled busts reared above me, hiding coyly under covers. A couple of eighteenth-century paintings, which I didn't rate much in value, rested against the brick wall as if the Tate accepted my judgment.

Poking around in these cellars was no problem. I was able to examine the part where the sewer tunnel should break out and was relieved to find that it came up inside the inner security check. I ran into a group of workmen working on the new wing. I backed off damned quick before they realized I wasn't one of them. It took a little time to find my way back to the locked double doors because the building is old and rambling. When I got there, from this side, I was able to unhitch the lock myself and returned to the Gents to remove my dungarees.

With my roll under my arm I went up the stairs and into the galleries. Each main gallery had openings both ends with minor galleries leading off. Between the main galleries were huge open flat-topped doorways, some marble-surrounded, some wooden. I could see no way of closing them. I had to be careful; every gallery, big or small, was manned by an alert custodian. I stood in one of the big marble-framed doorways so that I was between two galleries. I idly looked over the paintings on one side, then the other, as if undecided which gallery to enter. I then saw the hinges.

Inset into the green marble frames was a central, narrow strip of marble either side of the aperture and each was hinged. Which meant they opened. I had to wait awkwardly until both custodians were looking away from me, then I quickly flipped open the nearest panel. It opened easily to reveal a cavity the height of the frame. I caught my breath and flipped the panel back in place. In the cavity behind it I had seen a metal door that clearly slid from its sheath to meet another from the opposite frame. These were the doors that would be wired.

I continued to wander round to find that only certain doorways housed the secret doors. The pattern emerged that large sections housing several galleries could be sealed off in units, rather like watertight areas on a ship. It had been a productive trip.

I took myself off to Vauxhall to look at the depot at which the Arab was based. The gates were wide open leading into a cobbled yard. One of the Wedgwood-blue vans was in the yard, and a couple of flushers with yellow safety helmets were disappearing into an old brick building that looked as if it had grown up with the London sewer system. There was no one about at that moment, so I took a few seconds to have a quick look at the layout. There'd be no trouble here getting in or getting out with a van. This would be the easy part, which meant extra caution because the easy bits often spring surprises as if they didn't like being underrated.

On advice I'd received from the Arab I took off for the Bayswater Road and positioned myself near the Lancaster Gate Hotel opposite Kensington Gardens. I had a long wait with not much to look at but passing traffic and a scattering of pedestrians. Eventually a light-blue van trundled up on the opposite side of the road and stopped about two hundred yards away, its red and yellow diagonal warning marks quite visible from where I stood. I crossed the road and walked slowly toward the van. By the time I got there the street cover was open, one man was disappearing down the hole like a yellow beacon in the gloom of the sewer and another was holding the lid. I knew that the one on top would stay there.

"Hello, mate," I said. "Looks like rain."

He looked up at the tumbling clouds and pushed back his yellow helmet. "I 'ope not," he said cheerfully. "My mates won't like it."

I bent over to look down the hole. It was narrow, with a perpendicular steel ladder anchored to the wall, and disappeared from sight in total blackness. I could hear the swishing of water and faint, strangely hollow voices.

"Keep back," he said with a grin. "Wouldn't want to fish you out."

"How far down?" I asked.

"This one's about sixty feet."

I knew why he was there but chatted him up about his job and he was only too glad of a natter. In a little while the driver joined us and it became clear that these men took a pride in their job. It turned out that it wasn't as distasteful as it seemed. And there was historical interest. All the main sewers were old London rivers, long since sunken or built over with much of the original brickwork and bridges still visible below the surface; there were romantic names like the rivers Fleet and Tyburn.

I saw the reflection of torchlight on water far below and stepped back as the first helmet began to emerge. There were three of them; the Arab was the second one up, and although he knew that I intended to take in the scene at some point or other he nearly gave the game away when he saw me. As an old campaigner I ignored him and by this time had backed away to the wall separating the park. Ginger Douglas looked nothing like an Arab now. I watched as the manhole was closed and as the men turned on the tap of disinfectant at the back of the van and let the fluid run over their boots and long gloves. Then they traipsed inside the van for a cup of tea. As I walked on, the urge to see the Tate job through was almost compelling. The fact of being used to these attacks of compulsion made them no easier to deal with. I had repeatedly to remind myself that I was involved only for Dick. It helped a bit. I'd try a last ploy with Norman in getting a straight look at his place and if it didn't work I'd move in. It wouldn't help at all if I finished in the next cell to Dick; it would be like putting another five years on each of our sentences.

I saw the Arab again that evening. We met in the same fugg-filled cellar, and while I didn't like it I had to admit it was safe—in one respect—but as I'd now turned up twice some of the inmates began to get wrong ideas about me and I had to elbow my way to the corner. When I sat next to Ginger Douglas they backed off but hovered near the worm-eaten bar. I was scowling and bad-tempered by the time I turned to Ginger; he was back in his Jacob coat with the same bobbled beret.

"What's wrong with *you*? Why don't they pester *you*?" I snarled.

"Because they know me—duckie." He was grinning at me and I had to grin back and after a while I chuckled.

"You nearly let on today," I admonished him.

"Well, what a daft thing to do, turning up like that."

"I'd warned you. I needed the picture." I explained to him about the dimensions of the thermal gear and the length of the lances, but he was certain that there was sufficient space. We went through the whole routine from the moment I nicked the van and when we'd finished went over it again. The Arab had thought things through, and his service with the drainage people had paid dividends. He knew what he was talking about and I listened carefully. When I left him I asked myself why, if I didn't intend to do the job, I was being so thorough. Norman didn't need to know all this. I had to give him a general idea, but he didn't need to know the small details. I tried to face my question honestly, but I'll never know if my answer was evasive by omission; I could work no other way. My preparations had always been thorough. Even doing a dummy, as I believed this to be, I couldn't cut corners.

This meant that I had to see the unholy trio once more to tie up finally their end with the Arab's. They didn't know of his existence, of course; they didn't want to know. They didn't know of Norman, or at least not in this connection; nor did the Arab. But they all bloody well knew of me, and this was what I didn't like. Charlie and Slasher were rough but careful; they listened, if not with respect for me, then for the job. Big Fred listened too, but I could see his piggy little mind working in resentment, and as I didn't want trouble I said, "Look, fellers, we're onto a good one. A lot of money. Let's forget our likes and dislikes and do the job properly. O.K.?"

They nodded and grunted and mumbled agreement and Big Fred said "Right." It was the way he said it that left me in doubt.

Norman exhaled, pulled in his stomach as if he was trying to break his spine and held the position for six seconds while holding his breath. He explained to me that it was the one isometric exercise that required exhaling instead of inhaling. It kept the stomach in and he certainly had no pot, but with a man so vain he'd starve rather than lose his looks.

We were in the secret study of the house next door. The issue could have just as easily been discussed in the study of his main house, but there was some psychological blockage that suggested to him that if his family didn't know of the place they couldn't know his plans either. It gave him a tremendous feeling of security and of oneupmanship.

"It looks a reasonable risk," I said, "but there are weaknesses." Norman sat behind his desk and became attentive, but even as he listened he was making pressure of hand against hand. When he offered me a drink I surprised him by accepting, although all I wanted was to break him of his obsessional exercise.

"Continue," he said as he impatiently planted a cut-crystal spirit glass half full of Scotch into my unwilling paw.

"I don't think much of the thermal lance team. They remind me too much of Rex Reisen's strong-arm boys. And one of them, Big Fred, has a personal grudge against me. He's the sort of bloke who might show it at the crucial moment."

"I'll take care of him," said Norman, and I knew that he would. "But they're good boys, very highly rated."

I couldn't argue. "I can get in," I continued, "I'm sure of that. But we must have another man outside. With the amount of heat that'll be chucked out down there we could blow the whole bloody street to bits apart from ourselves. Which means opening the Thames-side manhole and the one outside the Tate."

Norman thought for a while and was stationary, his steely eyes looking hard at me without really seeing me. He wasn't going to argue; his astute mind was already sifting through likely candidates. Max would have argued. Eventually he nodded slowly. "That's no problem." And I knew that he already had a man earmarked. He ran his hands over his hair, careful not to dislodge a strand. He was eying me cagily when he said, "Something's upsetting you. What's on your mind?"

There are times when I wished I had features like Knocker Roberts, all wire wool and gristle. I gave too much away but it had to come out. "I'm not hitting anyone whatever the prize. These old boys are probably all ex-servicemen. I'm not so much as laying a finger on them if they get in the way."

Give him his due, Norman didn't flicker and he lied well. "I'm relieved to hear it. That's why I asked you. I know your form, Spider. No rough stuff. Excellent. So what are you going to do instead?"

Crafty devil. "I'll just have to try to avoid them. I can't believe they're sitting guard outside each gallery all night long. Patrol is the normal practice and that can be coped with—usually."

"Anything else?"

"I go into the galleries alone. I want nobody with me."

"Naturally. That's how I always envisaged it." He began to exercise his scalp and I reckoned that he thought I'd covered it all.

"Where do you want the paintings taken once they're nicked?" I asked.

"When you leave the sewer you all drive off in the van and continue along the Embankment. It won't take long to divest yourselves of your protective clothing en route. You turn up Villiers Street and park outside the Players Theater. Three cars will be waiting. One for you to hand over the paintings, the second to take you home and the third to disperse the thermal lance team. I'll give you a little more detail on the day."

I nodded. It seemed all right. "And which are the paintings?"

At last he smiled—carefully, so as not to create too many creases. Now the boring but necessary technical details were over he came alive. "There is an exhibition of modern painting by Francis Bacon. Not exactly my taste, but it is said of him that if he has a friend he wants to make wealthy he need only give him a painting. And this is true. Among living artists perhaps only Picasso can show him his heels. I can dispose of eight canvases without trouble, and that will bring about half a million pounds. The four others you'll find together and are all Picasso. They're all modern art—not your taste, I feel."

"When do we hit?"

"That's up to you." He risked a smile again. "But the exhibition finishes on Saturday."

Saturday. It was already Tuesday. I stared across at him in astonishment. He was still smiling.

9

My MIND was racing like the clappers. Saturday. It would be impossible to leave it until the last day; some of the exhibits might be removed immediately after closing. That left Wednesday, Thursday or Friday. The cunning bastard. My real shock was having the job thrust on me with little chance of escape. Suddenly it was real *and now*.

"We'd better set it up for Friday," I said. "We should be at work well before one, and if the unholy trio are as good as they make out we'll be inside before two and out by half three to four." I was insane. Yet I couldn't help myself. I wanted to do it.

Norman was disappointed. "You've covered all the angles. Why not before?"

"Because I'll cover them again," I insisted. "And again. I'll still be covering them all the way to Millbank."

He sat back resignedly. "I'll organize it," he promised.

"Now what about a pre-celebration drink and then a quick look round your delightful home?" I rubbed my hands together as if I was enjoying it all. In part I was.

Norman glanced at his watch and stood up sharply. "I didn't realize the time. I'm taking the family out. It's Ulla's birthday. May we postpone the drink? Make it a celebration drink on Sunday?"

No mention of a tour of inspection and I could understand why. When we were back in the main house I said, "Where are you taking them?"

"Oh, we're doing a show and then onto a club to meet up with some friends."

"You'll be back late," I commented as we went down the stairs.

"We're not really late-nighters. We'll be back before one."

We stood inside the hall and suddenly he shot out his hand. I took it.

"Good luck on Friday, Spider. It could make you a very rich man."

Or a lifer. Evidently we wouldn't meet again until after the job, and this worried me.

"Give me a ring," he said, "some time tomorrow evening after nine. I'll confirm that arrangements have been made as you want."

So that was that. I'd arrived playing dummies and was now up to my eyeballs in reality. His daughter came out, totally ignored me and informed Daddy that he was late. He didn't trouble to introduce me, but maybe he was pushed for time. I let myself out.

I arrived back at my flat to find Maggie had let herself in.

"You've been trying to avoid me," she accused, half hidden behind massive framed specs. I think she was wearing them of late to hide the smudges of privation round her eyes. Like the rest of us, Maggie was worried sick, but she wasn't good at riding it.

"You're a smasher," I said. "And I love you. Now push off; I've got a job to do and I must change."

"What sort of job?" She anxiously followed me into the bed-room while I started to peel off my clothes.

"The usual thing," I replied lightly. "I like that trouser suit. It suits you. Narrows the hips."

"Come off it, Willie. When you pay compliments you either

want something or are avoiding something."

"Not true," I said as I buttoned up a dark shirt. "You look lovely. You always do but more tonight."

She sat on the edge of the bed and there was weary defeatism in the simple act. "Whenever you see me through rose-tinted spectacles you're in danger. It's a reflex action, as if you're trying to cram me into your memory in case you don't see me again." She took off her glasses; I was right about the smudges under her eyes. "Who are you burglaring?"

I pulled up the zip of my operational dark trousers. "Not burglaring. I'm not stealing anything. I'm breaking into Norman's. They'll be away this evening."

"Oh, no. He'll have you killed if he finds out."

"He won't find out. He'll be out and it won't take me long."

"Must you?" she wailed, knowing that I must.

"There's evidence there. I've got to find it. Once I have I don't have to go on with the Tate job because old Norman will be nobbled."

"By the police?"

I detected her disbelief. "Of course by the police."

"Do you think Chrissie will leave it to them?"

"Come on, Meg," I protested. "That's what it's all about. If she wanted Norman knocked off she wouldn't wait for me or anybody. It's part of the bargain."

"I don't trust the sound of her," said Maggie illogically.

"I don't trust any of them, but she's offered me a partnership which I haven't refused. She'll have to keep her part of the bargain."

Maggie gave me an old-fashioned look.

"Well, what else can I do?" I was peeved at her attitude. "These are the people we're dealing with. I have to play it as I see it."

"That's two partnerships you've been offered, darling. You'll be detaching yourself from Norman's and refusing Chrissie's. That makes two formidable enemies."

131

I'd finished dressing and was looking for my clasp knife. I spun round to face her. "Then tell me what to do. My brother is on a murder charge."

"I haven't forgotten," she said quietly.

"You should leave me. I told you before. I attract trouble like—like a flypaper pulls in flies."

We each brooded for a while, tensed up by events not of our making. I found the knife and slipped it in my pocket.

"Do you want me to help you?" It was a small plea from Maggie.

I sat on the bed beside her and put my arm round her shoulders.

"No, love. There's no need."

She gazed at the wall and I said, "You know we're caught up and have to go on, don't you?"

Maggie nodded almost imperceptibly. I rose, went to the dressing table and coated my fingers with varnish. Whatever Norman would do he wouldn't call in the fuzz, but it's a good habit not to break good habits. You never know. "You should go back to your place," I suggested softly.

I put my hand on her head, gave it a little push and left.

I went by bus. I had enough time and I shouldn't be too late afterward to pick up a last bus or a taxi. To break in anywhere before midnight was crazy. There are always people up at that time. It needed only one person in the wrong place at the right time and I was doing another stretch. I detest operating against my better judgment.

When I stepped off the bus I was within half a mile of Norman's place, and most of that was through back streets, which tended to decrease my gloom. As it got quieter my mood blended more with the idea of the job. I turned into Norman's street.

There was a hall light on and in one of the upper rooms. They had no maid that I knew of. In Norman's precarious game it was more likely that Ulla employed daily help. The lights didn't worry me too much. Any villain knows the usefulness of leaving lights on; they suggest occupation, which is often a deterrent. I crossed the road to the house, looking both ways as if crossing a busy street. I cocked my head. Quiet. I opened the gate and went in. Suddenly it was all silence, as if the whole street was holding its breath, watching and waiting.

I went up the same drainpipe and opened the same window as before. Inside I kept the curtains drawn and used my pencil torch. I went to the bedroom and opened the wardrobe leading to the main house. I examined the clothes hanging on the rail. No additions, no deletions. I went through into Norman's study, where I switched on the lights after insuring that the curtains were across.

I had a good look round just in case I'd missed anything before. It was a quarter to midnight, so time was with me. Although the house was empty I still moved noiselessly. All his desk drawers opened and their contents were quite innocuous, as I expected of someone like Norman. He had nothing that the fuzz shouldn't see. I switched off the light and opened the door about a quarter of an inch.

Some light filtered up from the downstairs hall in a mellow, deceptively clear glow. I stepped onto the carpeted landing and quietly closed the door behind me.

On the top floor it was practically dark and I had to use my torch. In each room I pulled the curtains across and switched on the lights. This was largely the bedroom area apart from Norman's study.

There were no bronzes here, not that I'd expect to find them in bedrooms. I went down to the next floor. One of the rooms had the light on that I'd spotted outside. I put my ear to the wood and listened. I couldn't hear anything, but to play safe I decided to leave this room until last. As my escape route was on the top floor, I reversed my normal routine and went down to the ground floor.

The first reception room off the hall I already knew to be clear so didn't waste time on it. There was another larger reception room with brocaded armchairs and marble-topped occasional tables, with Chinese rugs scattered over a deep-pile carpet. It was like bouncing on sponge as I crossed to the curtains. Crystal chandeliers scattered light and color round, and two Georgian tea tables snugged up each side of the post-Adam fireplace.

There were bronzes in here—three pieces, a pair of figures and one huge Chinese warrior on horseback resting behind the door like a mandarin's doorstop. It was old and worth a bit, but I got my mind back to the job. There were no children on eagles' backs. Off with the light, back with the curtains, always slowly so that the runners didn't make a noise. It was tedious and fruitless. The dining room and the kitchen were as unrevealing.

I went back upstairs conscious of the time trickling away downhill at an increasing pace. I crept past the door with the light strip under it and slowly turned the handle of the next one. The blur of windows faced me across the room as I silently closed the door behind me. This, I realized, was a back room, so I risked using my torch. I pulled the curtains, then switched on the lights. Almost the first things I saw were the two bronzes.

The room was a library with an incongruous television set in one corner and leather armchairs facing it. Tambor doors were pulled across the ugly eye of the screen. Shelves and shelves of leather-bound books covered the walls. It hadn't been like this when I was librarian in Dartmoor. On twin onyx pedestals in each corner, either side of the windows, were the bronzes, the eagles facing the center of the room as if they were some superb make of acoustic equipment and music would issue from their open beaks. Each child balanced on one knee on a wing-spread back. They were superb. I joined Norman's tremendous admiration of them. One of them had killed Max, according to Chrissie.

I examined the one with the boy carefully. Any blood would have been removed long since, but I was looking for possible damage like a bent wing tip or an unlikely dent. Both were in excellent condition, and the feather work was magnificent, together with the proud poise of the birds. They'd have looked better without the children. Would Norman use one to kill and then bring it here?

I'd found them, yet I felt depressed. No wonder Chrissie had wanted to take matters into her own hands; it wouldn't be difficult for both her and Norman to produce barrowloads of witnesses each willing to testify possession. I was still engrossed on a last look, half examination, half appraisal, when the door opened.

I had only to turn my head to see who was there. It was far too late to think of cover. My first reaction was one of disgust for being caught flat-footed, although the quality of Norman's carpeting was really to blame. Young Peter Shaw stood in the doorway quivering from shock.

"Oh, my God," he ejected. He'd recognized me instantly, but it didn't alter the fact that he must have thought he had the house to himself and was scared out of his wits to find someone here. I thought he was about to yell when I said very quietly, "It's all right, Peter. You've got me bang to rights but I won't harm you."

"But you must have broken in," he gasped, his voice shaking.

"It wasn't difficult." I smiled, trying to calm him. "Your father should have the place sewn up."

I think he realized that I wouldn't thump him and his lower lip slowed up. Even in fear his supercilious whine was there. But he didn't know what to do. I knew one thing he wouldn't do—dare not do.

"Are you going to call the police?" I asked in a friendly sort of way.

His long pale face hovered beside the still open door and his distended eyes wavered. "How did you get in?"

"Through a window."

"But I didn't hear you."

"I didn't hear you either," I replied dryly. There was one thing stabbing at my mind. If he told his father I was done.

"I came to get a book," he said, as if that explained everything. From somewhere he found some courage. "You are supposed to be a friend of my father. This is treachery."

I nodded. "It must seem that way. I thought you were all going out for your mother's birthday."

"My stepmother. Yes. Well, I found I had some studying to do." He was hesitant. He wouldn't opt out of the family celebration for that reason. There were undercurrents in this lad I couldn't determine.

"Didn't you want to go? Tell them you felt ill?"

Ridiculously he looked embarrassed, but I needed his trust.

"Come right in, Peter. You've caught me. We might as well discuss it in comfort."

"What can we possibly discuss? You had better leave now."

"What do you intend to do?"

It was difficult for him to say it, not knowing how I would react, but he did it with a little nervousness and much dignity. "I will tell Father."

"That could be like killing me."

"Oh, don't be ridiculous." But he was shaken, unsure.

I didn't say anything, giving him time for it to sink in. Then he burst out, "Good Lord, what do you expect me to do?"

I kept quiet while he battled with himself, and the kid was under torture, like both forces of schizophrenia fighting for possession at the same time. "What you have done is despicable, yet you dare ask my help."

"I haven't asked for anything," I said reasonably.

"By implication," he insisted.

"The implication of silence?"

He frowned. "What did you come to steal?" His law training was emerging, and I wasn't sure that this was good.

I chuckled. It needed an effort. I wasn't out for Oscars, but if ever I had to convince someone, then it was now. "Would you believe me if I said nothing?"

"You don't break into someone's house for nothing."

"True. But it doesn't have to be theft." I was thinking quickly. "Have you any opinion of me?"

He looked surprised. "I don't know you. I've barely spoken to you until now."

"You must have some idea. Your father may have said things or you may have heard elsewhere."

"I seldom move in my father's circles and I don't listen to gossip. Just where is all this leading, Mr. Scott?"

He was gaining in confidence and this suited me. I wanted him to have a clear, logical head free of fear and uncertainty and not overshadowed.

"It's important that you have some opinions of me because it can determine whether I tell you something or nothing."

He came farther into the room, eying me in puzzlement, now more curious of me than the situation. I had to make a decision and, my word, it had to be the right one.

"Are you pleading with me?"

I liked him like this. He'd temporarily forgotten his father and was showing traces of what he might be if left alone.

"Yes," I said bluntly. "But not for mercy. I've never done that with anyone. I want your understanding."

He spread his hands. "But isn't that the same thing? You want me to understand you so as to see your point of view and thereby hold your secret. This is absurd."

I was trying to weigh him up and he was so basically complex that it was difficult. I had to gamble on my assessment of him, which was exactly what I was asking him to do of me. He had nothing to lose and could afford to be detached about it; I had everything to lose. He was going to tell his old man unless I made it good. I *had* to take a chance.

"I came here to find evidence against your father for murder."

137

10

PETER SHAW FROZE on the spot. Slowly his hand groped for a chair back like a blind man. He'd gone very white. I walked past him and he made no effort to stop me. I closed the door and came back into the room, placing him once again between me and the door. I was trying to show that I could be trusted, that I hadn't run out.

"You'd better sit down," I said.

"No, I'm all right." He was holding tightly onto the chair. "My father is not a murderer."

"No man knows what another man is. Few know themselves."

A delicately fingered hand passed over his eyes. "We'd better have that talk you wanted." He sat down wearily like an old man. Still pale, he looked across at me like a dog who's just been unjustly punished. It seemed to me that young Peter Shaw had received too many impacts in his short life. Now he'd had another one.

I was getting worried. "Won't the family be back soon?"

He shook his head slowly. "They never come when they say they will." He saw my doubt. "Please, Mr. Scott, get on with it. If they do come back they won't come up here, particularly if they think I'm working."

I wished I could be as sure. I had yet to get out. "Max Harris was murdered on the fourteenth," I said. "There is strong circumstantial evidence to suggest that your father visited him that night. The presumed murder weapon is in this room."

"Then why haven't the police arrested him?"

"Because we're talking about people who wouldn't give the police the time of day. They have their own justice."

He looked at me helplessly. I supposed studying law as he was, and having the father he had, it was difficult to understand the law outside the law. He was living some sort of nightmare and it wasn't due solely to finding me in the house.

"You say the murder weapon is here?"

"It's the bronze with the boy."

He smiled feebly. "Rather a large object to take from the house and bring back, wouldn't you say?"

"He didn't take it but he did bring it back. It was Max Harris's."

His long fingers twitched nervously and he didn't know what to do with his hands. He was puzzled. "Whether or not it was Mr. Harris's I cannot argue. What I do say is that both bronzes have been on those pedestals in this house for at least six months."

I felt the cold tap drip down my back. "You're a close-knit family," I said equably. "You're bound to protect your father."

He started to laugh jerkily. "That's rich." He laughed on until it was unhealthily high-pitched and I thought he was verging on hysteria. I started to rise when he got a grip on himself. "I'm sorry." He steadied to a halt, but his nerves were in shreds and I was afraid even to move in case he went over the edge. "You say the murder was on the fourteenth. At what time is it estimated?"

"About half eleven to midnight."

"How extraordinary. My father picked me up from a friend's house at eleven that night. He's very good like that; he had promised. It's a difficult area for taxis, and what with garaging and parking problems I don't run a car."

His voice was wavering and he was anything but comfortable, but if he was willing to testify in court, then Dick was going to stay where he was. Apart from fear of this happening there was the dread of him being right.

"Did your father actually call at the house? Did your friend see him?"

"No. When Father says he will call at a given time, then that is what he does. I didn't want my friend to suffer the embarrassment of feeling that he should invite Father in for a drink. Frankly, I wasn't keen on them meeting anyway. I made sure that I was outside when he arrived."

"So there's only your evidence of him picking you up."

"Indeed. But I'm not lying, Mr. Scott."

He saw something of my own confusion and it gave him strength.

"You're an extraordinary fellow. You break in here, yet expect me to believe your motive. When I myself make statements you immediately disbelieve me. Why on earth should I trust a man who does not trust me?"

How far could I go? If Norman found out it wouldn't make any difference what I said. He'd do his homework. "Be absolutely certain of what you're saying. Another man's future is at stake—a man I know for a certainty is innocent. That man is now under arrest." This wasn't going as it should; he had to be wrong or lying.

He seemed to be feeding on me, for as my confidence waned his grew.

"You still think I'm protecting my father? God forbid. Look at me, Mr. Scott. What do you see? The son of a villain who will shortly be taking his finals in law which I might well deliberately flunk because my father will want to use my knowledge in a way I couldn't allow. Do you imagine that I'm insensitive to my background? And how do you imagine I face my friends day after day? If I were like my father I would have no problems, for his education was no less than the one he provided for me. I can't explain why he's like he is except that he once lost a fortune. If I was like my sister

I could cope. She has the happy knack of wearing blinkers so that she sees no sordidness. She has trained herself to accept its advantages and to pretend the rest doesn't exist. So she has become the brittle creature you saw."

As he spoke I realized that I was probably the first person he had ever told this to. He couldn't tell his friends, and Ulla and Norman were too set in their ways to want to understand. He was alone in a family and didn't know which way to turn, so much so that he was at the moment finding solace in me. We formed a strange pair. Yet it was a plea, and although time was passing dangerously I had to listen.

"How can a man train for law when his own father is outside it? I take after my mother, you see. She was a very gentle person. When Father turned to crime, presumably to recoup his losses, she tried to tolerate it but eventually had a nervous breakdown. So she left him. The dreadful thing was that she lost the custody of us children. She was still too ill to cope and would never betray my father in court. Had she been of hardier stuff and less in love with him she might have survived. But she didn't. As young as I was, I remember. I always will remember. And if I ever tried to forget I have my father's presence to remind me daily. Yet he cannot do enough for any of us. It might be a love born of guilt; I doubt that he'd ever risk being introspective enough to find out."

His voice grew stronger and steadier as he went on, as if resolving something. His fingers fluttered to his chin in a private agony of despair. "You are lucky, Mr. Scott. Your issues are simple. Mine are tearing me apart, as they did my mother, and unless I find a solution they'll destroy me in the same way."

Suddenly I shot out of my chair as I heard a door bang downstairs. Christ! I stared at him in helpless appeal. "They're back," I groaned.

"Sit down, Mr. Scott, please. If they come here we'll both confess. I beg you to hear me out."

He was on the boil and I had to let the steam subside. I was sweating, but there was no stopping him now.

"I have little to thank my father for except a warped devotion. Whatever he has done and for whatever reason, he cares about us. Which is why he couldn't have killed Max Harris. Mr. Harris was no threat to the family, and my father would only kill if we were endangered. Then, I'm afraid, he would kill anyone. His family is his particular sheet anchor to justify his deeds. He can convince himself that what he has done he has done for his children. The need for him to grasp this basic lie as a matter of truth has become an obsession."

Even in my great concern to escape, to get out before Norman found me, I saw a flaw in his assertion. Max could easily have constituted a threat to Norman's family, but I had no intention of voicing it now. He saw my agitation and took comfort from it.

"You're afraid of being caught," he accused. "You should be like my father; he's been successful for so long that he thinks he's impregnable. He may well be because he's clever and careful. On the other hand, if he found you here it would shake his judgment of himself."

"And he would feel his family was being threatened," I put in pointedly. "You said it yourself—he'd kill to protect them."

But his thoughts were still introvert. "How ridiculous it will look if one day Father is convicted and I am his legal adviser. I wonder how they would view *that*."

My ears were straining to pick up movement downstairs. I was afraid to make a move for the door in case he created trouble. It wasn't healthy to have the doubts that he carried. It would be a long time before he could expound as now without fear of it reaching Norman, and he was more than reluctant to let me go.

"What do you think I should do, Mr. Scott? You're an impartial observer."

"Do?" God Almighty, I could hear a light tread on the stairs. "There's someone coming," I whispered.

He seemed impervious; after all, he wasn't risking much.

"About my studies. Do you think I should complete them, knowing how the costs are met?"

His voice was too loud, yet I knew that he wouldn't lower it. I took over the vocals, keeping a low key and hoping that I wouldn't be heard beyond the door. "You've gone so far," I pointed out. "You're already committed. It would be very stupid to back off now."

The footsteps were outside the door. I held my breath in the hope that he would catch the desperation of my mood and at least wait a few seconds. When he spoke it was as if he had no awareness of anything except the two of us and his myriad problems. It was like an orchestral crescendo in an empty room.

"But it's only comparatively recently that I've really discovered my father's involvement. I am rather a naïve person, even if I am academically stable."

I grabbed the conversation back as the footsteps continued on the upper stairs. My prayer must have been strong, for it was difficult to believe my luck. There were still two others below.

"You're not responsible for your father. There are plenty of sons who would retch if they examined some of their old men's unethical capers camouflaged by furled umbrellas and hidden under brushed bowlers. Don't worry so much, matey. Finish your education and then use it properly. Leave your old man or give him an ultimatum. Then do some good with what you've got."

He was about to argue the point; it was written all over his face. He *knew* about his father; others didn't. If I didn't stop him it would be endless. I took the biggest chance of all.

"What is the matter with you?" I snarled, still keeping my voice down. "Are you so gutless? You know what to do. What sort of a person asks a bloody villain about morals? Do you have to have someone to blame if it doesn't work out? If you

143

do, then get a more respectable prop than me. All right, I'm sorry for you if that's what you want. It's tough. But have some dignity. Tell your father to get stuffed and stand on your own feet. It's bloody marvelous for the spirit."

My calculated outburst at least brought him back to both of us and the room and why we were here at all. His stare contained anger and a little self-pity; I'd wounded what pride he had.

"If I were you," I added, "I'd have left home long ago. I'd have said, 'Dad, you're bent. Straighten out or I'm off and you know what you can do with your money.' You asked my opinion, I've given it." I didn't know where it was going to get me. He was little different from Ulla and his sister, except that he was bugged by conscience.

As he stared at me, head back, eyes steady, it was clear that some of this was passing through his own mind; it had probably done many times before but without someone looking him in the eye and telling him to pull himself up by the chin strap.

"Can I go now?" I asked, not as casually as I intended.

"I'm grateful to you, Mr. Scott. You have a strange honesty for a thief. You didn't spare me even at the possible cost of your own delicate position." He smiled a little whimsically. "I could suggest that you practice what you preach and that you face my father yourself, confront him with your views of him."

I'd been half expecting it. "I would if afterward I was allowed to go out and earn my own living." I tried again. "Can I go now?"

"You really are worried, aren't you?" He was enjoying getting back at me. My mouth dried as I heard someone on the stairs again.

"Scared is a better word. My head's on the block and you've got the ax. Take my word that Norman will have to do me."

When would the young fool grasp the situation? Suddenly he heard the footsteps himself and motioned me quickly behind the door. I was there before his finger had stopped indicating. I still had to know. "Are you going to tell him?" I flung out in a whisper. He appeared confused, as if forgetting how we'd come to be in this room together, then he whispered back, "I won't tell him provided you believe me. He *did* pick me up that night."

"I believe you," I groaned.

The footsteps, muffled by the carpet but like clogs on boards to me, stopped at the door. I stood behind it, back to the wall, watching the uncertain expression on Peter's pale face. He licked his lips. I felt like licking mine. I knew it was a woman outside but not which one. The door handle fascinated me as it turned and the door swung slowly toward me.

"Oh, there you are, darling. We wondered where on earth you were." Ulla, honey-toned with a degree of underlying malice. Perhaps she realized Norman's children didn't care for her. I saw her go past the crack of the door and wished she'd push it further back. She stepped into the room just beyond the door, looking striking in a low-backed evening gown. Even her back view was suggestive. If she turned her head I'd had it.

Peter, unused to the situation, was edgy and was having difficulty in keeping his eyes averted from me. Fortunately he seemed to detect Ulla's polite insult and it needled him.

"You mean you were concerned for *me*?" He moved toward Ulla, keeping her attention.

"Well, of course we were. You said you weren't feeling well."

He walked past her and out of my sight, but his high-pitched voice reached me clearly. "My dear Ulla, I've been studying. Shall *I* turn the light out?"

Suddenly I was in darkness and the door was shutting out the dull light from the landing. I stood there in the dark wondering if Peter would keep his word. He'd got rid of Ulla but had shown that he wasn't too strong on clear-cut issues; he might have second thoughts. The footsteps went downstairs, which meant that they weren't yet ready for bed. I'd better get it over.

I opened the door gradually and peered out. The hall lights

were still on. I stepped onto the landing with a lighter tread than Ulla's, closed the library door and went upstairs to Norman's study. I had to be quiet because I suspected that Belinda was somewhere on this floor. I entered as a door banged downstairs. The ponderous tread could only be Norman's. It took me a fraction of a second to make up my mind, but in that minuscule of time I was sweating.

I dived across the room, pulling out my torch and ruthlessly beaming it at the far wall. I skirted the desk and opened the record cabinet, afraid that I hadn't the time. The record shelves swung back as I heard Norman reach the landing, his footsteps almost inaudible as I entered the dark interior. I cut off the torch as the door handle rattled and clumsily swung round inside the wardrobe as the door started to open. I closed the door of the cabinet and light flooded in through the diminishing gap. Darkness cut in once more while I stayed like a hunchback, hoping to God that Norman hadn't seen the dying movements of the cabinet door. I was afraid to move in case he heard me. And yet if I didn't he might come through.

I couldn't hear a thing inside the wardrobe. It was like being in an airless cell. Clothes on the rail cuffed my head as I backed as far as I could. My feet hit the wardrobe doors as if I was trying to break them down. The back panel began to open and a widening shaft of light slid through, creeping over my feet and lower legs like slow-moving lava. It was too late to get out. Had Norman heard me? I did the only thing left for me to do. I fumbled my way to the end of the wardrobe, pushing past the clothes, well aware that the hangers rattled on the bar and simply praying that Norman wouldn't hear.

I reached the end, put both arms out to steady the clothes, then stood absolutely still behind the short row of garments. The light scythed a few inches in front of my feet. Norman crept in and by moving my head slightly I could see him bend as if searching for something. For a physical-exercise fanatic

146

he was breathing heavily, but it might have been exaggerated by my hearing pitching to danger level. He straightened, brushing against the clothes, forcing them into my face. But I didn't budge a fraction even when fabric fibers started irritating my nose. I could see him plainly in silhouette, his neckline middle-aged, his legs floodlit by the pool of light. I smelled spirit on his breath and thanked God I hadn't been drinking myself.

He opened the wardrobe doors and walked out, leaving them open. The room lights came on, and suddenly it wasn't dark at my end of the wardrobe any more. He came back while I tried a chameleon with the wood at my back and the clothes at my front. I held my breath. Norman reached back, his face suddenly bathed in subdued light, and closed the cabinet door. It was like switching off his face as it disappeared with the comparative gloom. But it was still far too light for me. He drew back and closed the wardrobe doors.

I was in darkness again but in a worse fix than before. It was too risky to go back into the main house with three others there, and I didn't know what Norman was up to the other side of the wardrobe. I moved toward the doors and listened. I pulled at one of the doors. The light was still on and sliced me in a vertical beam. I stepped out into the bedroom.

He wasn't here, which was immediate relief, but I was a long way from getting out, considering his study was my escape room. I closed the wardrobe doors.

While I looked round for a hiding place I considered getting out from a window on the lower level, but I couldn't be sure that he wouldn't hear the opening and closing of the window, particularly the catch. I reckoned my best bet was to locate him, then act.

I moved toward the stairs and started on down. There was something compelling in the risk I was taking, yet I couldn't help myself. Keeping to the edge of the stairs, I made slow progress and just prayed that he wouldn't emerge so soon after

147

arriving. I reached the landing and heard a voice from the library. Creeping nearer, I put my ear to the wood and heard Norman speaking into a telephone. I didn't know that he had a phone here. There wouldn't be a better chance. I went back upstairs to the study.

As I climbed down the pipe I was extra careful going past the library window.

If ever I needed a car it was then. I cursed the fact of having sold mine. I could have nicked one, but it seemed ridiculous to increase my crime figures when my mission was straight. I reached Chrissie's place after a hell of a lot of walking. It was now just after two o'clock, and I could have done with a donkey jacket to keep out the chill. It was bleak round here. A couple of moggies sat eying each other from opposite gateposts. The Daimler Sovereign stood out from the rest but was beginning to look neglected even under the inadequate street lighting. I doubted that it had been used since Max's murder, which was a pity because it was beginning to develop an inferiority complex, as if nobody wanted it.

Like the others, Chrissie's house was in complete darkness. I hoped she hadn't a man with her. I rang the bell for some seconds. I wasn't surprised when nothing happened. I pressed the button again and kept my thumb on it. After some time a window above me opened and I stepped back on the path to get a view. A curler-clamped head hung out, and even from where I stood I felt the full force of unspoken anger. The lamplight caught the fury in her eyes.

"Who the bloody hell's that?" Inbred caution kept her volume down, but it was an effort.

"Spider," I whispered up at her. "Your potential partner."

"What're you playing at?" she spat back at me. "Do you know what the stinking time is?" Her white face floated above me like an invoked spirit.

"That's not friendly, Chrissie. Let me in."

"Go to hell and come back at twelve." She started to withdraw her head.

"Chrissie," I cooed, "if it wasn't dead urgent I wouldn't be here. I want to sleep too. Now let me in before we wake the neighbors."

"You big creeping bastard." It was her final fling before she closed the window. She hadn't sounded like a partner. She kept me waiting a good twenty minutes. I guessed she'd eventually come because curiosity would get the better of her.

The only movement during that time, apart from me trying to keep my circulation flowing, was the two moggies descending from the gateposts and sizing up for a scrap as they realized they were both toms.

When I was ready to lean on the bell again the bolts were pulled back and a chain rattled. "Come in," Chrissie said irritably as she opened the door. "People will think I keep a knock shop."

I let it pass, as Chrissie wouldn't be too worried what anyone thought as long as it didn't cost her. She led the way into the lounge, which was almost as chill as outside, as she'd switched off the heating on going to bed. She was wearing mules and a bright yellow patterned silk housecoat. Why did she always wear such harsh colors? The curlers had gone and her hair was immaculately curled and lacquer-sprayed; I could taste the bitterness of the spirit. She'd put on some makeup and looked like a freshly carved ivory image. Apart from her sour expression she'd done a reasonable job on herself. She sat on the arm of the chair, heedless of the long leg that emerged through the gap of the housecoat. She knew, and I knew, that it wasn't for me, which spoke volumes for her attitude as a partner. But it was a good leg.

"Well?" she demanded. "You've got me up, so it'd better be good."

"You couldn't spare a hot drink? Coffee maybe? I've had a time of it."

"Get on with it, Spider. If it's urgent the coffee can wait."

"I finally had a good look round Norman's place. Both bronzes are there."

Her eyes lit up wildly. "What did I tell you?" she said triumphantly. "I told you, didn't I?"

"So you reckon that fixes Norman?"

"Of course it bloody fixes him. I'll let the fuzz know."

"There's a snag," I said, watching her closely.

Chrissie frosted up. "Don't try pulling anything, Spider."

I shook my head. "The son reckons that both bronzes have been there for six months. He caught me at it."

She stared at me in silence, her head full of questions while I wondered which one would explode first. I should have known that it wouldn't be concern for me.

"Well, he would, wouldn't he? He's bound to say that. The whole bloody weak-kneed family is bound to say it." Then with a sneer: "They'll all stick by Daddy who produces the bread." The simulated plum-in-mouth accent didn't quite come off.

"Maybe," I said noncommittally.

She rose slowly from the arm of the chair, and the leg disappeared in the folds of the housecoat. "You're not saying you believe this creep of a kid, are you?"

I shrugged. "I don't know. He seemed sincere enough."

Suddenly the second implication hit her. "Does Norman know? The kid will tell him. Have you mentioned me?"

Chrissie was predictably true to form. I smiled. I couldn't help it. If I went into partnership with her I'd need my brains scrambling. "Have you got round to thinking what would happen to me if Norman knew?"

She didn't answer but was dying to know if I'd brought her into it.

"You're safe," I said contemptuously. "I don't grass, though God knows why not."

"I should have remembered," she said in relief. "I forgot your reputation. Anyway so far as I'm concerned that clinches it. I'll fix Norman for doing Max."

"It had better stick," I pointed out. "Old Bill will need more than your evidence."

"He'll get it." There was a malicious twist to her mouth. "I can produce half a dozen people to swear that bronze was in this house up to the time of Max's murder."

"I've no doubt that he can produce another half dozen to swear that it wasn't."

Chrissie stepped toward me, eyes ablaze, and I thought she was going to swing at me. I stepped back but she stopped and shouted, "What's the matter with you? Are you chicken? You should be pleased that we're getting your brother off the hook; instead you sound as though you're trying to foul up the whole issue."

I shrugged. "Like I said. It's got to stick or the hook will pass right through my brother."

"It'll stick. Don't you worry, Spider boy. It'll stick."

Watching her then, I didn't doubt that she could make it stick. It made me uneasy, although I wasn't sure why. I wouldn't like to be her enemy and I wasn't that far off. She wasn't tired any more, nor angry at being wakened. She slowly paced the room, erratically smoking a cigarette and ignoring me as she thought things out. Chrissie appeared a very satisfied woman, which didn't satisfy me.

I never did get that coffee. When I left her I wondered whether Max's meanness was less his than hers. She was mean in a variety of ways, any one of which could be dangerous to underestimate. My final fling with her was to ask to borrow the Daimler to drive home as there was little hope of a cab and it was a hell of a walk. I'd return it in the morning. She trotted out some claptrap sob story about sentimentality and Max and how he'd been the only one to drive it and now it was to her a sort of a shrine. It wouldn't have sounded so bad if her face hadn't been frozen with revenge at the time.

I should have been as pleased as Chrissie about the bronzes. I wasn't. I was worried—more worried than at any time since Dick was tucked away by his own colleagues.

I wondered if it had been all for nothing; that all I was left with was the Tate job. If Chrissie was going to move against Norman I hoped that she'd do it before the job was scheduled, and even that disturbed me because it wasn't entirely an honest hope. Anyway, it was more than my life was worth to try to back down on that, and if I tried Norman would start to examine *my* motives. Either way he'd gun for me all the way.

11

THE NEXT MORNING I filled Maggie in as she made the coffee, standing behind her in the kitchen door. By the time she'd plonked down the cups on the small sofa tables I'd brought her pretty well up to date, leaving little out of this last development. She didn't interrupt me once, and it was marvelous how she kept up a cheerful bustle of movement, as if she was listening to my recounting a day at the office. But now we were seated we had to pick the bones. She looked almost as tired as I felt, but I kept it to myself. I didn't like Maggie aging through worry over me.

"Do you think Chrissie did it then?" she asked at last.

"I can't see how. The police have cleared her and they have nothing to love her for. They'd have dug deep to try to pin it on Chrissie, on anybody when the only other suspect is a copper." It was strange thinking of Dick in so detached a way, yet at the moment I couldn't get emotional about him.

Maggie eyed me carefully. "From the way you speak it seems that you're no longer sure that Norman did it."

"If I'm not, then it's because Chrissie's evidence is suspect. She *wants* to pin it on him. Now he may have done it; he's still chief suspect with me, but I think she might be rigging the bronze bit. And I don't think it will stick."

"You mean that she's convinced he did it and intends to do anything necessary to achieve a conviction?"

"Something like that."

Maggie put down her cup. She wasn't looking at me when she said, "You think that she may have another motive?"

Our gaze locked across the room for long seconds.

Maggie didn't say anything more for a while. She sipped slowly at her coffee, and I could just see green traces of eye beneath her lowered lashes. She put down her cup and started fingering her hair. "She's using you," she said at last.

"I know it."

"You've got to wriggle out of the Tate job," she said flatly.

"Meg, I can't. He'll never let me off the hook. It's too near and he's already spent too much on it."

"Then you must try. Talk to him. Tell him you're not confident."

Poor Maggie. She would always slip up on what made villains tick. She could never screw her mind sufficiently to see inside their nuts.

"I'll talk to him, Meg, but bear this in mind. He's already paid me two hundred and fifty pounds; he's been paying a man for working on the sewers for a year, and there are three other men on his payroll, apart from sundry expenses. Not only won't he write that off but he's expecting a vast fortune from this job. I'll be wasting my time."

"You never know," insisted Maggie. "He may decide to get someone else."

"Between now and Friday? What we've got to hope for," I said grimly, "is that young Peter Shaw keeps quiet."

I left her because we'd exhausted the subject. I knew that if I stayed there'd be no relaxation for either of us and that we'd go round and round, always finishing up at the same point and then starting off again like being lost in the bush.

The lift was on its way up when I rang for it. The doors slid open and out stepped Ron Healey, looking a little more cheerful than last time, his carrot hair still unruly but at least he'd combed it.

"Just coming to see you," he said.

"It's funny you always pitch up at Maggie's when you want to see me," I pointed out.

He grinned boyishly. "She is a dish, Spider. My luck might change."

"Not with what I've fed her about coppers it won't."

"You're forgetting Dick's one."

"An ex-one by the way things are going."

He looked surprised. "No luck your end?"

"Not the right kind of luck. Sideways progress."

"I can do better," he said. "That's why I'm here."

My ears rose like a terrier's. We stepped into the lift and I pressed the button for ground.

"We have a suspect under surveillance. Nothing more than that. Nothing proved, no real case but enough grounds to watch him." He gave me a hard look. "I'm trying to ease your misery and Dick's. If this leaks out I could lose my job."

"Anyone I know?"

"Don't be unreasonable."

We stepped out at the ground floor and went down the stone steps to the street and stood on the pavement.

"You must have picked up a clue or two," I probed.

"Or acted on information received. Don't pump me any more. I've said my lot."

It had to be Norman. Chrissie must have done her stuff. Watching Norman wouldn't help. And I had to see him to-morrow without the fuzz around. I wondered if his phone was tapped.

We strolled slowly down the street together. "Have you told Dick this?"

"No. And nor must you. It will only build up his hopes on thin grounds and will be worse for him if nothing comes of it. I just thought that you might have a contribution."

"Not long ago I thought I had. Now I'm not sure. Give me a little longer." I reflected on Chrissie and the bronzes and

155

backed my instinctive judgment by keeping quiet about them. "Are you looking for anything in particular? Point me in the right direction and I might be of use."

Ron Healey shook his head slowly. "Just hoping for whispers, a cough or two. It's the old game of patience."

I rang Norman as soon as I got back to my own flat. Ulla answered the phone, her voice going carefully flat when she knew it was me. I didn't mind her writing me off, provided she hadn't Chrissie's vindictiveness. If she had she'd use it more effectively. She was indifferently noncommittal and called Norman.

"Spider?" In that one word Norman conveyed an attitude. It was almost as though Ulla was still there but using his voice. Maybe I was getting too sensitive.

"Norman, I must meet you tomorrow. Can you lunch with me where we went before, say, twelve-thirty?"

"I can see no reason why we should meet until the weekend. It's unnecessary and possibly foolish."

"It could be foolish if you don't." I hadn't liked his tone; he'd always kept it friendly up to now.

"That sounds like a threat."

I groaned. "Norman, would I threaten you? It's just important that I see you before Friday."

"All right. Twelve-thirty. Don't be late." He hung up.

I leaned against the wall, blowing my cheeks uneasily. What had happened? Norman had changed. I could imagine what might have happened, but had it? If it had I was dead. I undressed slowly, wondering whether I should ring Maggie or leave it until I'd met Norman. I rang her. By the speed she answered I knew that she hadn't yet turned in.

"Meg, it's me." If she didn't know my voice by now she never would. "Have you a girlfriend somewhere in London who could put you up?"

"Why? What's happened?"

"Answer me, Meg."

"Pam Davies will always put me up. She lives at Ealing, a bit far out after here."

"Ring her up and fix it. Take a few things to the office with you tomorrow and go down to her place in the evening after work."

"I can't ring her at this time of night. Anyway, what on earth's happened?"

"Do as I say, for God's sake!" Worry was making me harsh. "Ring her now. Nothing's happened. It's just a suspicion. I want you out of it. If you stay you're adding to my problems, and don't go taking that the wrong way. For me, Meg. Please."

There was silence. Then I heard her breathing. "What about you?"

"I'm all right. I'm just being overcautious, but it's better to be. I'm relying on you, Meg. Don't let me down and don't ask questions. I don't have any answers."

She gave me Pam Davies' telephone number, and the way I was thinking I didn't write it down but memorized it. I'd have felt better if she'd taken a few days' leave from work, but I knew that she wouldn't. I hung up, leaving her fretting.

I took a look round; most tables were empty and Norman wasn't here. I went to the small bar and hunched myself over a stool, remaining half turned toward the door. I ordered a tomato juice with a dash of Worcestershire sauce but needed a treble Scotch. My head had to be clear if I wanted to keep it on my shoulders.

Three tomato juices later some of the tables had filled but Norman hadn't arrived. If I'd been drinking spirit I might have begun to relax enough to order more, lose the edge of my wits. It wouldn't be beyond Norman to think in these terms. At a quarter past one he still hadn't arrived and the place was fairly full. It looked as if he wasn't coming, but I had to sit it out because this was my last chance. It didn't do my nerves any good, but I resisted the urge for a stronger drink.

He pitched up at nearly half past one. I'd been waiting an hour. Seeing me wave, he came to the bar with a slightly silly smile on his face. "Sorry I'm late. I was held up. You must be a few drinks up on me."

"I am," I said soberly. "Tomato juices."

He looked vaguely disappointed. "I'd forgotten your tee-total habits." He hadn't. He'd merely hoped that I'd changed them under the strain. Last night's impression of a change in him returned strongly. Outwardly he was no different, his slight smile, his charm, but underneath it he was guarded, and its extent was indicated by it showing through, if only minutely. Norman could handle crises on his head, so whatever bugged him was deep. I ordered him a double Scotch; he briefly raised his glass.

"Well, what's so important that you've had to drag me out here?"

"We'd better sit over by the kitchens. It's the only isolated table left."

"My dear Spider, I have no time for lunch."

"We can't talk at the bar here." I led the way, knowing he would follow. "Have something quick and light," I suggested as we sat down. "An omelet perhaps."

He managed to keep a token smile on his face, but something was radically wrong. I didn't like the way he had to fight not to show it. In turn I had to pretend I hadn't noticed and hoped I did better.

"Well?" he said again. I could now see that he was drawn, a little gray and seemingly a little uncertain, as if someone had really pricked his vanity. If he'd found out about me that would've pricked it all right. There were no isometrics in him today, and coincidentally he looked his age for the first time since meeting him a few days ago.

"Something worrying you, Norman?"

I caught him on one leg, and his smile instinctively became defensive but, a professional to his fingertips, his reply wasn't delayed. "This job is imminent. I'm banking on it a great deal."

"But you've got enough bread," I scoffed.

"Who mentioned money? I have enough but I can't stagnate. I'm still waiting for your answer."

This was more difficult than I'd imagined. I had no prepared script; I had to play it off the top of my head. "I want to cry off," I said.

His face stiffened so much that I thought he was doing one of his exercises again, except that his eyes were fixed on me like rivets about to be hammered in. And he was breathing very shallowly.

"Cry off? You do mean from the job?" He couldn't believe it.

I nodded wretchedly. "The more I think about it the more I have to acknowledge the risk of violence. I just couldn't do it."

Norman was having a bad time. His well-trained mind upped its revs, seeking out the traps and impossibilities of what I'd said. "We've been through this," he muttered savagely. "As you well know. You don't have to use violence."

"That's what we agreed. But I couldn't stand by and watch the unholy trio using it either. It's not my scene."

The omelets arrived, and I could see Norman resisting the temptation to throw his at me. I don't think I'd ever seen him openly display temper before. A smile from him now would have to be chiseled out. I felt partly frozen myself.

"What's the real reason?" he suddenly snapped.

I looked down at the steaming ham-pitted eggs and reckoned they would choke me if I tried to eat. "I have an abhorrence of violence; I've told you before. I've thought round this job from every angle a score of times. I've reached the conclusion that it can't be done without someone getting hurt."

I was watching Norman closely. His features gradually relaxed as he used his considerable will power to bring himself under control. His words were controlled too as they emerged from his barely moving lips with the odd distortion of a talking weighing machine. "So you suggest that I get someone else?"

"If you can. I realize it's difficult."

"That's magnanimous of you. Twenty-four hours to find an expert to plug an important gap and absorb what it has taken you some time to learn. And then expect him to make no mistakes."

"You could delay it a little."

"The exhibition, my dear Spider, finishes this week, or have your suddenly chilled feet affected your memory too?" Chagrin was smoldering in him, yet he managed to smile again—like a sadist watching suffering.

"If you can produce someone," I said, "I'll spend the next twenty-four hours in briefing him."

He pushed his omelet away as if it offended him. "Who do you suggest?"

"I don't know." I shrugged. "You had this scheme in mind before I pitched up, so presumably you had someone then."

"The fellow I had in mind was already committed. Your arrival was fortuitous. Otherwise I would have had to put the whole scheme off for some considerable time and wait for an equally good exhibition. But Picasso and Bacon! I ask you. Ginger Douglas is getting restless working down sewers, and it's unlikely that the unholy trio, as you call them, will hang on forever; none of them are endowed with perception. They want their money now. To delay would mean a new team."

"Why don't you go yourself?" I suggested quietly. It was like heavily slapping his face. He reeled back and for a few seconds was stunned. Then he said, "I don't think that funny. I'm a planner, not an operator. No, I'm afraid it must be you, Spider."

I pushed my own plate away as if I was trying to checkmate his.

"I've explained," I said weakly. "Call it cold feet if you like, but you know that I've always worked alone."

"You still will once you're inside the Tate." Suddenly he leaned forward with a friendly little gesture. "Look here, Spider, I understand your feelings regarding violence. I even respect them, but have you considered my own point of view?" His voice was soft but threaded with steel. I wished I knew how much he'd found out about me, and it wasn't something I could ask him. His eyes were very indifferent as they locked on mine.

"Apart from anything else, I'm not prepared to lose face to those I've employed. I'm nothing if I don't hold respect; business drifts elsewhere. But that aside, I've spent far too much in time and money to lose it all now because you have qualms you should have voiced at the outset. You had the opportunity to think things over. Now it is too late. You'll do this job, Spider, because your life won't be worth living if you don't. There are a dozen ways I can get at you and I will. And when I think you've had enough I'll dispose of you. You've learned too much about me; you've seen too much. You came in of your own free will. You'll go out feet first because I would never be able to trust you again and I wouldn't want you around to remind me of my most serious mistake."

He wasn't bluffing. He hadn't stayed out of nick by being careless. Besides, I'd proved his judgment wrong and he'd never recover from that while I was around.

"There's nothing you could do to me," I said rashly.

His smile was spontaneous, the first genuine one he'd managed at this meeting. "No? Then what was Maggie Parsons doing taking a suitcase to the office this morning? You wouldn't have warned her to stay out of town for a while? If you did it was good thinking, Spider. But it won't help. And then there's your business; there's half a dozen ways I could bankrupt it. You're too young to die, Spider. You'll do the job all right—on the original terms; the partnership died when you got cold feet."

I couldn't run from him forever and he wouldn't want me loose. He'd been quick to spot Maggie as a way of getting at me. There was nothing more effective. There was at least a chance that he'd let me off the hook after the job, once I was committed. I was quiet for longer than I realized, for he broke in on my thoughts.

"Come now, Spider. You do the job properly and violence doesn't arise. You know you can do it."

"When did you put someone onto Maggie?" I asked flatly.

"After you telephoned last night."

I didn't believe him. I reckoned it was before that. I gazed at the cooling omelet. "O.K."

"Sensible fellow. Oh, and Spider, don't ball it up. If you do I shall consider it deliberate. But then you're too good a craftsman and much too intelligent to do something silly." He pushed back his chair, stood up and gave me a last quizzical stare. He wasn't all that happy. Neither was I.

After he'd gone I sat there for a bit with two untouched omelets, which upset the waiter when I paid the bill. I went back to the office to try to take my mind off things, but it didn't work. I was making out some air tickets for a pressed Charlie Hewitt when I was told Mrs. Harris wanted me on the phone. I hated taking these sort of calls with Lulu and her stand-in within earshot.

"That you, Chrissie?"

"Where've you been, you dirty stop-out? I've been trying to raise you for hours."

"You've got me now. What do you want?"

"I want you over here sharpish. There's something I want to know."

"Ask me now."

"You bloody well come straight over, Spider, or I'll send a couple of boys. That wouldn't look so good in front of your staff. You don't want blood over your ticket stock."

Suddenly everybody was threatening me. This partnership business didn't look too safe. "O.K. It'll take me half an hour or so." I finished the tickets, checked them, then passed them over to Charlie on the counter. He looked at me strangely. Maybe I was showing my age. I felt a hundred and five. I caught a bus from Shaftesbury Avenue and sat upstairs among the smokers, which was as near as I could get to getting away from it all. London passed by on a conveyor belt I'd just stepped off and wasn't likely to return to.

The Daimler was still there with a new cocoon of dirt and misted chrome; I felt for her. Chrissie opened the door like a fanfare, loud and brassy. Her hard eyes picked over me like a tattooist's needle, and I rubbed one arm subconsciously and walked past her into the hall and then into the lounge. She wore a flimsy light-blue creation that wasped her waist and a bra that pushed her breasts up high.

"Right," she said as she slammed the lounge door behind me. "What's your crafty game?"

I sank weakly into an armchair. "Which one?" I asked mildly.

"Don't you come funny with me. I offered you a partnership. Now I hear you're still doing jobs for Norman."

Her blond hair was so perfectly curled that I thought it must be a wig unless she used cement as a lacquer. I was getting lightheaded, a sure sign that the hoodoo was on me. "And just how did you expect me to win his confidence without getting friendly?"

"I didn't expect you to. All you had to do was search his drum and having done that finish with him."

"It's not that easy."

"Are you screwing for him or not?"

"I intended opting out. Now it's more than my life is worth to back down. He's got me over a barrel."

"So 'ave I. And don't forget it. *I know you visited Max the day he was murdered.* No one else seems to have found out. Now ain't that strange?"

My skin crawled. I'd seen her vindictiveness against Norman.

"I thought you wanted to land Norman with it."

163

"I will. But if you don't toe the line against him you'll be in with him. You're working with him. If I know that stupid bugger he's already given you bread. You came here that day and so did he. Maybe you came a second time—with him."

"You know better, Chrissie."

"I know I can drop the word that you came that day and that you've been seeing Norman."

"So what do you want of me?"

"I want your testimony that you have seen one of those bronzes here and after the murder at Norman's."

"You can get plenty of people to do that."

"Only the first part of it. In return I'm willing to say that you broke in for me to establish proof. You won't even get a fine. And then you can have that partnership."

How much of a case could she bring against me? My record would condemn me; so would my silence on visiting Max; so would my sudden association with Norman. A few perjurers thrown in could sew me up. Ironically, if she did this Dick would be released. But I've always sworn that I'd top myself rather than do another long stretch. And Chrissie knew it.

"I'll take my chances," I said.

Chrissie laughed like a smoker's cough. Her follow-up smile was brittle. "You should be more convincing. How would you like Norman to know you have a brother who's a jack?"

"Someone's already tipped him," I said. "If not that, then at least that I broke in and why."

That took her out of her stride for a couple of seconds. Then: "You wouldn't be that cool. If Norman knows that, you're dead."

I was already feeling it. I shrugged. When you're in a slough between towering catastrophes what else can you do except pray—and I hadn't ruled that out.

"How long did you knock it off with Norman?" I asked slowly.

It was the best reaction of the day. Chrissie went so white

that her powder appeared detached from her skin. The pale red nails of one hand clawed viciously into the fabric of her chair. Her jaw sagged as if it had taken a physical blow, and her bright eyes went vacant with shock.

"What did you say?" she asked hoarsely.

"You know very well what I said. I've seen your dress in his secret pad: Jean Varon."

"You bastard." She rose slowly, trying to control her slow, heavy breathing in the tight bodice, and her fingers clutched into barbed balls of sinew and nail. Her vacant stare was slowly replaced by venom that spat hate straight at me. She realized that her reactions had completely given her away; it was too late for denials. Yet in spite of her fury there was something pathetic in her stance.

"How would you like me to drop the word in the right quarter? The fuzz would find it interesting."

Her lip trembled, and I mistook its meaning. I really thought I was going to see hard-boiled Chrissie cry. It was unbelievable and I should have known better, but it looked like it. She was bursting with barely controlled emotion and her eyes were filmed by moisture. Then her fingers unfurled as if controlled by clockwork, and her long talons were raised. She threw herself at me with a choked cry of fury and caught me unprepared.

It was too late to attempt to get out of the chair, so I did the next best thing. As her nails spread to rake my face I pushed hard with my feet and toppled the chair over. One nail nicked a channel from my upper lip, and I felt the stickiness of blood on my tongue as I landed on my back with Chrissie sprawled between my raised legs.

I made a frantic grab at her wrists as her distorting, snarling face hung just over mine. My fingers met my thumbs around her narrow wrists, but it was like holding electrified cable. She fought with the savagery of the gutter, and I clung on for life, for those nails of hers would make a razor slash look like insect bites. She bit deep into the back of my hand, and I roared but still managed to hold on. She wriggled with a feline fury that did all but break away. If I let go I'd go down in a bloodbath and probably sightless at that, for she was already trying to claw my eyes out.

We rolled over until I was on top of her, trying to kneel on exposed thighs and press her arms back to the floor while she struggled in desperate, sensuous movement, like a rape scene. She tried to head-butt me, claw, kick and bite, and she was not entirely unsuccessful in any of these. All I could do was to hang on until she lost steam. My nose felt as if it had caved in.

She suddenly went limp on me and I needed the respite. I wasn't stupid enough to relax my grip, but in the next second she was at me again and broke one wrist free. I brought my shoulder up quickly to cover my face, so she grabbed my hair and had me yelling my head off. I clamped her wrist again and we were off, and it was me doing the weakening. We rolled as she squirmed under me, and she brought a stockinged knee hard into my crotch. I doubled from pain, instinctively humping like a hedgehog and covering my face and head with hands and arms.

She'd hit me so hard I couldn't have moved if I'd wanted to; the pain seared through my groin and I heard myself moaning. I had to take what she dished out. She kicked me, scratched at the back of my hands, tearing at the flesh and drawing the blood she needed for satisfaction. I took it until I was numb, but I had to remain until the pain eased off. When she started to hack a hole in my head with the stiletto heel of a shoe I lashed out blindly with one arm and flung her sideways. I straightened as much as I could but was still on my knees. So was she as she scrabbled up. Her eyes were mad as she swung the shoe at my ear. I ducked awkwardly, did a painful shuffle forward on my knees, then thumped her straight on the jaw. She crumpled like a doll.

Christ! I bent double again, breathing like a pair of old bellows. Scruples: I should have thumped her at the outset. I took a quick squint at Chrissie. Her jaw was already swelling. Incredibly, her hair was hardly displaced. I stayed there panting for a while, then climbed unsteadily to my feet. With difficulty, and ridiculously, I bent to pull her dress down. Burning pokers had seared my hands, and as I held them shakily out I saw the red bars of blood from wrists to knuckles. I saw the shreds of flesh under her nails and felt sick.

12

I SANK ONTO A CHAIR and wondered what the hell happened next. At least I knew for certain that the bomb she carried in her was fused by Norman. If her passion for him was anything like her anger for me he must have had a pretty torrid time. So Chrissie knew how to love but not how to let go. I looked down at her shallowly breathing figure, completely soft and feminine in repose, and realized that I couldn't leave her like that. I didn't like the shape of her jaw; nor did I like the idea of bringing her round. I rose, righted the other chair, then found the bathroom.

I looked a sight. Blood trickled through my hair and down my forehead. My nose was gushing and my lip was still bleeding. Where she'd rained kicks at me was now beginning to ache. But the backs of my hands were the worst. I washed in cold water and poured some over my head. When I'd dried off the towel looked as if it had been badly dyed. I searched for some styptic that Max might have used but found none. I did find some bandages in a first-aid kit and bound my hands; the rest would have to congeal. I was a mess.

Back in the lounge, Chrissie was still out but breathing more normally. I did another search and found a row of keys hanging up on hooks in a china pantry. I lifted an ignition key with a Daimler tag from its hook and went back to Chrissie.

She was stirring and groaning. I suppose I should have helped her up, but I'd had enough of getting too close to her foraging talons. I sat down and waited. Her eyes fluttered open, the mad glare replaced by one of puzzlement. Her breathing became heavy again as emotion flooded through her with consciousness. I rose. I wasn't being caught squatting a second time. Apart from the unlikely tidiness of her hair, she looked ravaged and the jaw swelling had discolored. She gave a huge, painful sigh and half sat up, leaning on one elbow. A hand came up tenderly to explore her face and she grunted. As I was standing slightly behind her, I don't think she saw me. She gazed listlessly round the floor and then suddenly burst into tears.

Chrissie sobbing was almost unique. I wouldn't have wagered sorrow against self-pity. It wasn't through pain—Chrissie would have taken that with blasphemy on her lips—and it wasn't remorse. Great gulping sobs burst out of her, as if she had a bone in her throat. I just stood there watching the flood of tears staining her face and carpet without being able to raise pity for her. It looked as if her fury was spent, but I wasn't gambling on it. The shelf of her breasts darkened as the tears flowed. I waited quietly, reminded of what had led up to this by my own aches and pains and burning hands.

When she eventually stopped she rolled onto her knees with her hands forward, her head hanging down dejectedly between hunched shoulders. Her dress was torn along the hem and was ripped at the back, revealing clear skin and part of her bra. She began to sniff back the tears.

"Feeling better?" I ventured.

Her body stiffened instantly, and although her head barely moved I could tell that she could see my feet. She told me what to do with myself and any attempt at polishing it would have sounded wrong from her. She climbed to her feet, and I didn't make the mistake of helping her. Her head came up, her eyes still tear-filled but baleful. "Sod off," she said more politely.

"You'd better get that chin seen to."

Runnels of tears streaked down her face, funneling her powder like drying riverbeds in a desert. She wouldn't forgive me for seeing her like this, but what was a bit more malice.

"You wouldn't understand, would you?" she rasped. "You and that simpering marshmallow bitch Maggie Parsons. We were both already married when we met. We couldn't help that. But there were no problems when his first wife was alive. Everything was wonderful. What Norman and I had for each other was real. *Real.* Until that money-grabbing cow Ulla came along. My God, I'll fix her one day."

"But not until you've fixed him. Or does fixing him fix both?"

She stared uncomprehendingly, then said, "Don't you understand? Toward the end Max found out about us. That's why they broke partnership. Max didn't like it because he had to work with Norman daily. After they parted Max tried to ruin Norman. So Norman did the only thing left. He killed Max. He killed him," she repeated dully, "and took away the only thing left to me. Max had his faults but he stood by me. Now I've nobody while Norman still has that crafty bitch spending his money for him—and those two uppity kids."

"You'll have to learn to live with it," I said.

Her eyes blazed again. "Don't you believe it. He's not getting away with it and nor are you. If you don't help me I'll make bloody sure that you're not around to help him."

"I'm not perjuring myself for you or anybody."

"Then you'll pay the price." She swung round on me and I backed off, thinking she was going to start all over again. She sneered. "Afraid of a woman? A creeper who says he won't lie? You're a nothing. A nobody. A cream puff. Max would have wiped the floor with you."

I held up the ignition key. "I'm borrowing the Daimler," I explained quietly. "You've made such a mess of me that I'll get picked up unless I get out of sight."

Her eyes became shifty; it wasn't difficult to read. I said, "If

170

you report a stolen car I'll shop you. I'll explain to the fuzz about you and Norman. That should get them crawling all over you."

Her gaze hardened again. "I'll fix you, Spider Scott. I'll fix you good. Go on, enjoy your ride; it's the only one you're going to get. I'll lift the keys off your corpse."

I moved backward to the door while she stood slightly swaying as if drunk. Her arms came up and her bloodied fingertips began to explore her curls. She was getting back to normal, which wasn't going to help anyone. She cast another glance at me, a cocktail of contempt and viciousness, and moved toward the phone. There was something in the way she did it that included me in the motion. Chrissie wasn't going to waste any time. I got out quick.

The interior of the Daimler was cold and damp and musty. I opened the window, switched on and had to give the button several thumpings to start her. She turned over, spluttered a few times, then picked up gratefully. I pressed the button for the bonnet air vent, then eased her carefully from the row of cars in which she'd been locked so long. The car purred away, glad of the airing and responding beautifully, but I was sick to the core.

It was now the evening rush hour. I got caught up in a stock of traffic that did my nerves no good and attracted more than a few curious stares at traffic lights. I wasn't sure how much more blood had flowed since bathing my face. My immediate worry was Chrissie. Norman wanted the paintings, so whatever he might have in store for me would wait until after the job. But Chrissie was different; she was so intent on getting Norman, whether he'd knocked off Max or not, that she'd remove anyone who was a threat to that aim. She certainly saw me as that. She'd gone beyond the bounds of love or possessiveness. Chrissie had gone over the edge; my searing hands confirmed it.

There was no letup in the traffic, and the engine began to drink petrol as if making up for the days of neglect. I switched tanks, relieved to find the second one full. When I finally reached my block I found a sudden hesitancy at going into my own flat. I don't know why; but I don't ignore warnings. I swung away from the pavement as I'd been pulling in, and someone gave me a long, deserved blast of horn. I edged back into the flow and headed for Maggie's place. It took a long time to cover the short distance, but by the time I finally parked I was glad I'd changed my mind.

I went up to her flat and let myself in. As soon as I entered the hall I felt her presence. She wasn't there, but her personality remained and even a faint fresh smell of her lingered in the bedroom. It was like coming home to a friendly ghost. I missed her. When detached from Maggie I always did, but when those detachments were forced, and they often were, it was painful because I worried about her. I am getting older and softer and maybe it's time. Everything about the flat was bound to remind me of her, and I found it rewarding and unsettling at the same time.

I bathed, patched myself up, raided the small freezer and hashed up a meal with a jugful of coffee. I sat in her favorite chair, very aware of her, and reached for a small red leather, gold-tooled book on a console table one side of the fireplace. Shakespeare's sonnets. In one movement I'd displayed the gulf between Maggie and me. Shakespeare. I didn't dig this bloke's stuff on the telly, never mind the written word. But Maggie could lose herself in him. I flicked through the pages trying to pick up the magic Maggie felt. I started reading and began to probe some of the sense, the perception.

I rang Maggie about eight o'clock, kept it light and assured her that everything was just fine. We both kept up the act, knowing that tomorrow was Friday, the great day. She didn't even mention it. Nor did I. I watched some television without really seeing it, which isn't difficult for me, and I considered how I might finally squeeze out of the contract with Norman and still stay in one piece. Then I thought about Maggie staying in one piece and got off the subject. I went to bed, taking the sonnets book with me.

Sitting up against Maggie's pillows emphasized her absence. I began to feel really lonely. I was tired without being able to sleep. I picked up the little red book again.

Is it thy will thy image should keep open
My heavy eyelids to the weary night?
Does thou desire my slumbers should be broken,
While shadows like to thee do mock my sight?—

Oh, Maggie.

I must have drifted off at that point. I can remember the difficulty I had over the last line, the words blurring repeatedly and each time I dragged my mind back to semi-consciousness to start the line again only for it to fade out. Going back over it like that was as hypnotic as counting sheep. Sleep grabbed me and I blanked out on the final try.

It was the softest of noises that had my eyes open wide. I kept still and listened. No sound. My neck ached, suggesting that I'd been sleeping in an awkward position for some time. The book of sonnets had fallen from my hands onto the cover-let. I closed it quietly and put it on the bedside table. The time was almost midnight. I switched off the light because I hear better in the dark. I carefully climbed out of bed, groped in my pocket for my pencil torch and crept to the door.

They were having trouble with the outside lock. Maggie's old lock was so easily opened with a piece of mica that I'd made her change it long ago. I'd also made her fit a chain on the door, which I hadn't fastened before turning in. I quickly pushed the two pillows under the blankets and crossed the room barefoot. I opened the bedroom door and entered the lounge. Now I could hear them more clearly—just odd scratches of sound but completely familiar to me. I hoped I wasn't so noisy on a job.

173

To give myself time I crossed the carpeted lounge floor, avoiding the furniture by instinct, then silently fastened the chain with just the right touch. It wasn't too soon. The lock clicked back. I dashed back to close the bedroom door, then felt my way to the kitchen as the front door slowly opened, to be halted by the chain. That wouldn't stop them for long if they were properly equipped. Out of keyhole range, I used my torch sparingly in the kitchen, finding a hammer in a toolbox in one of the cabinets. It was nice and heavily reassuring in my hand. Almost closing the kitchen door, I peeped through the slit into the living room.

A sharp click and rattle informed me that they'd cut the chain and the door opened wide and closed again. They kept still as I would have done, listening before using light. A torch clicked on, its beam cutting the darkness in harsh brightness. I squinted as the beam traversed the room. Two of them— dark hunched shapes pulled noiselessly across the room by a shortening beam. They knew their job and headed for the bedroom. I followed.

They stopped outside the bedroom while I crouched behind a chair. One of them put his ear to the door. Neither spoke a word. I had the impression that they'd worked together before. The bedroom door was opened slowly after dousing the torch. I gained a few feet to kneel behind the settee. The bedroom light came on, and one of them swore viciously. The light from the bedroom overflowed into the lounge, but I was all right if I didn't move. They started throwing the bedclothes about and the one who'd sworn yelled out, "Where the bloody 'ell is she? She must've been expecting us."

Then his mate, calmer, more observant, said, "The bed's been slept in. It's still warm."

They rushed back into the lounge flashing the torch round wildly until the calmer one had the sense to switch on the light. I was still hidden unless they came my way to the kitchen. But in any event I couldn't move. I was chilled solid and wanted to be sick. They'd come for Maggie, not me. My stomach went as hollow as if I hadn't eaten for a week. When that phase eased I was flooded by a burning reckless violence. Sense, guile, none of it mattered any more. The hammer was in my hand and I was trying to squeeze the wood to pulp. I stood up, using the settee for leverage, very aware that my legs were shaking in anger.

As I appeared they both swung round, and one of them had an automatic that centered swiftly on my chest. "Spider Scott!" He was the bigger of the two, the swearer. The gun fitted his coarse face and cruel lips. His hair was prison-cropped. His was a face I vaguely remembered but would now never forget. He misread my pallor and grinned crookedly. "Where's the girl? In the kitchen, is she?"

His companion read the scene better. His sharp intelligent face and rat black eyes froze as I straightened. "Careful, Lennie." The warning emerged from straight lips that didn't move. But Lennie had the gun; he could be brave. "What're yer going to do with that then? Hammer the bullets as they come?" He still wore his twisted grin. But he wasn't quite so sure of himself as I came slowly round the settee. I wasn't thinking of his gun; I was thinking that these two bastards had come to harm Maggie on account of me. Lennie didn't take his eyes off me, but his lopsided grin wavered into a sick caricature.

"Don't try, Spider Man, or I'll stop you."

That got through to me but didn't change my mood, though it prevented his head coming within hammer range as I stayed still and he regained a little confidence. Without shifting his gaze he said to his mate, "Check the rest of the flat." Chummy gave me a doubtful look and left Lennie with me. It didn't take him long. He came back puzzled. "She's not here."

Lennie gave me a long thoughtful look, which appeared painful for him. These boys could do a job as long as it went to plan; complications were usually solved by reflex action which in them meant violence because it was positive and got them off the scene. I could see Lennie trying to work it out. I was a little calmer now, but the hammer in my hand was still asking to be used and I wasn't going to forget these jokers.

"Where is she?" demanded Lennie.

"You've just heard. She isn't here."

Lennie's face twisted into a snarl. "Don't be funny with me, mate. How would you like to stop one right in the crotch? She wouldn't be much use to you then, would she?"

I very nearly threw the hammer at him and he sensed it, for the automatic came down at an angle as he concentrated on an aim.

"You're a berk, Lennie." Rat-eyes put in his bit. "He's riling you."

"He ain't going to rile anyone else." His trigger finger tightened, and I was just about to throw myself behind the settee when rat-eyes put in another argument for me.

"You won't get paid for knocking him off. He's not the contract. You'll wake the whole bloody block. And he's a friend of Knocker Roberts. Use your loaf." I almost warmed to rat-eyes; he had a sharp brain and he probably saved me, for Lennie relaxed a little. I wasn't sure until then whether or not he'd been bluffing.

Rat-eyes said to me, "It was closer than you thought, mate. So the bint didn't stay 'ere tonight?"

"Tonight or any night. I've taken over the flat—until Chrissie's off my back."

Rat-eyes smiled bleakly. "Naughty. So where is she?"

I played with the hammer. "You really expect me to tell you?"

"You'd better," blustered Lennie. "We ain't much time." He waved the gun at me, but his chance had gone and the rot of discretion had set in.

I looked to rat-eyes for intelligent answers. "What were you going to do to her?"

"Naughty again," he said. "You know better." He now tried a friendly smile. "Look, Spider, there are two of us. Lennie gets very nasty when he's upset, as you've seen. We don't want to move in on you, but we must find the girl. She can't mean that much to you."

It was his first mistake; his briefing had been bad.

"The first one to come near me gets a smashed skull. And you both know I mean it." They stood quite still, Lennie now appearing ridiculous with the leveled gun. He was the sort of man who had to have the comfort of one, like a baby with a dummy.

I knew why they were holding off. Rat-eyes had said it.

"Knocker and I were on the Moor together. He has an attachment for me. You know—always reckoning he owes me favors. Chrissie should have told you that as well."

If a villain didn't know of Knocker's reputation he didn't know much of anything. I didn't want to hide behind it but swallowed pride for Maggie. Ironically she loathed Knocker. I could see they both wanted to go. Rat-eyes realized that wouldn't be enough. "Look," he explained, "we were going to take the girl and 'old 'er. She wouldn't 'ave been harmed. It was to make you toe the line."

I opened the front door for them and they weren't slow in moving toward it. They stopped when I raised the hammer. "This isn't the end of it," I said. "You made the mistake of your lives when you agreed to get Maggie Parsons. And Chrissie knows that. If I were you I'd sort it out with her. Tell her I said you're to be paid anyway."

They looked bewildered but didn't argue. Maybe they didn't know of Chrissie's acute meanness. It would be like a body blow to her to shell out for failure. After they'd gone I locked the door and rammed a chair under the handle. I sat down still holding the hammer and a shiver went through me. Maggie had never been in this sort of danger before. It shook me to my roots.

I bought a new chain and a padlock as soon as the shops were open. Chains are O.K. for all normal purposes, and I didn't want Maggie to be scared out of her wits by finding a cut one. This was T day and I'd resigned myself to accepting that there was no way out that wouldn't complicate matters further. Last night had shaken me; Norman wouldn't make the mess-up Chrissie had. It was likely that he already knew where Maggie was.

During the course of the day I tried to get Chrissie on the phone from my own flat, but it was mid-afternoon before she replied. I warned her that if she ever tried to get at Maggie again I'd shop her to every copper in sight and to Norman as well. Maggie's safety was the one issue that would probably induce me to grass. I think she got the message, for she used a rapid succession of profanities that would have finished up in the Guinness Book of Records if they'd been printable. It wouldn't stop her. In the mood she was in, guaranteed porridge wouldn't stop her, provided she satisfied her lust for revenge. But it might take her focus away from Maggie and back to me.

In the evening I didn't know whether to ring Maggie or not, then she rang me and I joked my way through the whole situation. She saw me getting an extended ten stretch for something I didn't want to do and finishing up beside Dick. It all seemed crazy now, but it hadn't when I'd first set about it. All my eggs had been in one basket and I'd dropped the lot.

I selected a pair of fine pliers, a hardy clasp knife and a long-handled pair of metal clippers. A cranium saw, plasticine and rubber-soled shoes completed my equipment. I took the end spring clips off my crocodile clip and replaced them with small metal spatulas. At half eleven I left the block. I nicked a car a good half mile from my flat and drove off toward Vauxhall.

Now that I was on the move again the job attracted me strongly. I couldn't help myself. I was looking forward to it and was afraid of it at the same time. I would have found it difficult to stop myself now whatever happened.

Clouds tumbled before a high wind, blacking out most of the sky. Normally it wouldn't worry me, but if we had rain on this job while down a sewer it wouldn't be funny. There was still plenty of traffic about, which gave me a cozy feeling of being loosely packed in and unobtrusive. I glanced at the petrol gauge. A few gallons left. Plenty. I kept her at thirty and drove like a demonstrator of good road manners.

I glided into Bessborough Gardens, went round the square a couple of times before finding a darkened gap to park. I got out regretting that I couldn't return chummy's car to him, but when you're on a job, that's it. It is a pleasant square surrounding a railinged green. And it was quiet. I stepped out toward Grosvenor Road.

The scene became shabbier as I neared the river. Old brickwork stained with age and abused by scrawled chalked signs, fronted dilapidated buildings that should have been torn down long since. There was one big advantage to me: People didn't linger in an area like this. I was on my own, my rubber soles making no noise, leaving my ears flapping for the heavy pad of coppers. Seedy districts like this understood stealth and contributed with an aura of decay and neglect and stagnant smell. I entered the long slow curve of Grosvenor Road, so different from adjacent Millbank. I crossed to the opposite side and followed a dingy brick wall ruptured here and there by metal gates. I was following the line of a wharf and glimpsed a long building with broken windows slinking behind the wall as if trying to hide, ashamed even in darkness. It was lonely and empty and lifeless and I was grateful.

The depot gates came into view across the road. They were solid and set into sound yet old brickwork. From almost every angle it was ideal. The immediate district was strictly non-residential, and it was a part where the clock of progress was set right back. There was no obvious hiding place but plenty of shadow—more shadow than light. I stood opposite, listening and looking, relying more on my hearing than sight. I crossed the road, took hold of the padlock on the gates, stretched my ears once more, then took out the clippers hanging down my trousers leg. I stood back for leverage and applied full pressure. The lock was old-fashioned and strong, and I had to have several attempts. It snapped like a shot. I whipped off the old lock, pulled back the bar and pushed the gates wide open.

I was vulnerable, so worked fast. I crossed the cobbled courtyard to the old building. Big, slide-back doors held another padlock, which I clipped as quickly as I could. The sweat was beginning to flow. I needed bigger clippers but had sacrificed them for mobility. Tearing the padlock off, I pulled back the doors on their runners. Three big Wedgwood-blue vans faced me, their diagonal mauve and yellow stripes clear even in the bad light.

I opened the rear doors of the right-hand van and climbed in. I flashed my pencil torch. There was a central table with a bench each side for the flushers to sit. To the right of the door was a store cupboard. I opened it. The Arab had done his part. It was full of heavy waders, long woolen seamen's socks, coveralls, safety belts, helmets, a safety lamp and some big battery lamps. I closed the doors and climbed out. At one side of the garage were storerooms facing onto the courtyard. The Arab had told me which one. Using the handle of the clippers as a jimmy, I splintered the door round the lock and levered. It flew open with an enormous crunch. The idea was to make it look like a break-in. The Arab had saved me time by sorting it out and putting it in the van. I dashed round to the front of the van. The Arab had gone as far as could be expected; the ignition key was in. It wasn't imperative but it saved time.

I heard the double tread as I was about to climb into the cab. I couldn't quite place it. People say the beat copper is a dead loss, but you can take it from me that they can cause problems. Every so often they're going to pitch up.

I crossed to the outside gates and closed them. There was no padlock, and the haft might be sticking out. I had to take the chance. Just inside the gates and to their left was a lowish building and a wall. I climbed up, all the time listening to the approaching heavy tread. From here I shinned up the stack to the roof of the higher one. I could now see the coppers approaching slowly on the other side of the road.

Inch by inch, so as not to attract attention, I eased my way down again to the low-building level. From the Arab's description I knew that the main building straddled the old River Tyburn, which emerged dejectedly from underground as if bewildered at man's savage sentence to condemn it from human sight. With the history that old flowing stream carried with it I could understand its disgust. Anyway, it might offer me a way out if I had to move. I keyed up my hearing and waited, ready to bolt.

They padded past: clump, clump, yak, yak, all nice subdued stuff that gave me an early break. I watched the darkening sky moving with the restlessness of cloudbanks gathering for a wet weekend. The lighter patches had deepened to exclude the earlier translucent glow of moon. I could *smell* rain. And that worried me more than the coppers who had marched on without so much as shining a lamp.

I waited until I couldn't hear them, then reopened the main gates and climbed into the cab. With my foot on the clutch I sorted out the gears, then backed her into the yard. I climbed out, closed the big blue sliding doors, then slipped the broken padlock over the loop of the haft. I now backed the van into the street, stopped again, on double yellow lines which gave me a childish satisfaction, then closed the two main gates. I slipped the bar across and padlocked it with the new lock I'd bought that morning. I threw the key over the wall. Outwardly everything was now back to normal. If the coppers came back on this side they'd notice nothing wrong.

The Tate Gallery was conveniently near to the depot, but I still had a call to make nearby. By choosing my streets carefully I kept to the neglected ones and pulled onto the Chelsea Bridge to head south of the river. I was actually going away from the Tate but had decided it better to risk only myself at the outset rather than the whole team. With Battersea Park on my right I pulled left off Queenstown Road, not far from the Battersea Power Station; the stacks looked like huge cigars spewing into the turbulent cloud, padding them with dark pollution. I pulled up near a derelict warehouse. There was a small recessed yard, its rickety gates open, which I backed into.

They must have been watching for me. Big Fred came out of a side door like a crouching gorilla. Give him credit: He had the rear van doors open before I'd switched off. I climbed down to help them, and Slasher, Charlie and another man were already loading the first cylinder of oxygen. I went with Fred to fetch another. We made a couple of trips before we had all the cylinders and thermal lances on board. There was a little trouble with the lances, which were awkward to store because of their length, but eventually everything bedded down. The fourth character was called Sid, a small, starved-face man with a gray stubble and the restless hands of a dip who so far as I was concerned was needed only for the bit part I'd envisaged. We then took off our shoes and slipped into the thick socks and the sole-weighted waders. We fixed our safety belts and sorted out the yellow crash helmets and red rubber gloves so that we each had our own handy. While we were getting ready I noticed that I wasn't the only one glancing anxiously at the sky.

We'd hardly spoken. The professional in each one of us simply got on with the job as quickly as possible to leave sufficient time for the real work. I pointed out the safety lamp so that they could get it ready to test for gas when the time came. We were all moving awkwardly because of the weight of the boots, which were unusually heavy on the foot and pitted with studs presumably to grip the wet, slippery brickwork of the sewers. I shepherded them inside the van and, when they were seated round the table, closed the doors. I went back to the cab and pulled myself up as clumsily as a deep-sea diver. I sacrificed a few seconds trying to make sense of the clutch, brake and accelerator pedals through the thick soles of the waders. It was worse than I'd thought.

I backed slowly out of the yard in a series of jerks that must have upset the boys in the van, climbed out, closed the gates and got back in again. It was better moving forward but was still like driving with no feeling in the feet. I took it carefully, wanting no undue attention now. I took her back the way I'd come, over Chelsea Bridge, along the miserable loneliness of Grosvenor Road and past the depot again to carry straight on to Millbank, following the slow turns of the Thames. We virtually had the place to ourselves. I pulled into the recess outside the pale ghostliness of the Tate, left the sidelights on and climbed out. I was getting a little better at it.

The rear doors were already open when I reached them, and the boys were climbing out awkwardly. I whipped a turnkey from the cupboard and signaled Sid to follow me with the safety lamp. We crossed the wide deserted road to the Thames side and located the sewer cover. It's amazing how many different lids pockmark the pavement—electricity, gas, water, telephones, and drainage; they all had their patch. We pulled back the metal cover and looked down. It was black, but we could hear the flow of water and a gaseous, paraffin kind of smell emerged, not offensive but slightly sickly. I lowered the lamp on a cord and saw the light brighten as it hit the darkness. Unless we wanted to blow ourselves into the quickly flowing Thames there was no hurrying this bit. It was now after twelve-thirty.

I pulled up the lamp. The lead acetate paper hadn't changed color. I said to Sid, "All you have to do is to stay here. Leave the lid open and kick it hard twice if there's rain." We both looked up at the tumbling sky but neither commented. "If the fuzz come, signal me and tell them there's an emergency and refer them to the inspector over the road. That'll be me. My name's Jones. Got it? That's all you have to do. You stay here until I say you can go."

Sid nodded and took up position. I looked across the road at the little tableau, then glanced beyond them to the stubby serenity of the Tate and felt vaguely sorry. The old lady was about to be ravaged.

13

I CLUMPED ACROSS THE ROAD to the unholy trio. Their faces were shadowed under their helmets, but there was a kind of uncharacteristic submissiveness I didn't expect from them. It was a pity I didn't give it more thought, but there was no time and there was a job to do.

"Get the gear out," I instructed and no one argued. They pulled out the first cylinder while I took to the steel vertical ladder fixed to the wall of the tunnel, which was about three feet by three. The ladder was so close to the bricked wall that I couldn't get all my foot through but quickly found that splaying out my knees made it a little easier. It was so narrow the wall brushed my back. The tunnel went straight down and ended in a chamber, which added another three feet to the width and six feet to the length of the tunnel. Immediately I felt the strong tug of water. If I backed into the downstream of the horizontal tunnel that flowed from the chamber there would be sufficient room for the length of the thermal lances. I traversed the lamp to get the general layout. The beam reflected on walls and water, creating illusive nuances of light and shadow at once claustrophobic.

Most of the main sewers are old rivers; the tributaries are largely man-made and of concrete. The walls of the chamber and of the main sewer leading from it were brick. The sewer itself was round but for a couple of feet of flat, uneven brickwork to walk on. The heavy boots at last made sense and more so as I was standing in a fast-moving stream of about thirty inches depth. It was too deep, but we'd have to cope. The water was unexpectedly clear and the smell of paraffin much stronger now. Someone must have tipped some down a drain somewhere, for it cloyed the stale air, refusing to budge. As I turned the beam downstream I saw a protrusion that was obviously an old bridge and had been left as a support. I briefly felt a twinge of sadness that history could be buried so.

There was barely enough room. I turned to face the chamber again and shone the lamp on the wall to be cut. Eight brick heights above the water level would be the center of the aperture; it was all so tight. I looked up at the small square of light above me. It was just a lighter shade of darkness as three faces almost blocked it. I did a careful calculation. We dare not bore at any point that wasn't a good eight feet down from street level. Above that point we could expect gas mains and electricity.

Someone above tapped the metal cover, and the clang filled the sewer, answering the adequacy of the sound as a danger signal. The noise swelled and echoed and I suddenly felt lonely down here in so much darkness and eerie solitude. They were getting impatient above but I had to be sure. I again shone the lamp beam on the damp, ancient brickwork and looked for a water mark. When I found it I didn't feel too good; it was above my head. I knew from the Arab that the sewers had been known to fill but didn't dwell on the thought, for I also knew that with heavy rain they could fill disastrously quickly. For all other purposes the one thing we had was plenty of head room; it was the least important requirement. I started up the ladder conscious of the weight of the boots against gravitational pull. With the close confinement of the shaft and my own bulk it was more difficult than I was prepared for.

Helping hands pulled me onto the pavement, and I reflected how greed could effectively close ranks against dissension. None

186

of us wanted it to go wrong. The only thing that perturbed me was the way Big Fred half avoided my eyes when I turned to thank him. It made me uneasy in too familiar a way. As I'd intended keeping an eye on Fred anyway, I left it at that; there was nothing else I could do. I gave them the general layout and explained that one of them would have to hold the oxygen cylinder in use upright so that its valve was above water level. I then went to the rear of the van, turned on the tap low down on the near side and thoroughly rinsed my waders and gloves under the disinfected water. You never knew who might be watching and this was part of the routine.

We made sure the road was clear, then started lowering the gear. Fred and Slasher went down, with Charlie and myself helping to lower the first cylinder, the lance holder, the blow lamp to get the lance tip going and the lance itself. They had trouble below with the length of the lance, and I could see their lamp beams crisscrossing like searchlights while they sorted themselves out. I could hear them splashing about and swearing, their expletives bursting up the shaft like pressured audio bubbles. It was no time to remonstrate; they had problems. Finally Fred's croaked "O.K." floated up, bouncing off the narrow walls and reaching us like a hoarse, distorted whisper. I nodded to Charlie. He slipped on a pair of goggles to protect his eyes against molten splashback, as the others would have done by now, and started off down. With his slight frame he didn't have the same difficulties Big Fred or I'd had. He didn't use his lamp, and the others shone theirs up the shaft to help him. They were going to be pretty tight down there.

I looked across the road to Sid, who had the most boring job of all, but important. It all had to be just right. He touched his helmet in acknowledgment and I gave him a nod back. There was no room for me down the shaft; my job, for the moment, was to deal with any problems on top. Big Fred knew where to bore and he was expert at his job. Things had quietened down below. I imagined that Charlie would hold the cylinder while Big Fred and Slasher worked on the lance. Sensibly they were conserving lamp lives by using only one, and I saw the sudden flash of the blow lamp as they got it started.

In spite of the precautions we had taken I was relieved that nothing happened as they heated the lance end. There had been no sign of gases, but the two open sewers must have played their part in letting out what there might have been. Charlie turned on the oxygen and the fusion started at the lance point. With Charlie holding the cylinder and directing the beam the strong glow of the heated lance was minimized, but what I wasn't prepared for was the smoke.

It came billowing up the shaft as if there was a fire below. At first I thought the unholy trio would be asphyxiated, then remembered that they were well back in the downstream tunnel and that the air draft would suck the smoke up through the hole.

After a couple of minutes I kicked the metal cover twice quickly. Charlie must have turned off the oxygen immediately, for the glow disappeared and there was sudden silence. The smoke began to dissipate. I made sure the road was still clear, then hoofed it down the ladder, pulling up just above the water line and remaining on the ladder. I looked down at a pile of molten slag still tumbling into the water like slow-flowing lava, hissing and steaming and squirming in tortured death throes as it toppled down from the part cavity already burned out. It was the first time I'd seen the devastating efficiency of a thermal lance, and for a moment I was impressed into silent awe as the slag heaped up under the water. Fortunately the boring was on the north wall of the chamber so that the slag did not form a dam that would raise the water level. The hissing continued as the slimy mass spewed down, sending up long tapering springs of steam and smoke as it hit the water.

"What the hell's the matter?" For the first time Big Fred showed his truculence. He stood in the main sewer, the lance held in both hands, his goggles pushed up on his sweating forehead. He was baleful and surly and I preferred him like this because I understood him better.

"There's clouds of smoke pouring out at the top. It's not going to be easy to explain when Old Bill pitches up—and he will."

Fred wiped his face with the back of his rubber glove. They looked a weird bunch with the water gushing about their knees in the uncertain light. They were all sweating.

"That's your problem," growled Fred. "You're the smart boy. You sort it out."

"I just want to warn you to respond in a split second to another signal and disperse the smoke as best you can, but at once."

I thought Big Fred was going to give a choice retort and the other two glanced at him, but he said sullenly, "You do your job, we'll do ours. Now we've got to ignite this bloody thing again."

I went back up thinking that really Charlie couldn't have reacted more quickly than he had. All they could do was to try to waft the smoke into the main sewer and shorten the odds. As I reached the pavement I called down and shortly the smoke came ballooning as I looked anxiously about me.

It began to spit with rain—no more than that, but worrying. The trouble was that I couldn't be sure that it wasn't raining heavier elsewhere. The buildup in the sewers didn't have to start on the spot; it could gush in without warning from another area. The sound of each drop amplified on the plastic helmet. The pavement began to mottle in dark patches. Should I tell the men? Sid was looking across at me and was obviously thinking the same.

I looked up at the sky—one continuous dark canopy with the night glow of London reflecting dully beneath it. The tumbling clouds had merged and flattened, slatelike, and looked set for a long time. The men hadn't far to come up. It wasn't as if they were halfway along some long, main sewer. On the other hand,

I guessed that the chamber would fill up very quickly if the weather got worse. I decided to let it ride for a while. If it worsened I'd get them up.

Although I was troubled, my reflexes still operated. I spotted the patrol car some distance away. Two things helped me—an almost infallible instinct for the presence of coppers and a streetlight reflecting on the blue bubble of the car roof. I gave the cover an almighty kick and the smoke started thinning instantly. "Just stay put," I called down the shaft. "The fuzz are here."

It came cruising along on Sid's side of the road at no more than thirty, which meant there was nothing special on. I was tempted to waft the smoke away with my hands but held back, ignoring the car, which approached slowly. I knew it would stop because they were time-killing. And it did. It U-turned and eased up behind the van, doused its headlights and a uniformed sergeant and a constable climbed unhurriedly out.

"Hello, mate." They casually joined me. "Putting in overtime then?"

"Hello," I said with a grin. "Emergency."

"Lucky it's stopped raining," said the sergeant. They both peered down the shaft, but I knew they wouldn't see anything but a black hole. The boys had the torch off.

"Hell of a smell of smoke. What's going on?" The sergeant straightened, twitching his nose.

"Welding," I lied. I pointed across the road to Sid. "There's a flaw toward the Thames. The sewer's cracked and there's seepage. Not funny, I tell you."

"You mean you've only just found it out?" The sergeant wasn't suspicious, but he would be if I messed up the answer.

"Naw. We don't work at night generally. We found the crack on a routine inspection earlier today. But it needs special support and braces to be welded on. Like on an old house when the wall bulges. Takes time to get that gear. But we daren't leave it till morning. A drop of rain and the street could lift."

"As bad as that?"

"Worse. Your electric cables and main water pipes are only a few feet above the sewer. Once you get seepage it creeps into every crack and loose joint there is."

The sergeant listened. He was interested. He didn't look a fool, but I was gambling that his knowledge of sewers was less than mine.

"What about the Tate?" he asked. "All those paintings. Could it get in the cellars?"

I couldn't judge whether it was a loaded question or plain curiosity. Both coppers wore blank faces beneath their flat peaked caps. "Does it have cellars? Anyway, they wouldn't keep paintings in cellars, would they? What about damp?"

The sergeant shrugged. "If there's a risk, I ought to report it."

I shrugged. "If that's your only problem I wouldn't worry, mate." I pointed to the island in the middle of the road. "The fracture is just beyond there, and the sewer runs from us to Sid over there, then it follows the line of the river for a bit. The Tate's in no danger."

He nodded. "Interesting. I'd like to go down."

"You can make application," I said helpfully. "You have to be kitted out and you have to sign an indemnity."

"Indemnity?"

"In case you slip and hurt yourself or catch a disease. There's some queer diseases down there. We get sort of immune, although Sid was laid up for a couple of months last year. A fever and a peculiar rash it was. You know these bloody doctors; they didn't know, did they? Old Sid was looking like a boiled lobster with black pepper sprinkled all over it. He had a rough time, and the quacks gave it some fancy names, but they didn't do any good. Never been quite the same has Sid."

The coppers looked over at Sid, who was keeping his nerve and looking over the parapet at the Thames, which he was just tall enough to do.

"Look at the weight he's lost," I added, as if expecting them to know.

The sergeant said, "We can demand to go down in the line of duty." It was half bluff, half self-assertion.

"If you force the point you can borrow my coverall and waders," I offered. "Give me a little chit for me to show to my boss. But for God's sake don't slip, for there's a lot to slip on. Don't let it get in your lungs whatever you do."

He knew I was exaggerating and I gave him a wide grin. He grinned back and gave me a friendly push on the shoulder. "Hope you sort it out," he said. "Come on, Chalky."

I gave them a wave. They waved back from the car. Norman hadn't been so dumb; he knew I enjoyed a battle of wits with the law. It had been reasonably easy because I'd taken the trouble to do my homework with the Arab. I called down. "O.K."

Fred's voice came up. "We need another lance. This one packed up just before you signaled." Which accounted for the quick dissipation of the smoke. You need a little luck. I got the lance from the van and slid it down to Fred, who came up the ladder to meet it.

I saw the flash of the blow lamp again and the smoke started clouding up the shaft and mushrooming into a slight breeze that now caught it, toyed with it, then gradually thinned it in capricious eddies above my head. I was glad the rain had stopped, but the sky was still thick, ready to burst. I unhappily wondered if the thermal team would need the remaining cylinders and lances. They did. As I lowered them at intervals I worried about having brought enough. If they couldn't finish it we'd pack up and go home, having risked a long stretch for nothing. I was getting edgy.

When the yell came from below I was down those steel rungs, coughing through the smoke, because it had been a cry of triumph.

Three lamp beams cut through the dissipating smoke and fastened on the hole they'd cut through four feet of concrete. It wasn't a big hole, just big enough to crawl through. The slag was still toppling onto a heap that rose above the water level, sliding, at its peak, back into the water with the now familiar hiss. I turned to Big Fred. "Nice work. Do you want any of the gear back up?"

He was too pleased with himself to be resentful. Grime rimmed his goggles and face, but for the moment he was happy. He knew his job; he'd done it well. Slasher and Charlie were grinning in triumph, their goggles pushed high. "I'll need the lance holder," replied Fred. "The cylinders can stay 'ere. I can get more." I didn't ask him where. The last lance was about half used and he decided to leave that too, with the blow lamp. These boys only believed in hanging onto gear difficult to replace, and it was obvious that they wanted to travel light on the return journey.

I told them what had happened above and instructed Fred on what to do and say if the fuzz returned. I wanted him on top as the one most likely to cope with it. He listened, eyes down, retrieved the thermal lance holder, then started on up. He was back to avoiding my gaze. I told Charlie and Slasher that they'd have to stay down here until I came back. I'd considered letting them into the back of the van, but if the coppers returned—and it might not be the same pair—and asked awkward questions and then looked in the van, I had no confidence that all three would satisfy them. They'd probably react like the old lags they were. Big Fred could be sullen, but I backed him to carry it through. They didn't like it, but I knew that Fred would back me on it if only to save his own skin. I handed Charlie my helmet and forced my way the short distance upstream to the cavity.

The slag heap was now in the way, directly in front of the hole. I leaned forward and with my rubber-gloved hand scooped out the rapidly cooling remnants of molten concrete into the stream. I got a foothold at the base of the underwater slag and leaned forward, thrusting one arm and my head into the hole. With the slag impeding me it was difficult with the hole so small. I couldn't get purchase. I kicked at the slag, but, cooled off by the water, it was already solidifying.

"You'll have to push me through," I told the other two. "While I'm limp carry on, if I kick my feet ease up; it'll mean I'm in trouble."

They positioned themselves either side of the slag and I leaned forward again. They lifted my feet and slowly pushed me into the rough-hewn hole. I scraped my hands on rough concrete but managed to keep my face out of trouble and let them continue pushing me through. My head emerged into darkness, but I knew it to be free. I kicked my legs and Charlie and Slasher stopped pushing. Easing my lamp forward, I switched it on and flashed the beam down. I almost laughed with relief. The cellar floor was just beneath my gaze—about six inches from the rim of the hole. Fred wouldn't have thanked me if he'd found himself boring into the floor. I let the relief seep through me, then scrabbled through. I sat down with my back against the cellar wall and pulled off my waders and gloves and stood up with my long woolen socks still pulled up above my knees; they were ideal for silent movement. I opened the front of my coverall so that I might more easily grope for the instruments I would need. I stood my waders against the wall near the hole so that I could pick them up on my return and had the numbing thought that if the water level rose the cellars would be flooded and I'd be trapped inside the Tate.

It was the nudge I needed to get going. I swung the lamp beam round, recognizing the cellar, the squat pillars up to the ceiling and the shrouded sculptures over by the far wall. Because of its bulk I left the lamp and used my own pencil torch and hurried across the bare brick floor and entered an open corridor which ran off the cellar to join another. Halfway along an average-sized wooden door opened into another cellar at the far side of which were stone steps leading up. These, I knew, would take me to the sub-basement, where the restaurant and administrative offices were and beyond them some galleries. From the moment I opened the door at the top of the steps I knew that I'd have to have eyes all round my head. It was not new to me, but there was an awful lot of visual ground to cover. I stepped into a corridor in total darkness, closed the door and stood with my back to it for some seconds. It was pitch-black.

I looked at my luminous watch—half past one. Not bad— plenty of time. There'd be occasional routine checks, and this was the insoluble at the moment. I was willing to bet that they'd be on the hour or half hour; at what intervals it was impossible to guess.

Lights suddenly came on at the other end of the corridor. Without hesitating I opened the door behind me and went through, closed it and crouched at the keyhole. More lights came on. I wanted to remain at the keyhole but was ready to move quickly if the door opened. There were footsteps—one man moving slowly, but I guessed there'd be others elsewhere. He went past the keyhole at a measured pace, doing, night after night, what must have become an immeasurable bore. Who'd rob the Tate? I was poised, ready to jump behind the door, but he continued on and all I could do was wait. So it was on the half hour. I was lucky to find out so quickly.

It was some time before the lights went out, and I gave it another ten minutes after that. I opened the door and stepped out again, listening, trying to penetrate every corner, and in the Tate there are a multitude of them. With the strange open plan of the place and the very high ceilings there was a feeling of abject emptiness, but I already knew the lie to that. I crept out, risking my torch as the lesser evil of that or knocking into the unexpected. My stockinged feet made no sound at all.

I knew exactly where to go. I turned right, took the wide curving stairs up to the ground floor. I turned left, noting the sealed gallery to my left, continued toward the rear of the gallery and came to my first obstacle: metal doors shut off the entrance to the gallery. The biggest problem was so much open space.

195

I faced the metal doors, looking out of place, ejecting as they did from the green marble arches. It was like using a quality frame for a hack painting. I shone my torch round the lock and then the whole of the frame. There was no trace of wiring, but in view of the fact that the doors slid back out of sight into hidden recesses an alarm could easily be fixed direct from the lock, which was bound to be a hooked variety. Opening the doors would break the circuit. And so would breaking the lock.

I pulled out my crocodile clip and inserted both spatula ends into the crack between the doors, insuring that both spatulas touched the lock. I then plasticined them in place.

The wire between the spatulas looped down, leaving me room to work. All I now had to do was to saw the lock between the spatulas, a space of about a sixteenth of an inch. I fingered my jacket lapel and pulled out the thread of cranium saw. I hadn't used it since the Chinese legation job. Keeping it in the collar kept it curved, an essential requirement for the next step. I pushed one end through the crack of the doors just above the lock. It looped down naturally enough, but I had to fiddle with it before the end reappeared through the crack beneath the lock. I now fixed on a wooden grip at each end, very careful not to dislodge the crocodile clip through the movement of the saw. I fixed the torch between my teeth and, keeping it as steady as I could, started to saw.

It wasn't easy in the shifting beam. I knew that if, when the lock was cut, the spatulas lost contact, the alarm would raise the roof, so I had to keep sight of that terribly small gap and to watch the spatulas all the time. The sweat started dropping at my feet.

14

It was impossible to saw like this without some noise, but at least there wasn't the metallic whine of an ordinary metal saw. I just kept up a seesaw motion, pulling with either hand and making sure that the very fine, cheese-wire-like saw bit deep into the lock. The risk was when the lock parted into two pieces. When I judged I'd got halfway I carefully let the saw dangle, then examined the crocodile clip. I removed both spatulas and rammed them together into the narrow slit I'd cut into the lock. This was safer, for the fit was very tight and would also help prevent the freed end of the lock shifting once it was cut through. Using my knife, I managed to squeeze some plasticine through the gap to help stick the spatulas down. I'd left myself sufficient room under the spatulas to saw without danger. I got back to the grind.

The last fraction of an inch of uncut lock was dicey. I could feel it moving and had to take it very carefully. Finally it was severed and the cranium saw came through intact. The free end of the lock hadn't sufficient room to fall out, but there was enough room for it to fall forward fractionally and break contact. I thrust my knife into the slit and kept it in position. At the same time I pushed the door back by about a foot. The wire on the crocodile clip began to stretch, but I was holding the one spatula in place with the knife, pressing it into the free end of the lock. I'd already checked that the other end was secure.

I pushed the door until I had sufficient working room, then spread plasticine over the whole lock area on both doors so that the spatulas were held tightly and the two halves of the lock kept firmly in position. While I worked I had the strong feeling that the whole Tate security force was breathing down my neck, just waiting for me to finish before grabbing me. Satisfied that the circuit was safe, I pushed the doors as far apart as the crocodile clip would comfortably allow, got down on my knees, blew the metal filings into the gallery, then eased my way through, careful not to touch the stretched loop of wire. I was in. On the other side I rose, gradually pushed the doors together again, pulling the lengthening loop of wire through to this side so that it would not be seen by the guards.

I shone my torch fairly freely down the wide gallery, coming to an unbarred archway at its end which simply widened out into a further gallery. Turners. Huge paintings on the walls which would have caught my admiration at any other time. In front of the next archway was erected a massive seascape, the waves living under the moving torchbeam. I was grateful then that Norman hadn't wanted Turners. Some of the canvases were so large that I knew I'd have had trouble with them. I passed through into the third open-planned gallery to the Picassos. I wasted no time and went quickly round the walls checking with my list those that Norman wanted. He had done his homework; they were all of reasonable size.

Every frame was screwed to the walls. I have a great respect for art, but I didn't have the time to unscrew the frames and remove the canvases from the backs. I felt like a vandal wantonly destroying beauty and in this sensitive mood could feel the emanations of anger pouring from the silent paintings as they observed and brooded over my actions. My covered razor blade with its short wooden handle enabled me to get slightly inside the frames so that there was little or no reduction of picture size.

I hadn't heard a further security check and was banking that the doors weren't opened but merely scrutinized for tampering. The doors I'd opened would pass all but the minutest check. While I was here I was reasonably safe. Getting out would be different. Yet this logic couldn't dispel the feeling of being watched nor the atmosphere of great sadness that communicated to me from the walls each time I used the blade. It was desecration, but I continued the slaughtering as fast and as carefully as I could. When I had them all down I placed the biggest at the bottom, the smallest on top, then rolled them up into a manageable size. I placed the roll by the wall and went into the next gallery. I gave a last look round the series of vast, night-shrouded caverns and went down the wooden staircase.

The stairs were solid, without loose boards, but from habit I took them slowly and kept to the sides. At the bottom I was back on sub-basement level. Each gallery was clearly marked showing the name of the artist, and I made a beeline for Francis Bacon. I'd viewed his paintings before but somehow, in the beam of the limited torchlight with darkness engulfing all but that pale focusing channel flitting briefly from canvas to canvas, they looked immense—some of them certainly six feet high. At an approximate value of sixty thousand pounds each, who was I to argue? I uttered a futile apology and started my butchering again. It was almost as bad as being cruel to animals, but I stuck at it, being as kind as I could. Under the fading torchlight they moved and writhed as if in silent agony. I felt each delicate slash of the razor myself.

As I worked, the remonstrative silence deepened about me in a depressive, cloying way that had me partially disoriented. The gradual loss of light added to the darkening gallery a strong feeling of suspension and of ethereal intrusion. Something was working against me, unseen yet communicating in vibrations that were both fanciful yet utterly real in the sense that I couldn't shake off the feeling of forces gathering to strike at me. I had offended, and I was left in no doubt of it. People who mutilated paintings, if only minutely as I was doing, could make no claim to being art lovers, yet I was one, had always been, and was now betraying the gift of appreciation as a musician or writer or painter betrays his basic talents for avarice. I was always my worst enemy when it came to self-criticism, a fact that had never been of use to me in front of a judge. I'd have opted out of this deal right then but for the danger to Maggie and, I must admit, to myself.

I got on with it. My torch had considerably dimmed, but I knew that it would see me through, and anyway its decreasing strength gave my eyes a chance to adjust slowly. I had finished. I rolled them up and took them upstairs, retrieved the Picassos and rolled the whole lot up, tying them with string from my waistband.

I followed the pale torchbeam through arches and galleries and pitched up where I'd started. I was unhappy about pulling the two doors apart in case one blob of plasticine adhered to the wrong door, pulling away one or both of the spatulas and breaking the circuit. I inserted the knife blade between the doors and tried to cut down cleanly to separate the plasticine and keep the spatulas in place. The lights came on beyond the doors before I could withdraw the knife. All I could see was a bright strip of light down the crack of the door. The gallery remained in darkness. I kept my head and stood absolutely still, one hand on the knife.

There were several pairs of footsteps, as if this was a focal point before the custodians split up to do their rounds. The knife blade was poking through the other side of the door. If I left it there it must be seen; if I moved it, the movement might attract attention. One thing I couldn't do was to wait and see. Holding my breath, I gradually began to draw the knife back a fraction at a time. To free it from the tacky plasticine I needed to wiggle the blade, but that was out of the question. I had to pull it straight and hope that it would come.

It came so far and no more. The plasticine gathered with the tugging motion and built up around the blade. I could have released it with a vigorous movement I dared not apply. Standing stock-still, feeling impotent and tensed, I tried to figure it out. It was almost impossible to judge how much blade might be exposed the other side of the doors. I could only wait and see with my hand still on the knife to make sure it didn't move.

The footsteps were scattering, and I could hear some going upstairs. There were others on this floor, but echoes confused direction. I had to sweat it out. I glanced at my watch: three-thirty. I'd been two hours. I could imagine what Big Fred and the boys thought of that. The time had passed quickly because I'd been occupied and the lock had taken some time, but the few minutes the custodians took over their rounds seemed eternal and I dared not move in case the knife shifted. But the canvases were becoming a weight. With one hand I slowly let them roll down my leg onto the floor.

Footsteps became more pronounced again, and now there were voices as the men regrouped; they reverberated in the lofty hall and corridors, distorting words into unrecognizable, amplified sounds that magnified the number so that they collected in depth outside the doors. I strained to isolate meaning in the jumble of overlapping sounds and managed to pinpoint odd words which on their own were meaningless. Footsteps cut discordantly through the echoing word jungle, and then I heard laughter which struck at every wall, booming off ceilings as deep hollow sounds, as if scattered from a central speaker.

Laughter. A good sign. I hung on grimly to the knife. Don't move now for God's sake! Then someone tapped on the metal door and I nearly hit the roof. The knife moved and I froze too late. What the hell was I supposed to do? I'd let go of the knife in shock, but although the handle had dropped there was no risk of it falling. Rat-a-tat-tat sharply on the metal and then footsteps following suit on the floor.

And then, thank God, more laughter. Someone was playing the fool, rapping the door and doing a little tap dance. I was drenched with the sweat of shock and relief. What about the knife? The lights were still on and the custodians still there. What was going on? I risked an eye to the crack between the doors, but an eighth-of-an-inch width coupled with a two-inch depth showed nothing but a light strip occasionally blacked out in patches.

A voice, authoritative above the jumble, called out and produced retreating footsteps which took with them intermittent laughter, and the sounds began to fade. One pair of footsteps roamed outside, as if someone was making a final inspection. I held my breath again. The footsteps went the way of the others, then a minute or two later the lights went out.

I still had to wait it out. From the last echo of footsteps I judged that they'd retreated in the general direction that I had to go. It was too soon to follow. Charlie and Slasher would have to continue to endure the gradual numbing effect of standing in water. I gave it fifteen soul-destroying minutes. I wanted to get out quickly, a feeling I'd learned to control, but although I was used to this it was one facet of creeping that never became easier. Even so, my self-discipline was rigid. After fifteen minutes I gave it another two with my ear to the door.

I now moved the knife up and down until it came free. I switched on the torch, and the feeble beam seemed to have lost strength even while it was out. Slowly I pulled back one door at a time, careful not to tauten the wire. I pushed the roll of canvases through and crawled through after them. I quickly considered leaving the doors as they were, then backed the idea that the later the discovery of theft the better. Pushing the doors together and trying to keep the wire on the gallery side of them created problems but was eventually done. I picked up my bundle and crept round to the corridor, realizing that there was an outer sealed area even beyond this one, otherwise the side door to the basement would have been protected. Norman's patient perseverance and outlay was on the verge of paying immense dividends.

The nape of my neck was prickling all the way down the corridor. Somewhere to my left I heard sudden laughter but could see no lights to warn me of precise location. The sound was probably nearer to me than volume indicated; the doors were thick and solid and would mute any noise. But it worked both ways. I kept going. When I reached my exit door I went through it with relief, down the steps, across the basement floor and through the second door that led me to the cellar through which we'd bored.

It was like coming home, the sense of relief enormous. I padded across the floor, knelt down, put my head in the hole and whispered loudly, "I'm back. Just putting my boots on."

"About ——— time. What sort of bloody creeper are yer? We're frozen solid and it's pouring up top." This was Slasher, back to being tough now the job was done. But there was something else in his tone other than coarse anger that I didn't like —a contemptuous insubordination that held me to no account. I felt the burning of slow anger and tried to sit on it. Holding the torch into the short tunnel, I was dismayed to see the dull reflection of heaving water only just below the lip. The water must have risen considerably, and I could now hear its powerful current racing down toward the Thames. I pulled my waders on quickly. Pushing the roll of canvases ahead of me, I crawled into the tunnel from a horizontal position on the cellar floor. When the roll reached the lip I called out, "Take these. For God's sake don't let the water get at them."

By now my torch was almost useless, but one of the others used his lamp and I could see someone splashing forward— Charlie, I think—and red rubber-gloved hands came forward to grasp the rolled canvases and carefully withdraw them. The lamplight showed more clearly the new pace and depth of the current, and I could imagine how the two men in the sewer must have felt over the last two hours as the level and power of the stream gradually increased. I pulled myself through head first, having difficulty at the end, as I had to get my feet down first. I called out for some help, someone to steady me while I hooked my legs through, but nobody took notice.

This annoyed me and I swore forcibly. Dammit, I'd nicked a

fortune that was going to put more money in their pockets than probably they'd ever had. "Give me a hand, damn you." I could see them now in their own lamplight, standing on either side of the steel rings laughing at my efforts. "You bastards." I backed out into the cellar and slid into the tunnel again feet first on my belly. I was smoldering. I exploratively lowered my legs into the stream, groping round the now completely sub-merged slag heap and feeling the strong pull of the flow. No one came to help. Anger swept through me in furious waves, aggravated by the release of tension and now anticlimax. I struggled upright with difficulty against the powerful current, still groping for a secure foothold and holding onto the tunnel lip for support. Inside the chamber the noise of gushing water was uncomfortably ominous. I hadn't arrived too soon.

I stood there steadying myself, then turned awkwardly to face the shaft. Slasher and Charlie were still standing either side of the ladder, the stream swirling round their thighs, more noticeably on Charlie, the shorter, who was having diffi-culty in hanging on. It didn't stop his malicious smile, how-ever, which crept out of the shadow from the overhang of his helmet. Slasher, too, was enjoying himself at my expense. I was still fuming, and what made it worse was the sight of Big Fred coming down after putting the canvases in the van. He stood on the ladder, his feet just low enough to be submerged in ris-ing foam, and looked down at me with the same sort of inso-lent grin as the others. I felt the cold shoot right through me, and it wasn't from the icy water.

"What the hell are you doing down here? You should be on top." My own snarl startled me. Something about these three was terribly wrong.

"Sid's on top," said Big Fred easily. He was just daring me to challenge him.

"Sid should be the other side. What're you playing at?"

Big Fred widened his grin, which wasn't intended to be friendly. "I brought 'im over 'ere. I've closed the other entrance.

Right?" I stared at them while they played their lamps on me. The reflected light shone under their faces, deepening cheeks and eye sockets, creating cavities of their stretched mouths. They looked evil and I could feel it strongly in the chamber.

"You bloody fool," I said. "You'll ruin the whole jaunt. Get up there quick, all of you, and give me a hand across." I'd demanded help as an effort to restore authority, but in the pit of my guts I already knew that it wouldn't work.

"Why?" sneered Fred. "You ain't going anywhere."

Now we were coming to it. Their earlier behavior made sense. I had to try to preserve sanity, to keep it calm. They obviously intended taking the van and leaving me. I'd done my job and now had been cut out of the deal, the sweet revenge of Norman.

"Making me hike back won't solve anything. If I get picked up, so might you."

"That's right." Big Fred's laughter mingled with the growing roar of flood water. "So we make bloody certain you don't get picked up, eh, Spider—mate?"

I think I'd guessed earlier, but the impact hit me then, hard in the hollow of my stomach. My mouth dried instantly. "They'll look for you—flat out."

Fred was enjoying himself. "We've been lucky then. The fuzz called again but didn't stop. You're the only one who's been seen, Spider boy. Sid tells me he was watching the Thames while they spoke to you. If you're not around, who's to tell them about us? Right?"

I reckoned Big Fred could fix me on his own although I could try him. But three of them? They had me and it showed. This was a bonus to them.

"Why?" I tried. "What have I done to you three except line your pockets with those paintings?" I couldn't plead and was careful to keep my tone demanding, but I had to know.

Fred stopped grinning. He'd had his share of fun. "Because we're being paid a dirty big sum to do you, Spider old cockey.

You big-'eaded creep. You could've done nothing without us making the 'ole."

I lunged across the gap that divided us, but the current was so strong that but for the heavy boots I'd have been swept off my feet. I kept going, lurching, arms out to maintain balance and to grip the nearest throat that came within reach of my clutching fingers. Slasher and Charlie lost their smiles and became apprehensive. But whatever I tried, it could be only a token gesture. I swung at the two in the stream, and Big Fred's studded boot rose out of the water, dripping black, moving ponderously but too quick for me as the other two tried to grab my arms and I toppled forward. The boot clipped my chin, and it was like being hit with a crowbar. My knees gave and, only partly conscious, I felt the surge at my waist tugging me into the main sewer.

Hands gripped me and I fought feebly, a half-conscious effort at self-preservation. I started to beat back the woolen blanket draping my mind but was now smothered by the three of them. They forced my arms behind me while I tried to kick out, but the boots plus the weight of water kept the force from my straining muscles, and anyway the unholy trio had anticipated the kicks and kept well to the side. Suddenly they let me go. I had a blurred impression of Big Fred grabbing Charlie as the current caught him and of Slasher clinging desperately to the side of the ladder. Seeing my chance, I brought my arms forward and nearly dislocated my shoulders. They'd tied my wrists to one of the rungs.

"Get up there, you two. Scarper quick." Slasher and Charlie didn't need urging. They shoved their boots into the rungs, pushing me aside so that I swung outward and not caring that they kicked me blue while they groped for the ladder. One of them used my shoulder as a rung, and blood gushed from my ear where the toecap split it. The strain on my roped wrists was agonizing as I was forced away from the ladder. I swung there for a bit and only vaguely saw Fred at the side.

"The boss man wants you to 'ave time to think what you've done to 'im," he shouted in my injured ear. "I don't know what it is, mate, but at the rate he's shelling out to us you must've really upset 'im." He shook me by my sore shoulder when he thought I hadn't heard. "I'm setting a time fuse on a stick of gelly above your nut. It'll give us an hour to get clear before it blasts you into the drink. They'll never find you, mate. They'll think whoever it was made a mistake with explosives when they see the 'ole—if there's any 'ole left apart from a bloody big one. Right?"

It was all crazy. I snarled at him. "You big ignorant fool. You have only to leave me and I'll drown."

Fred was not put out. "It might stop raining," he said cheerfully. "Anyway, boss man wants you in little pieces. Rat food. Right? Now you think about it like 'e said. So long, mug."

I heard his heavy footsteps on the steel rungs. He pushed my head with a boot as he went past, not hard enough to put me out—he didn't want that—but sufficiently hard to send a searing pain behind my eyes and to give me a throbbing headache. I was already fruitlessly struggling before he reached the top. His big feet clumped on the pavement above my head, and he shone his lamp down the shaft to take one last satisfying look at me. He must have been well pleased. I used the last moments of light to locate the explosive; it was tied just above my head and was wrapped in oilskin. Then the lid clanged down and drove spasms of pain through my head, but even worse was the sudden total darkness.

Not a sliver of light penetrated the place. I'd been in plenty of darkened places in my time but never like this. It was utterly black without any degree of vision. I might as well be blind. The claustrophobic effect was immediate, for the swelling roar of the angry, gushing water filled the sewer because it had nowhere to escape, so that there was just darkness and sound at once emphasizing to a frightening degree the confinement of the place and the decreasing space for air as the water level rose. I was standing in a raging torrent with my head stuck in an enormous seashell that cut my sight and filled my ears with the roar of a storm. I knew that I had to get a quick grip of myself or I'd go out of my mind. I could feel the water swirling at my upper thighs, I could feel rough brickwork under the studs of my boots and I could feel the steel ladder behind my back. I clung to these things to avoid becoming disoriented and thereby bewildered. I was startled to realize that my bound hands were already below the cascading surface. Water was already spilling into the top of my waders to add to my misery.

Yet the discomfort, the agony of my head and ear, the terror of the stygian darkness and compressing air, the changing smells from paraffin to a peculiar sour sweetness, then to a strong smell of petrol that made me heave, the difficulty of keeping my feet without free use of my hands gave me something to combat and try to cope with, partly occupying my mind and dispelling just a little of my terror. I tried to consider what to do. What was my chief danger? Oh, Maggie, help me, please. My cry was to her because I'd always been on the wrong side of the fence to impose on God. And she was tangible, someone easy to recognize and to reach out for in moments of dire stress. If she had some contact with Him, then He might get to know about it because I'd long since relinquished all right to any attempt at direct approach. My mind was forced into these half-baked philosophies only when the chips were down and I was staring at death, and I well realized the weakness of my own case. I wasn't going to cringe or beg for mercy now, and I tried to throw all this out to Maggie in desperate thought waves. She'd understand.

Having convinced myself I wasn't worth saving, I got round to thinking how it could be done. If only there was light. The water was still rising and at a new alarming rate with increasing strength. With one foot I groped for the bottom rung of the ladder, found it, hooked my heel over it and pushed myself up as far as my bonds would allow. I leaned awkwardly sideways, and my face brushed the oilskin covering of the explosive and its fuse. I had to search with my lips and tongue, almost pulling my hands off as I stretched the rope to full play. I located the cord that bound the package to the ladder and followed it with my tongue until I found the knot. Gelignite has a terrible reputation for unpredictability. There wasn't much in it for me either way, so what did it matter? I couldn't see how the cord was tied, so I pulled at it with my teeth.

Two things were against me: the knot was tight and I couldn't make out what type of knot it was; the other was that any effort to grip it with my teeth kept moving it and I had to start again. This happened so often that it began to drive me slowly mad. I kept biting my lip when my teeth slipped off the cord, and I was chafing both lips and gums. I'd have given anything for just a glimmer of light. I kept at it, trying to keep my head, biting back the continued frustration and far too conscious of the passing of time and the continually rising flood level. It wasn't doing my wrists any good either, but they were so numb by now that I didn't know if they were bleeding or not.

When I got a grip with my teeth it was usually on the wrong part of the knot and served no purpose except to flay my nerve ends and bring tears of frustration. There was no one to see me here, so I just let them flow, which was better than screaming my head off. Still I kept pecking, while the noise level increased as though there was a giant waterfall every few feet. During an insane moment while I temporarily gave up uselessly gashing my teeth, I perceived that the traditional acceptance of hell was fallacy. It wasn't an eternal fire in the center of the earth; it was a raging torrent swelling by the second without the illumination that fire could give. This hell would quench a traditional hell in seconds; it was darkness and wetness and isolation and despair and drawn-out death of the weakening mind before the body too succumbed. Hell was down here in a sewer, and in another world above, sleeping heads knew nothing of its existence, enjoying sweet dreams, unhearing of the anguished screams from the doomed, agonized souls beneath them.

Maybe I did scream; I don't know. I'd been sticking at the knot, but it was three steps backward and none forward at each craze-making attempt. I gave it up, licking blood from my lips, until my spirit almost broke, then listlessly, hopelessly, started again. The more casual approach brought a better result. My teeth gripped a loop I must have eased at my last attempt. It gave me the courage to continue, and by gripping hard with my teeth and pulling back my head I was able to release part of the knot. I had a distance to go, I knew, but it was minor success and a start I so badly needed.

After that I just kept biting quietly, without real hope but with the will to continue and gradually enlarging on my initial success. The only way I could judge time was by the fact that the gelignite hadn't exploded. It seemed well over an hour of hard, restless and sometimes reckless effort, but it couldn't be. Nor could it be far off. As I nibbled away I wondered if I would be granted at least the brief vision of the explosion flash before I disintegrated. I knew that I must be so near to the time factor now that even terror was numbed. Suddenly the package wasn't there any more. I desperately rubbed my face up and down the steel but there was nothing. I hadn't heard a splash because the roar was all round me, yet it must have fallen in.

I lowered myself the one rung to the base of the chamber, and the water came up my body another few inches. I couldn't care just then. I leaned back in weariness, triumph and relief, unable to move for some seconds, swaying with the current and at the back of my mind wondering if it would still go off. The package had been covered in oilskin. Would the water penetrate and if it did what would happen? I started on my wrists, waiting for the bang.

15

WHILE I FIDDLED with my wrists I groped about with my boots, trying to locate the package. It was difficult moving my feet because the fast current repeatedly tried to tug me off balance. The only thing I located was one of the discarded oxygen cylinders, and I finally gave up, concentrating solely on my bound wrists. My previous struggling had given me a little play so that the bonds weren't uncomfortably tight but not sufficiently loose for me to slip out of them. Adversely the straining against the rope had tightened the knots, and the fiber had swollen in the water to make it even worse. I groped for the knot with my fingers but realized that I wasn't going to get anywhere that way. That left me one course open: friction. I started rubbing them up and down on the upright edge of the steel ladder, which wasn't exactly sharp but was all I had. My movement was limited, but I just kept going.

I had one advantage: my hands were so numb that I felt no pain, but my arms started to ache. It became a question of whether I'd break the cord before the water closed over my head. The level was rising all the time, and if it wasn't for the bonds I'd have been swept off my feet long since. Wet through, I could now feel flecks of foam sprinkling my face as the torrent gushed and frothed about my chest. I recalled the watermark above my head and put more energy into my movements. The strength of the flow was almost unbelievable when I remembered its original placid progress and few inches of depth. The noise, strangely, although still shattering, had subsided somewhat with the rising level. The significance of this eluded me for a while, then struck me hard. The flood tunnels opening into the main sewer were now under the water level so there was no longer the powerful noise of raging cataracts. The flood water was still pouring in but underneath, gurgling in undercurrent flows.

Suddenly I shot forward. I was out in the middle of the stream before I could do a thing to save myself. But for the weight of my boots I would have been below the surface, but even now I was still fighting for my life. I hadn't realized that the rope had been on the point of breaking. I made a belated grab at the ladder but was far too late and the current too strong for me to get back to it. I was floundering fast, unsure, fighting to stay on my feet. I had no choice but to let the current take me toward the Thames, where I knew it changed direction.

With the water up to my armpits, pushing me forward relentlessly, I kept up a clumsy breast stroke, dragging my feet and terrified of going under. I was floundering against a force I couldn't hope to combat, yet I knew that my chance would come soon but not when. I craved sight again, just a glimmer, but time in the terrible darkness hadn't provided me with a sliver of vision. I couldn't slow my pace. I had little control at all and was lucky not to have drowned already. I had cursed the weight of these boots; now I saw the wisdom of their design.

I used my hearing in lieu of sight and tried to judge the situation. There was a tremendous roar up ahead where the flow thrashed the old brick walls as they turned the corner. I could feel a conflict of current that tugged and tore at me while I swayed this way and that, expecting to be dragged down. My ears began to hurt at the increase of sound, the snarling, savage fury of an enraged flood temporarily impeded.

It smacked and spat and thundered and backwashed and swirled in all directions at once, and I found myself going. I was suddenly in the center of watery madness and knew that even the comparative stability of the boots could no longer save me. While I still had partial contact with the bed of the sewer I lunged to my right, pushing with my feet as hard as I could. They left the ground and I splashed down hard, arms flailing wildly. I tried to bring my feet under me to create a balance, and they stubbed into a ledge of some kind and I lurched forward, my head diving into the flow.

I had the presence of mind to realize what the obstruction might be, held my breath, felt the current redirecting me, then lunged again with everything I had. I was still under water and pushed my arms out blindly. Rough brickwork tore my knuckles, but it was the last-chance signal I needed. I threshed and desperately groped, then clung hard to the steel rung I'd hoped to find. In one upward movement I pulled myself above the surface, water cascading off me, and gasped for breath. My feet found the bottom rung and I started climbing up as fast as I could, grateful beyond measure that I'd tripped over the step that led to the exit shaft that Sid had been guarding.

I went up so quickly, exhausted though I was, that I hit my head on the metal cover. In my excitement even that didn't register except as additional general pain. I pushed up the cover and breathed in the air of life. *And I could see.* It was teeming with rain, the pavements awash with it; it battered my head and face and stung my skin. It was marvelous.

I hadn't time to revel. I staggered to the Thames parapet still gasping but half laughing at the same time. The street was completely empty, which didn't surprise me, and the depth of rain reduced visibility to water streaks round lampposts, but after what I'd suffered it was all heaven. I dragged off my waders, long socks and coverall and tossed them over the wall into the river. My helmet and gloves were in the sewer with the rest of the dumped gear. My clothes and hair were plastered to my skin; I was a walking sponge. My shoes had been left in the van, and Fred had probably dumped them where I'd just dumped the rest. In my thin socks and soaked through, I squelched in search of an easy car to nick.

I dumped the car on double yellow lines so that it would be quickly picked up and returned to its owner. I walked the hundred yards or so to my block, never believing that I could have enjoyed this sort of weather without shoes or coat. But I was still in dire trouble from at least two directions, maybe more. I went up the stairs to my rooms, leaving a watery trail that time would dry. When I reached the landing I stopped dead, eying the figure squatting outside my door, head lowered onto drawn-up knees and apparently asleep. I couldn't see his face; I didn't need to. My stomach flipped and I didn't know what to think. My first reaction was pleasure, but this quickly turned to alarm.

Approaching warily, I gave him a little shake, the water running down my sleeve and onto his thick, polo-necked sweater. Dick's head came up at once, his eyes immediately alert as they quickly focused on me.

"Spider!" He shot to his feet with a huge grin, then saw my state and his expression changed. "Christ! Look at you."

I gave him a sickly grin. "Never mind me. Just don't ask questions, not yet." I stood before him like a Monday wash, for the first time feeling real discomfort. "Dick, it's great to see you, but I hope you haven't broken out."

Dick saw my concern and laughed. "You're joking. I've been waiting here all night. I'm free. They got the bloke. They let me go. I couldn't get round fast enough to tell you. I tried Maggie, but she doesn't answer. I thought you must be out together."

I stood gaping at him while a slow pool gathered round my feet. Had this been all for nothing? I couldn't take it in. He saw I was bewildered. "Look, Spider, get out of those clothes.

O.K.?" He held up his hands. "I won't ask. You've been in the drink and have no shoes, but I won't ask. I'm a copper, right? But I'm also your brother, so for the moment I've seen nothing. You tell me in your own good time, but get out of those clothes now."

I unlocked the door and Dick went straight through and put the kettle on. I was wondering what his reaction would be if he knew that I'd just done the Tate. When the news came out he wouldn't be slow to realize. And then what? While he made a very welcome coffee I stripped and had a bath. He brought the coffee in to me while I was still in the steaming water. I'd been in water most of the night, but this was luxury. He sat on the bath stool, cup in hand, and filled me in. After so many shocks this night, the one of seeing him still left me stunned. I listened to him in a semi-daze.

"I'm still under suspension," he explained, "but they can't hold me inside for that. The inquiry will still go on. But they caught the bloke who topped Max Harris and largely thanks to you."

What was a little more surprise now? I didn't raise an eyebrow, but I did when he continued.

"It was Detective Sergeant Newton. He was on Max's payroll. They searched his flat and enough came to light to pin him. He was pushing Max for more. They argued and Max got rough. It was self-defense, but it won't help him much with corruption charges on top. Do you remember telling Ron Healey that Newton called on you? It was what got it going. Ron knew that Newton wasn't on the murder squad. What we don't know, and you'll have to help us here, is why Newton called on you. When we really moved in on him he cracked; he couldn't have been far off before."

I recalled Newton's strain and began to see a few pieces slotting in. I had to be sure and I had to get myself out of the mess that was going to burst round my ears when the Tate job was discovered. I gulped my coffee and climbed from the bath.

"Dick," I said as I toweled down, "push off. It's great seeing you. Really great. But I've something urgent to do that can affect this whole issue."

"You in trouble?" he asked worriedly.

"I will be if I don't get moving. And don't forget you're still in trouble yourself. Give me a few hours and I might wrap it up. But I've got to move fast. Meanwhile don't—"

"—ask questions," he finished for me. "I know. But I owe you something, Spider. This brotherly stuff doesn't only work one way."

"Not at the expense of your career. Now wrap up or we'll become involved. Stick round your flat and I'll contact you." I thought quickly. "Later, ring Maggie at her office. She'll be delighted to hear from you. And, Dick, tell her I'm all right, eh? Use your loaf."

He wasn't happy about it; nor was I. I was placing him in a new kind of danger. Right now I was far worse off than when we started and so was Dick but didn't realize it. Dick wasn't a fool, but he was my brother. "Take care," he said. "I don't know what you're up to, but I'm glad you're not operating in my manor." He smiled. "Helps salve my conscience."

Dawn was fluttering in uncertain yellow streaks when I hung on the doorbell of Norman Shaw's house. I held on so long that I must have wakened the household. Lights flashed on upstairs and finally a window opened and Norman's head appeared. He hadn't combed his hair, which showed how agitated he was. He recognized me and he was shaken.

"Let me in," I called up.

"You must be mad," he said. "I've no intention of letting you in. You're wakening the neighborhood."

"Let me in or I'll come in the other way. I might break a window on the way."

He still hesitated, perhaps thinking that I'd come to do him.

"I want to talk," I added. "No rough stuff."

The window closed and seconds later he appeared at the door in a dressing gown, his hair still ruffled, his face gray with stubble. He looked years older, but I didn't stir it up by telling him.

"Everyone's awake, damn you. They'll wonder what's happening."

"Good," I said. "I want the whole family in on this act. There's something they all should know."

Ulla appeared at the top of the stairs in a diaphanous negligee. Miraculously she appeared as if she was just going to bed rather than having just left it. "Good morning," I greeted. "I'm glad you're up. Get the kids. This concerns you all."

"What're you playing at?" Norman turned on me, his eyes blazing, then he looked up at Ulla. "Go back to bed and make sure that the children stay in their rooms. This is between Scott and me."

"But only for the moment," I acquiesced.

Ulla went away looking worried, and I followed Norman up the stairs to his front study. He locked the door.

"After what you've done to me tonight you're taking a chance locking the door," I said.

He was still angry. "Not so much, I think. They all know you're here."

He went to the small mirror, took a comb from his dressing-gown pocket and meticulously tidied his hair; he was getting back to normal.

"The paintings have got to go back," I said.

He didn't move but I could see his anger turn to amusement.

"You ordered my topping tonight," I went on. "Why?"

"Because you asked for it. You tried to pin Max's murder on me, you bastard. You'd have seen me do life for it just to save your brother."

It wasn't quite what I'd expected. I thought round it. "I'd have pinned you with it if you'd done it. I wouldn't have put a fix on you."

He glared at me. "Don't be so innocent. You tried just that."
Something was wrong; this hadn't come from Peter Shaw.

"Norman," I said reasonably, "if I'd wanted to fix you I
would've. Chrissie was trying to make me do just that, and I
refused—which cost me."

"Chrissie?" I had his attention. His expression became
guarded, his eyes flicking over mine, uncertain of what I knew
and afraid to put his foot in it.

"Yes, Chrissie," I repeated. "Your old girl friend. The one
you used to lay in the love nest next door. She's been simmer-
ing for a long time. She wants revenge."

I'd stunned him, which meant Chrissie hadn't put the boot
in on me. "Detective Sergeant Newton spun you the yarn," I
guessed. "He came over to you after Max had gone." I thought
quickly; it was all tumbling into my mind haphazardly. "Newton was scared of our relationship; he knew my brother was
inside and it suited him. He didn't know what I was up to with
you and he was worried sick."

But Norman was still feeling his way, not sure where this
was leading. He was standing near the mirror, sleek again but
for his unshaven chin, his hands in his dressing-gown pockets
and eying me suspiciously. I had to get him off the fence.

"Do you know that Newton has been nicked for doing Max?"

"What?" That got through.

"My brother has been released; he was waiting for me when
I got back tonight."

Norman went very pale and groped for a chair. He sat down
shakily, still eying me uncertainly.

"I'm not lying," I said. "Newton saw me visiting you and
jumped in with both feet. You didn't know I had a brother in
the police; he must have told you. Then he fed you the story
that I'd pin it on you at all costs in order to save my brother.
With me out of it and Dick still pinned for something he
didn't do, Newton was sitting pretty." I watched Norman's
expression change from incredulity to belief and added, "I

thought you did it, all right. With my own suspicions and what Chrissie fed me, you were a cert. But Chrissie pushed too hard; she finished up convincing me that you were clean. I went ahead with the Tate job so that you would never know why I had really contacted you. And that's a fact."

Norman looked across at me with more understanding but with no liking. I'd fooled him and it hit his vanity hard; he'd never forgive me for that. He rubbed his face wearily and rose like a very old man. He crossed to the mirror again, saw an unbearable moment of truth and turned away from it quickly.

"Chrissie killed Max," he said flatly. "She didn't use the weapon, that's all. When I dropped her to marry Ulla she threatened to tell Max of our relationship unless I kept her going, and finally she did. Max had a simple mind. We had to split. Both of us would have been reasonably happy to continue like that, but Chrissie wouldn't let go. She applied all sorts of pressures to squeeze me out until I approached Max direct to sort something out. The way she was playing the game I needed police protection quick. Max held a monopoly in that direction. I needed some of his force, so I offered Newton and another more money than Max and Chrissie were paying to get them over to me. I don't know if Chrissie twigged it and did something about it but they refused to play." Norman stared at me belligerently, as if it was all my fault.

"So I applied psychological pressure. I told them that I'd indirectly report them as bent. I explained how. They didn't believe me. They saw Max and Chrissie as the more powerful force and me as on the way out. So I had to prove my point. I told them that if I could implicate an innocent policeman by dropping indirect advice to a certain newspaperman, how much easier it would be to fix a couple who were really guilty. I knew that I could force a police inquiry with ease. I had no idea that it was your brother I'd fixed. Newton and his friend came over to me with some speed."

I stared at him in disbelief, my anger swelling. "You bastard," I snarled heatedly. "You caused Dick all this trouble . . ." Cold fury gripped me.

"I didn't know he was your brother," he repeated dully. "It's a common name."

Norman paused, very strained now, still pale. "I suppose Newton went back to Max to force him to raise the ante, perhaps to draw from both sources. Max wouldn't have taken kindly to that sort of pressure." He looked across at me. "I can't say that I'm sorry. You deserved what you got."

"And if I'd snuffed it?"

He hesitated. "The gelignite was a dummy. I wanted to scare the pants off you."

I laughed, although it didn't sound like one. "That's easy to say, isn't it? But we'll never know, will we? I nearly drowned in flood water."

He didn't answer. Anyway, I didn't believe him.

"The paintings are going back," I said.

"That's impossible. I have buyers in Japan, not art collectors —long-term investors. They don't need to take them out to gloat over them. It's unlikely that they'd know one from another, but they do know that they will appreciate in value and that they are investing for their children and grandchildren."

I stood up. "They're going back, Norman. The way you tried to fix me tonight cancels the deal. I was seen on the job and I've been seen by my own brother in such a state that he must connect me with it. We have a thing between us, my brother and me. I'll make bloody certain that he doesn't protect me. If they go back he can back-pedal on his morals to the extent that he can turn a blind eye."

Norman shook his head slowly. "You can have your share back, but they can't be returned."

"Then I'll leave you with this thought," I said. "If they're not back in six hours from now, I'm going to tell Ulla of your little place next door and who you've been sharing it with. And I'll tell Chrissie that Ulla doesn't know it exists. If Ulla sees Chrissie I think you'll agree that Chrissie will give her a bonus of malicious detail and convince her you've still been using it. You told me your family mean everything to you; you'd better be sure you meant it." I didn't enlighten him that Ulla would have still clung to him for his money. But I did know that he wouldn't want his image to Ulla destroyed; he really did love her. I put in the boot again.

"You tried to top me after I'd done a job for you. I'm willing to grass because of that. You'd better reflect on Ulla on the rampage while you're doing your first stretch. And if you want a second attempt at knocking me off you've only a few hours left to do it." I knew he wouldn't try it here.

I went to the door. "And another thing. You'd better get haul off your press contact and reverse that suspicion about my brother damned quick. I'll see myself out." I left him puzzled and annoyed but recognized that he needed time to think.

Ulla was waiting on the landing as I came out. She was worried, but it wasn't about paintings or Dick. I wondered if she'd been listening. I came straight out with it.

"Norman has some paintings nicked from the Tate Gallery. Make sure he returns them by midday or I'll tell him about the evening you took me home. Neither of you need the money; he can stand the losses."

I went down the stairs seriously wondering whether my days of non-grassing were over. Ulla could have hung that one on me; I thought she had, but she'd lost her chance now.

I got back to the flat and rang Chrissie, dragging her from bed. When she realized it was me she tried it on, but I curtly cut through her invective.

"They've got Max's killer. Newton—you know him. Any more nonsense from you and I'll tip Norman that you tried to fix him." I was ladling out the blackmail strong and thick. I couldn't see the point of telling her that Norman already knew; she deserved to sweat on it and it would probably keep her off Norman's back. "And the fuzz too," I added as an afterthought. I hung up as she was using a completely new and interesting expletive.

I cooked myself breakfast, hung around impatiently and listened to the radio news of the Tate job; it had caused a sensation. More disturbing was the accurate description of myself as a man wanted by the police to help them in their inquiries. The fuzz would want to put the record right with me; the car coppers wouldn't like being made to look stupid. I rang Maggie about midmorning. Dick had already been on to her, so much of the ice was broken. We arranged to meet that evening, and she was moving back into her own flat. It was the best moment of the day.

Just after one Dick and his friend Ron Healey called. They entered my flat as only coppers can with that slow, all-embracing stare that missed nothing and in this case contained something not unpleasant but not quite humorous.

"Hiya," they said in chorus and sat themselves down, looking at each other for direction.

"The Tate was broken into last night," Ron Healey said uncomfortably.

"The Tate?" I queried. "The sugar people?"

They grinned sheepishly. "Remarkable thing," continued Ron Healey. "The paintings were picked up in a phone booth following an anonymous tip-off. Sort of takes the heat off it a bit."

"Get away," I said. "Why tell me?"

"You're an art lover," said Healey slowly. "Thought you'd be interested. It was your type of job—good, neat except for a bloody big hole. The cellars were flooded, but luckily nothing of value was down there. Thought you'd like to know that you've got a rival." Again they exchanged glances.

"Another strange thing," said Dick. "My inquiry has been quashed—suddenly like someone had made a dirty big blunder. That should please you."

"Marvelous," I said. "Absolutely marvelous."

All this play had been without emotion as we fenced with each other, each knowing, each avoiding the real issue.

Ron Healey said, "Thought you might like to come out and have a drink with us tonight. You know, over Dick's release."

I began to relax. I grinned. "Tonight I'm with Maggie. What about tomorrow if you don't mind being seen with an old lag?"

They rose, looked at each other again and nodded. "We'll chance it. We can always make it look like we're nicking you." Dick wanted to say more but couldn't. They were happy enough.

Ron Healey shook my hand warmly. He was grateful. "Funny about those paintings being returned," he said as he went to the door.